Once

Upon a

Time

Barbara Fradkin

Once Upon a Time

An Inspector Green Mystery

Barbara Fradkin

RENDEZVOUS
PRESS

Text © 2002 Barbara Fradkin

LE CONSEIL DES ARTS DU CANADA DEPUIS 1957 | THE CANADA COUNCIL FOR THE ARTS SINCE 1957

We gratefully acknowledge the support of the Canada Council for the Arts for our publishing program.

Napoleon Publishing/RendezVous Press
Toronto, Ontario, Canada
www.rendezvouspress.com

Printed in Canada

06 05 04 03 02   5 4 3 2 1

National Library of Canada Cataloguing in Publication

Fradkin, Barbara Fraser, date—
    Once upon a time / Barbara Fradkin

"An Inspector Green Mystery"
ISBN 0-929141-84-9

I. Title.

PS8561.R233O52 2002   C813'.6   C2002-902965-1
PR9199.3.F64O52 2002

Acknowledgements

I am grateful for the contribution of many people in helping to bring *Once Upon a Time* to life. First, to my late husband Arnie, whose work as a War Crimes prosecutor provided the inspiration for this story and whose critical reading of the earliest draft helped me stay true. Secondly to the many experts who answered my questions; Renfrew historian Carol McCuaig, Sergeant Don Sweet of the Forensics Identification Unit of the Ottawa Police, Constable Brian Patterson of the Renfrew O.P.P. Detachment and Doug Davie of Davie's Antiques in Harriston. Thirdly, to Constable Mark Cartwright of the Ottawa Police for his ongoing advice and expertise in police matters, and to Jane Ann Tun, Madona Skaff and Robin Harlick for their feedback and support. Fourthly, to my editor Allister Thompson and my publisher Sylvia McConnell for their continued belief in my work.

And most of all to my children Leslie, Dana and Jeremy, for being there when I emerged from the dark places to which I had to go.

One

September 2nd, 1939

I hear her footsteps on the mossy riverbank
See the sun-flamed red of her hair
As it swoops in rhythm to her run.
She tilts her head, shields her eyes.
But still I hide, drunk with hope and disbelief.
She has come to me, my rebel princess.
Slipped the sentinel gaze of the village,
huddled in its uneasy rest.
Run across the cornfields behind the mill
And out to meet her poet.
Nothing to offer her but words spun into shimmering webs,
to catch her lofty dreams.
She spots me then and smiles,
And I open up my arms.

After fifteen minutes of waiting, the old man pulled the sweaty tuque off his head and scowled at the snow through the window. His long plaid scarf pricked his neck, adding to his annoyance. He could see little through the pale wintery light in the room, but he could hear his wife thumping around in his bedroom upstairs. Drawers opened and closed.

What the hell was the woman doing up there! He felt a surge of alarm as he remembered the letter. How stupid of him to leave it in his desk drawer. He should have burned it as soon as he got it. When they got back home tonight, he would. Once today's ordeal was over.

He looked around the room at the refuge he had sought to create. A modest parlour with a crumbling brick fireplace, a scratched piano and shelves haphazardly stacked with books. All he had ever wanted was this little cottage in the country, his pipe, his whiskey and an armchair by the fire. A retirement cottage, he had told his wife. Far from cruel strangers and prying eyes, from a past that still lurked in his head.

Yet in the end he had not escaped. He leaned back in the armchair and willed away the sudden tears that filled his eyes. She would see them—nothing escaped her—and she would fuss. Not overtly, for she knew better, but quietly, fluttering around the kitchen to make him tea, watching him with silent, questioning eyes. And now, because of that monstrous letter, how long before she knew?

A final thud roused him, and he looked up to see her descend the stairs, pulling a pair of thick woollen gloves over her gnarled hands. She frowned at him as she came across the room, picked up his tuque from the window ledge and pulled it firmly back down on his head.

"I'll get the car and pick you up out front," she said.

He heard the thump of her cane as she shuffled through the kitchen and pushed open the screen door against the thick snow on the porch. He glanced at his watch impatiently. Of all days for snow! She'll take forever crossing the yard, so scared she'll fall and break something again. And then she won't be able to start the car.

He heard the shriek of the shed door, the thud of the car

2

door, and finally the screech of the ignition. He cursed her aloud. Too heavy handed, no feel for an engine. But then he heard a hoarse, reluctant cough as the old Dodge came to life, and he hauled himself to his feet.

Outside, he squinted against the stinging snow as he watched her inch the car across the yard. She will think it's too cold for me to stay in the car. She'll want me to go into the clinic with her and wait in a room full of creaky old women. More complications.

He surveyed the white fields in silence as they drove down the long lane to the highway. They were going to be late, perhaps too late. But once they were on the highway, the driving was good. The roads were salted a glistening black, and the trip to Ottawa took only two hours, even at her cautious seventy kilometres an hour. The windshield wipers beat a steady rhythm against the snow, and he stared out the window at the passing farms, his thoughts lost in winters long ago. Wondering, worrying…

"If I'm through in time," she said, "we'll drop by Margaret's for early tea."

Her intrusion into his thoughts startled him. "We just saw her on the weekend."

"But they're on our way home, and she's expecting us."

"I want to get back," he replied peevishly. He felt her eyes upon him with their questions, but thankfully she said nothing.

It was eleven-thirty when she pulled into the parking lot at the hospital, and the wind whipped the snow about. He made no move, and when she turned to him questioningly, he said, "I'll wait here."

"But it's cold outside today. And I'm not sure how long I'll be."

"Leave me the keys. I'll start the car if I have to."

She seemed about to argue, so he closed his eyes and feigned fatigue. A moment later the door opened, and he felt a frigid blast of air. Halfway out, she paused, hunched against the swirling snow, and turned to him.

"Get out, woman!"

Pressing her lips shut, she pulled herself out and slammed the door. He watched her battle the drifts with her cane as she crept across the road to the clinic door, then he reached inside his duffel coat for his small flask. With a grunt of pleasure he brought the flask to his lips and took a long swallow. Maybe that will keep trouble away, he thought, and glanced at his watch. 11:37. He peered out through the frosted front windshield. Nothing moved. Not a car, not a solitary soul. He'd never put much stake in hope, but he allowed a faint stirring of it as he settled down to wait.

* * *

When the call came in to Major Crimes, Ottawa Police, Inspector Michael Green had been in his office battling paperwork for over four hours, and his mind was mush. The time was 1:43 p.m. He heard the phone ring on Sergeant Brian Sullivan's desk, heard a brief exchange of words, and then Sullivan's brisk trademark: "On my way."

Green waited three minutes to allow Sullivan to check in with the Staff Sergeant—no point in treading on too many toes—then headed out of his office, hoping for a casual interception. But the squad room was empty. Sullivan's desk was locked, and his duffel coat was gone from its peg. Damn.

Restlessly, Green wandered down the hall to the coffee machine and returned with his fifth cup of pallid fluid. He left the door to his little alcove office ajar, inviting someone to interrupt him as he returned to his monthly report.

Some time later, his phone rang, and he pounced on it, hoping it was Sullivan asking for his help. Or Superintendent Jules, head of Criminal Investigations, saying a call had just come in on a multiple homicide in Rockcliffe Park. Not even that. He'd settle for a wino who had rolled into the Rideau Canal.

But it was his wife Sharon, who had a day off from the hospital. She sounded cheerful, and in the background he could hear his infant son babbling excitedly.

"I just wanted to warn you the roads are really slippery, honey. And the driveway has six inches of fresh, fluffy snow on it. Pristine and untouched. To celebrate our first snowfall in our new house, I bought you a shovel at Canadian Tire."

Ah, the joys of home ownership, he thought. My very own stretch of asphalt from the street to the Dreaded Vinyl Cube in the cow pastures of Barrhaven. He could almost see the twinkle in her eye, but at this point even shovelling would be a welcome relief. "Don't worry, I'm coming home early tonight. Maybe even five o'clock."

There was silence on her end of the line, followed by a chuckle. "Five o'clock? Inspector Green is coming home at five o'clock?"

"We're having a temporary lull in murders in this town. It's too damn cold even for the crooks. I'm doing nothing but supervision and paperwork."

"Paperwork!" He could hear her astonishment. "Boy, you must really be desperate. Next thing I know, you'll be inventing a murder!"

He was still laughing when he hung up, but the smile faded quickly at the sight before him. Piles and piles of jumbled phone messages, computer print-outs and unread articles. He had not joined the force to push paper, but in the past couple of years, he'd felt himself being edged farther and farther from the streets and into committee rooms. He was drowning in paperwork and its electronic cousin, e-mail. At the click of a mouse, minutes of meetings and drafts of endless policies could be sent whizzing off to every middle manager on the force, whether they wanted to read them or needed to know them. All to prove how important and busy the sender was.

The Chief of Detectives, Adam Jules, knew better than to expect Green to respond in kind, but Green's job as administrator required some minimal output of paper. Annual reports were nearing, and the new Police Chief liked neat arrays of statistics to take to City Hall. He liked stats such as types of crimes reported, solvency rates, crimes by district, etc. To Green, homicide investigation was the cream of police work, as well as the only work he was good at, but to Chief Shea it was a mere footnote in his vast law enforcement vision. Fortunately, the press and the public loved homicides, which was why Jules forgave Green his abysmal administrative skills. Seeing his potential fifteen years ago, Jules had yanked Green off the streets, where he'd been mediocre at best, and into criminal investigations, where his tenacious drive and intuitive intelligence had given him one of the highest solution rates on the force.

But that was before amalgamation with the outlying forces had turned a tightly-knit, street level police force into a lumbering bureaucracy, and himself into little more than a cog. He sighed. How long since he'd been out on a call?

Some time later, his phone rang again, but this time it was Jules' clerk, wondering when she might expect his report. She had a gaping hole in her computer screen where his Major Crime statistics were supposed to fit. He toyed with suggesting that she make up whatever she wanted, provided it made him look good, but decided against it. Jules' clerk was very young and pretty, but she had absolutely no sense of humour. Choosing the wiser course, he mumbled vague promises and hung up—just in time to see Brian Sullivan emerge from the elevator and stride to his desk, shedding his heavy duffel coat. His face was ruddy from the cold. Casually, Green drifted over.

Despite the difference in their ranks, he and Sullivan had been friends for over twenty years, ever since they'd been rookies together on the streets, and there were many times Green longed to trade places with him, so that he could roam the streets again while Sullivan sat on committees tossing around words like "vision" and "strategic plan."

"So, how's it going?" Green asked.

Sullivan looked up from the notebook he had just opened. "It's a bitch out there. Crazy for November. What will it be like by January?"

"Tropical. You know this country, we wouldn't want to be boring." Green sat on the edge of Sullivan's desk. "What was the call?"

Sullivan shrugged and scribbled a few notes absently. "Oh, nothing much. An old man was found frozen to death in the parking lot at the Civic hospital. I went out to the scene, talked to the parking lot attendant and the man's family, but it looks like natural causes. I was just going to write it up, pending MacPhail's report."

"What does MacPhail say?"

"There were no real signs of violence, so one of the regular coroners attended the scene. But MacPhail will do the autopsy tomorrow."

"What do you mean 'no *real* signs'?"

"He has a small gash on his forehead. But not enough to

7

knock him out, let alone kill him. This was a big guy. He was old, but he must have been quite something in his youth, and even today it would take a lot to knock him down."

"What did the family say? Where did he get the gash?"

"They don't know. But he probably got it as he fell. The wife said he'd been sick for months. Short of breath, lousy colour. She'd been trying to get him to see her GP."

"All the same, did you check motives?"

A scowl flitted across Sullivan's face as he turned to Green. Standing, he was at least five inches taller and almost twice as broad. His linebacker physique had expanded to hang slightly over his belt, and high blood pressure was just beginning to mottle his handsome face. "How long since I made detective, Green? Twelve years? You think I don't cover the bases? The guy had no enemies and no money to brag about. But he was a drunk, it was written all over him. He probably stepped out of the car, passed out and never knew what hit him. End of story."

"End of an old man, too."

"I know that. I'm just reporting the facts, I'm not passing judgment." Sullivan's scowl softened. "It's fifteen below out there today. You know better than anybody what that kind of cold can do to someone with heart disease. He might have gone outside, taken a deep breath and dropped like a stone. I'm telling you there's nothing here. This is just another sick old drunk whose number finally came up."

Maybe so, thought Green. Disembowelled dead bodies were not his favourite part of a murder investigation, but by tomorrow morning, when the autopsy was scheduled, he might be in need of a small break from his paperwork

* * *

8

Dr. Alexander MacPhail was a tall, rangy Scot with a shock of wild grey hair atop a long, pockmarked face. He grinned as he pulled off a pair of surgical gloves, tossed them into a bin nearby and clapped Green on the shoulder. His rich Scottish brogue boomed in the empty basement hall of the hospital.

"Hello, there, laddie! I haven't seen you in a while. How's the air up there in the upper echelons these days?"

"Stifling."

"Aye, hot air tends to be." The pathologist cast him a mischievous glance. "So would you just be down here for the fun of watching me work, or would you be wanting something?"

Green grinned. "You know what I think about your work."

"A dirty job, but someone has to do it."

"I'm just curious about the old man in the Civic parking lot yesterday. Any information on him yet?"

MacPhail gestured to the closed door marked MORGUE but painted an unlikely lime green. "Do you want to come in and meet him? I've just sewn him back up."

"No thanks." Green hoped he didn't sound too hasty. "What does it look like?"

"Well...actual cause of death was hypothermia. But the old bugger had a whole book full of medical problems. Chronic hypertension, arteriosclerosis in both coronary and cerebral arteries, cirrhosis of the liver, some atrophy to the brain. Any one of his parts could have failed him temporarily at that moment."

"What about the contusion? Brian said he had a gash on his forehead."

MacPhail chuckled. "Sorry to disappoint you, laddie, but it wasn't enough to kill him. Stun him, perhaps. He could have slipped in the snow and struck his head. In a man his age, that might have been enough to disorient him. He may have lain there resting, not even aware he was cold."

"Was it a fresh wound, then?"

"Inflicted shortly before death, yes."

"What kind of instrument? Sharp, blunt, big, small?"

"A smooth, rounded object about an inch wide." MacPhail used his hands to demonstrate the size and shape. "Not much bleeding, and it didn't get any chance to swell before he landed face down in the snow."

"Is it consistent with someone trying to strike him?

The pathologist's eyes twinkled. "More consistent with hitting his head against a hard object—probably the car mirror—as he was falling."

Curiosity outweighed his distaste. Bracing himself, Green nodded towards the morgue door. "Can I see him?"

The morgue was a brightly lit room painted the same incongruous chartreuse as the door and filled with huge stainless steel receptacles. MacPhail had the consideration to pull a sheet over the body, but Green could tell from the contours of the sheet that the man had been big, probably once muscular. MacPhail had replaced the cranium expertly, but the face was mottled red and white. It was a large, beefy face topped by thinning strands of white-blonde hair. Glazed in death, the eyes were a pallid brown run through with red. Green focussed on the gash on his forehead.

"Strange shape for a car mirror."

"Car mirrors come in all shapes. Laddie, trust me. This one is a natural causes."

Probably, Green acknowledged, but he'd seen enough blunt instrument traumas in his career to feel a twinge of doubt.

* * *

10

It wasn't much to mark the passing of a life—a name, age, address and next of kin. Eugene Walker, eighty. Home was a rural route number in the rolling farmlands of the Ottawa Valley between Renfrew and Eganville, about a hundred kilometres west of Ottawa. But MacPhail's notes indicated that until the funeral, his widow was staying at her daughter Margaret's home here in the city.

Even when he pulled up to Margaret Reid's elegant west-end home, Green wasn't sure exactly what he was looking for. Three cars stood in the double drive—an aging Dodge, a small hatchback and a shiny silver BMW. He extracted his police badge and held it in readiness, but even so, the look of surprise was blatant on the face of the man who answered the door. Green suppressed a smile. He never tired of that look, which reassured him that he was not growing staid and inspectorish. He was forty-one years old, but because of his light build, his youthful face, and the fine spray of freckles across his nose, he looked barely thirty. His baggy trousers and navy blue parka gave more the impression of a city postman than a high-ranking police investigator. Green had learned to cultivate this lack of physical presence. Like a good spy, it allowed him to move and observe unseen.

Still, at times he would have appreciated a more authoritative bearing. As now, when grieving relatives needed someone to lean on, although the relative standing before him did not appear about to crumple into his arms. The man looked in his mid forties, dark-haired and probably handsome at one time, but now baggy-eyed and gone to seed. His eyes were slightly bloodshot, but that was his only concession to grief. He frowned as if Green were a pesky vacuum salesman interrupting his busy day.

Green introduced himself briskly, apologized for the

intrusion and asked to see Ruth Walker.

"Is this really necessary, Inspector? She's resting, and she already spoke to a police officer yesterday."

"Yes, Sergeant Sullivan. I'm just following up. Your name is?"

"What's this for? The old man had a heart attack, he's dead. It was quick and painless. What else is there to know?"

"Routine. Are you Donald Reid, his son-in-law?"

"I don't see why you need to know, but yes." He blinked several times. When Green continued to stand in the doorway, he stepped back with a scowl.

"Very well. Come in."

Mrs. Walker took about five minutes to come downstairs, and in the meantime Green absorbed impressions about the house. It was a quiet house, not just hushed in grief, but constrained. Everything had its place. The living room was furnished in expensive woods, testimony to the family's material success. Colour-coordinated watercolours adorned the walls, and china figurines sat on the mahogany table tops. Not a room for children, Green thought, although he had glimpsed a flash of teenage boys in the kitchen as he passed by.

When Mrs. Walker entered, she was leaning on a younger woman whom Green assumed to be her daughter. Dressed in red slacks and a red and white striped sweater, with not a strand of her cropped black hair out of place, Margaret Reid was the image of her living room. She perched emotionless on the edge of her chair.

Her mother, on the other hand, wore an old beige cardigan and ill-fitting tweed skirt. Her hair billowed in a cloud of grey curls, and her face was blotched with tears. Green had expected a broad, heavy farmer's face, but Mrs. Walker was delicately boned, with deep-set blue eyes and a finely pointed chin.

"How do you do, Inspector? I'm Ruth Walker. How may I help you?"

Green was not an authority on British accents, but he had watched enough *Masterpiece Theatre* productions to recognize this one as rich, precise and public school. The tilt of her head and the grace with which she extended her hand made him feel shabby. He drew out his notebook and summoned all the dignity his cheap parka permitted.

"First of all, let me extend my condolences on the death of your husband. The way he died so unexpectedly must have been a shock."

She eased herself stiffly into a heavy velvet chair opposite him. Her blue eyes held his, but he thought they moistened.

"Yes, it was. Although I suppose I ought to have seen it coming. I've known for some time he wasn't well."

"In what way? Dizzy spells?"

"Not exactly. More shortness of breath."

"Had he ever fallen before?"

She hesitated, and in her instant of discomfiture, the surly son-in-law snorted. "Lots of times. He always had one bruise or another. It means nothing, detective."

Green kept his eyes on the widow. "Had he seen a doctor recently?"

Ruth looked across the coffee table at him. Through the veil of grief, he saw a faint smile. "One didn't take Eugene anywhere. If he chose to go, that was fine. But he didn't choose to."

"Why?"

"I expect because he didn't want to hear the bad news. He was from the old country, Inspector. They're rather more fatalistic than you are over here. When it's time, it's time. No use fighting it with pills and machines."

"Do you think he was depressed?"

"No, not exactly depressed. I mean, he was ready to go. I think he had..." A spasm crossed her face but disappeared before he could analyze it. "...made his peace."

"Almost as if he were waiting for death?"

Her eyes fixed his intently. "Exactly. It was always Eugene's dream to retire to the country, and once he did, he rarely left the house. He spent most of his day in his chair, just looking out the window."

He smiled. "Dreaming about Trafalgar Square, probably. Or his favourite country pub."

Out of the corner of his eye, Green saw Margaret open her mouth, but Ruth shot her a quick glance which silenced her. "Eugene liked to say that his life began when he came to Canada," Ruth said. "All that happened before was best put behind us. He never talked about it."

It jarred with the picture Green had begun to paint. He thought of his own father, who also spent his days sitting in a chair, but who had his own reasons for not wanting to relive the past. Green wondered what Walker's reasons were, and if Ruth's glance at Margaret had been meant to silence her. "Odd," he mused casually. "Most elderly people love to reminisce. Sometimes the old days are all they talk about, especially if, like your husband, they have little else they can do now but sit in a chair."

She didn't rise to the bait. "Yes, a disheartening way for a strong, proud man to spend his last days."

There was a quiet finality to her words, as if she were closing the door. Respecting that, he moved on. "Can you run through what happened yesterday?

At this point the surly son-in-law, who had subsided in the corner, re-entered the fray. "Inspector, I really don't see the point

14

in this. Ruth, you don't need to put yourself through this."

"I don't mind, Don. He has a job to do."

Green admired her quiet dignity. With barely a quiver, she recounted the events of yesterday from their departure to her discovery of the body at one o'clock. Only when she described the sight of him did she falter, pressing her fingers to her lips. Green sensed Don beginning to rise, and he held up a warning hand.

"Where was he in relation to the car?"

"I'm not sure. He—" She broke off, her hands fluttering up to her face at the memory. "He...he was lying alongside the car, his head towards the front wheel, I think."

In perfect position beneath the side mirror, he thought. "Driver's side?"

"Oh, no, passenger's side. Eugene hadn't driven in years."

"I'd like to look at the car. Is it one of the cars outside?"

"Yes, Don fetched it." She turned. "Don, could you...?"

Seeming relieved to be rid of him, Don led Green outside to the Dodge Aries. Despite its age, there was little rust, but mud coated its sides. Salt stains from the recent drive into the city formed an irregular splatter pattern over the mud, but there were no unusual marks on the passenger side of the car. Nor were there any protruding edges; even the door handles were recessed.

But even more importantly, because it was such an old car, it had no mirror on the passenger side.

Two

September 2nd, 1939

The sun is sinking, soon the village will stir.
She curls in the nook of my arm,
her hips soft against mine,
And her skin like silk beneath my touch.
Copper tassels of cornfield dance in the sunset
And a breeze ripples the birches overhead.
Far off I hear muffled thuds,
catch a glint of silver in the sky.
Then a plume of smoke, a second, a third.
She lifts her head. "Our village?"
No, what would they want with our village?

"I don't remember nothing about no fucking cars, man! That was the worst day of my life! I remember the body— fuck, I'll never forget the body. Worst nightmare you could ever have, finding a stiff in your own lot. I was so freaked, I don't remember nothing else."

Green's small mid-morning break had now extended into his lunch hour, and he knew the clock was ticking on his freedom. He had traced the parking lot attendant to a small clapboard shanty on a narrow, crowded back street of

16

Mechanicsville. The young man had called in sick to recover from the upset of yesterday, and he ushered Green into the dingy living room, kicking newspapers and clothes aside to make a passage. The sweet odour of marijuana clung in the air. He gave a nervous whinny.

"It's my brother's place. I'm just staying here till I can get my own."

It took some coaxing, and a small shot of the whiskey Green found on the counter, to get Chad Leroux to retrieve his scattered memories. The young man rocked back and forth on the couch, smoking incessantly and talking in staccato bursts.

"I was checking a couple of cars. Out, like. It was fucking cold, booth's got no heater. Had my hood on my parka up, so I couldn't see shit. This guy in the car—he pointed out the old lady to me."

"Was the lot busy?"

Chad shook his head vigorously. "Most days noon is really busy, but nobody was going out that didn't have to. 'Cause of the storm, you know? The lot was plowed, but it was still tricky."

"Was it slippery?"

"Was it ever! And you never knew where, with the snow on top. I saw one poor old guy with a cane go right down on his ass earlier."

One more point for MacPhail's theory, Green thought ruefully as he invited Chad to continue.

"That's all! The guy in the car says 'Something's wrong with that lady over there'. I turn around, I see her way down near the end of the lot, waving her arms all about and screaming 'my husband, my husband', and—" Chad broke off, sucking in cigarette smoke to ward off the panic. "Fuck, I never did like bodies."

"No one does," Green muttered drily. "Were there other

cars near hers? Can you describe them?"

Chad rolled his eyes and blew smoke out his nose. "Who the fuck noticed!"

Green leaned forward, his eyes fixed on Chad's. "It's important. Concentrate! Picture yourself back there in the snow, the old woman screaming—"

Chad's head whipped back and forth. "I can't, man! I don't remember nothing! I know I should have noticed stuff like that, but I just thought 'Shit, the guy's croaked! And maybe somebody's going to blame me!'"

"Nobody's blaming you, Chad," Green soothed. "It's quite normal to forget everything else, but it's there, somewhere in your mind. I want you to lean back on the couch and shut your eyes." Green waited until the young man was ready, then dropped his voice. "Take three deep, slow breaths. Now I want you to picture yourself in the parking lot. It's cold, the wind is blowing in your face. You're walking through the snow, the old lady is up ahead screaming at you... Are you there?"

Chad had closed his eyes dutifully, but his body twitched, and his breathing was erratic. It took a few moments of further coaxing to get him properly focussed on the cars nearby.

"There's mostly empty spaces." Chad wet his lips. "But right next to her, there's one—no, two cars."

"Good. Can you describe the car right beside hers?"

"Medium sized. It's dark—maybe dark blue or charcoal grey, maybe even black. Sedan, four-door type. Nice and shiny."

"All right, concentrate on it. Describe anything—make, licence—anything."

Chad tried to oblige. His eyelids fluttered as he searched the invisible scene. "It was like the shape of the Aries, only newer. Like a Lumina or one of them GM family cars, but fancy. Buick LeSabre, maybe? Tinted windows."

"Okay, that's great, you can open your eyes."

Chad sat forward, eyes alight. "Hey, that's something! It really works. Did you—like—hypnotize me?"

Green smiled. "Nothing that exotic. I just helped you eliminate the distractions." He stood up, and Chad followed him with obvious relief. "Tell me, Chad, do some of the vehicles park in the lot on a regular basis?"

Chad looked blank for a moment, trying to translate. "You mean every day like? Oh, sure. Doctors, nurses and them. They use the lot, pay by the month."

"And do they have their favourite spots?"

"Some of them."

It was a slim hope, but a hope nonetheless, Green thought as he headed towards the Civic Hospital. Maybe in the parking lot he would find the dark, shiny sedan which had parked next to Walker's on the day of his death. And against which Walker must have smashed his head as he fell to the ground.

But ten minutes later he found himself in the parking lot amid endless rows of dark, shiny new sedans. The attendant on duty walked him down to the end of the lot and showed him where the body had been found. The whole area had been so trampled that it was useless as a crime scene, and there were no cars parked in the immediate vicinity and no dark sedans within fifty feet. Nonetheless, mainly to impress the parking attendant who hovered nearby, he crouched in the snow and sifted through it with his fingers. It told him nothing.

This is pointless, Green. The old guy hit his head on something, stunned himself and froze to death. You've wasted enough of the department's time. There is no mystery here. *Nada, bopkes*, zip. What was it Sharon had said? Invent a murder?

The breath of freedom is over, Inspector. Your paperwork awaits.

*　*　*

Reluctantly, Green headed back towards the office. No fresh snow had fallen since the day before, but the temperature had stayed low, and the snow showed no inclination to melt. Ottawa's efficient salt trucks had cleared the main streets, but the sidewalks and small roads were still rutted with ice. That, and a rash of fender benders caused by hotshots who'd forgotten how to drive in the winter, had slowed traffic to a crawl. Slipping in a CD of soft rock, Green let his mind drift over the case. Something puzzled him, not so much about the manner of the old man's death as about the reclusive old man himself. And about his widow, a gracious, elegant lady who Green suspected had put up with a good deal.

It made a small, poignant tale of a marriage, compelling from a human interest standpoint, but, he acknowledged grudgingly as he pulled into the station parking lot, from a major crimes standpoint, it was not much to get excited about.

Back behind his desk, he turned on his computer and obediently settled down to his report. After an eternity, his phone rang. It was Sharon. He glanced at his watch instinctively, but it was barely four o'clock. Time crawled when you were having fun.

"I'm leaving in half an hour," he promised.

She chuckled. "I don't think I can stand this new suburban you. And actually, I think you should swing by the synagogue and take your Dad home first before you come home."

"Dad?" His mind drew a blank.

"It's Thursday—his pinochle afternoon. It's too cold and icy for him to walk home. He's pretty frail, and I think those pinochle games are getting really depressing. Sort of like, let's see who's left standing this week."

The image of Eugene Walker's frozen body face down in the snow was incentive enough, and Green abandoned his desk gratefully at the stroke of five. Sid Green lived in a seniors' residence in Sandy Hill just off Rideau Street, barely a mile from the tenement where Green had grown up. For the past fifteen years, Sid had walked up Rideau first to the old Jewish Community Centre, and when that closed, to the adjacent synagogue to play pinochle with a handful of elderly immigrant Jews like himself. For fifteen years, a touch of *shtetl* Poland had flourished in the middle of Ottawa.

Now, as most of them passed eighty and various parts of their bodies failed them, the number was slowly dwindling, and when Green pulled up outside the synagogue, his father's scowl told him that today had not been a success. In a daily life of so few successes, his father had little optimism to spare.

"I want you to take me to Bernie's house," Sid said as Green guided him into the car.

Green was reaching for the seat belt and stopped abruptly. "Why?"

"He didn't come to the game today."

"Maybe it was too cold for him."

Sid waved an impatient hand. His white hair stood in thin tufts, and his eyes watered from the cold. He drew his coat tightly around his throat. "Bernie never missed a game."

Green started the car. "So call him."

"Marv did. There was no answer."

"Dad, he was probably just out visiting friends."

Sid snorted. "And who are we, chopped liver? We're all he's got. Where would he go?" He stole a glance at Green's set profile, and his voice dropped. "Something is wrong, Mishka. Bernie is looking very bad these past weeks."

With resignation, Green steered the car in the direction of

21

Bernie Mendelsohn's apartment, which was a crumbling low-rise mainly occupied by the elderly poor. He left his father in what passed for a foyer and went in search of the building superintendent. They were just jiggling the lock of Mendelsohn's apartment when the door cracked open, and an old man in pyjamas peered out.

"Bernie!" Sid exclaimed. "Why didn't you answer our call?"

"What call?"

"You missed cards! Marv tried to call."

Mendelsohn closed his eyes briefly, then turned to make his way back inside. Green noticed that his hands shook, and he limped badly. Quickly, he thanked the super and followed his father inside. The apartment was barely fifteen feet square and lit with a single yellow bulb hanging from the ceiling. Clothes were scattered everywhere, and open food cans were piled haphazardly by the sink. Green had only been there once before, but he remembered it as scrupulously clean. Like Sid, Mendelsohn had been widowed for nearly twenty years and had his set routines.

"I didn't hear the phone," Mendelsohn was saying. "I'm sorry, I was asleep." He sat down on the edge of his bed, and Sid took the rickety white kitchen chair. As there was no other place to sit, Green leaned against the wall and waited. Both men were frail, but his father, even with his heart condition, looked far healthier. Mendelsohn's skin had a yellowish cast and hung on his frame in folds. A quick glance around the room revealed a collection of prescription bottles by the bed. While the two friends bickered, Green went over for a closer look.

"You think I don't have eyes?" Sid demanded. "I can't see you look bad?"

"I'm eighty-four years old. You think you look so good?"

"Bernie—" Green interrupted, holding up a vial. "These are pretty strong painkillers."

Mendelsohn snatched the vial away with trembling hands. He shoved it into his pyjama pocket and took a deep breath. "Michael, I have a few aches and pains. Tell your father to leave an old man in peace."

Sid rose and came across the dimly lit room to peer at Mendelsohn. His wheezing was erratic in the stillness. "Aches and pains nothing. You think I don't recognize cancer? My Hannah took ten years to die, Bernie. And near the end, when it was in her liver and bones, she looked like you."

"Well," replied Mendelsohn quietly, "I won't be that long. Not ten years. Not even one."

Green stepped instinctively forward to take his father's arm, but Sid did not waver. He flinched but kept his gaze on his friend.

"When did you learn?"

"Three weeks ago. The painkillers are strong, and they make me sleep a lot. But it won't be so long. Thank God it won't be long."

"So…" Sid murmured. "Bernie. Don't you think it's time to call Irving?"

"Irving? Why should I call Irving?"

"Because he's your son."

"Son! Sure. What do you think, Sid? That everyone has a son like Mishka here?" Mendelsohn wet his lips and drew a palsied hand across his chin. For a moment his eyes misted. "I should be so lucky. Mishka would not have left an old man to die alone. But not Irving Bigshot Mendelsohn. He had to go to the United States, no law firms good enough for him here in Canada. I know his kind. Only what they want matters, and the hell with the weak old father who just gets in the way."

So great was his bitterness that even Sid was alarmed. He looked pale when they left the apartment some minutes later. As he buckled his father into the car, Green picked his words carefully.

"I didn't know Irving very well because he was a couple of years ahead of me in school, but I seem to remember he was always a *putz*."

Sid sighed. "Yes, Irving had a big head, but it was not easy always to be Bernie's son."

Green glanced at him, wondering whether he should even stir up the memories. The two elderly men had more in common than widowhood; both had been in the camps, both had lost children there. "You mean Bernie's second son."

Green held his breath until his father replied. "Bernie doesn't talk about it, but they are there, always in his memory."

"They must have been very little when they died."

"And that makes them easier to forget?"

"No," Green soothed hastily. "What I meant was—how does he know how they would have turned out?"

"You have dreams for your child. You will see. You see in the baby the man he will become. Bernie has always loved you, Mishka. He sees you like the little boy he lost."

"What exactly did happen to his kids?"

As he asked, Green kept his eyes casually on the road, but he heard his father's breath catch in his throat. For a moment, Green thought he was actually going to answer, but then his father waved a peevish hand. "Watch the puddle. I don't want to step out in a puddle."

Skirting the slush, Green drew the car to a stop outside his father's apartment and got out to help him. The senior citizens' building was a bulky low-rise conveniently placed between a bakery and a drugstore. Sid had moved there under

24

protest eight years earlier when he could no longer manage the stairs, but his heart still lay with the little brick tenement in Lowertown where his son had grown up and his wife had slowly slipped away. Sid scowled now at the squat, ugly cube as if it were an alien thing.

"Are you going to be okay, Dad?"

"Sure, sure. Eighty-three years old. All my friends are dying. I can't walk even one block. My hands shake, I can't open a door. A man should thank God for such a life."

*   *   *

Green was surprised how unnerved he was by his father's words. Both his parents were Holocaust survivors who had lost all their family in the war, but as an only child Green had seen nothing bizarre about the strange hours of silence and the lonely isolation of the home in which he'd been raised. He'd seen their fatalism and their protective paranoia as an irritating restriction on his youthful urge for adventure, and it was only when he'd started reading about the Holocaust as an adult that he'd begun to wonder about the depths of their pain. But all his parents had ever afforded him, as now, was a distant glimpse.

Later that evening, once their son had been securely tucked into his crib, Green fixed Sharon and himself a cup of Earl Grey tea. With a grateful sigh he sank down beside her on the sofa and drew her into his arms. Slowly, between soothing sips of tea, he told her about the visit to Mendelsohn's apartment and his father's reaction.

"He almost talked about it, honey," he said. "It's the closest he's ever come to telling me anything, to saying he never forgets."

She snuggled against his chest and cradled her cup of tea.

Her eyes were half shut with fatigue, but her black curls bounced vigorously as she shook her head. "I'm sure he doesn't. I couldn't imagine losing Tony. I'd lose my mind. But your father, he's had loss after loss after loss."

The thought unsettled him, and he sipped his tea a moment to ponder. He remembered his father's reaction to the long months of his mother's dying. His mother had talked non-stop, even refusing morphine in order to stay alert, so desperate was she to cram twenty years of motherly advice into nine months. But his father had spent long, unnecessary hours at the factory and ceased to talk almost entirely. It was from his mother that Green had received his first glimpse into his father's past.

"Don't stop him from working," she said. "That's how he was in the camp after the war. Busy, busy, everything had to be just so. You stop, you think."

After her death, his father had sunk into a deep apathy from which he'd been roused only briefly by the birth of Green's daughter by his first marriage, who was named Hannah in her grandmother's memory. When Green's self-absorption torpedoed that marriage, Hannah had been yanked from both their lives by Green's irate first wife before either man had much chance to know her. Green winced now as he thought how he himself had been responsible for that loss.

Bit by bit, Green, with the help of the hopeful widows in the Jewish seniors' club, had coaxed his father back into a meagre social existence and into the companionship of his card-playing friends. And now even that was proving a mixed blessing.

Green sighed. "I hope Dad can bounce back. It must be hard watching everyone dying around you."

"And poor Bernie. He's had such a life too, and what a way to end it. With a crummy apartment, a handful of grumpy cronies and a son who doesn't care."

"I don't know that Irving doesn't care. He's got his own life, and Bernie's not the most approachable guy in the world. His motto was always 'You think God cares?' I know he's gone through a lot, but as a father I'm not sure he was the best."

"Was yours?" she countered. "For that matter, are you? Even without the scars of the Holocaust, we fail each other in so many ways. Because of our pride and our hurts. Bernie fails his son, his son fails him. Even me—am I everything I should be to my poor parents? They want to come up for Tony's birthday, and I put them off till Chanukah, because I don't have the energy to deal with them. We all have needs that no one can fill. People get busy with their own lives, so in the end, one way or another, the old all face death alone."

That thought stayed with him, reminding him of Eugene Walker, who had faced death alone at one o'clock in the afternoon in the middle of a busy hospital parking lot. Sullivan had dismissed him as just another old drunk, Donald Reid had called it a quick and painless heart attack, MacPhail a simple "natural causes." It was true it wasn't top priority on the major crimes docket, but there was still that niggling mystery of the head wound, and surely the end of a man's life—and the cause of that end—should be worth at least asking a few questions.

Three

November 7nd, 1939

Winter is young, just gathering strength.
It hurls through the flimsy walls
into the shed where we huddle at the end of the day.
Six strangers, made brothers by the whims of war.
We rouse the reluctant fire, and by its flame
I see my thoughts and fears in the strangers' eyes.
We are not safe, even here.
Rumours fly eastward on the wind,
of hangings, houses burning and young men,
Poles and Jews alike, kidnapped off the streets,
to stoke the Aryan madness.
She droops against my chest, too weary for words.
Sickness hollows her cheeks and dulls the flame of her hair.
I am fine, she says, and the women laugh.
Laugh. While outside, the Nazi winter descends.

"Mike, it's goddamn natural causes!" Brian Sullivan
exclaimed the next morning. "I closed the case yesterday."

"Did you or did you not get photos of the scene?"

"Ident did. Of course."

"Then just give me a peek. I'm not questioning your

28

judgment. I'm just playing inspector, okay? Reviewing the file. What's the problem?"

"Your imagination," Sullivan replied. "You've got that look in your eye."

"It's just a hunch, a piece missing in the puzzle. Humour me."

Sullivan gave him a long, wary look, then booted up his computer, inserted a CD and pulled up the photo file. Green scanned the photos quickly. Some were closeups of the body, others of the larger area. One gave a clear overview of the death scene, showing the placement of the body and the surrounding cars. Green squinted intently.

Chad had been right. The car next to the Dodge was a dark sedan, at first glance probably something GM. The licence plate was visible but too small to read even with maximum enlargement.

Within seconds he had the Ident Unit on the line, and a few minutes later, he was examining a digital enhancement of the licence plate. Triumphantly he ran the number through the computer and jotted down a name and address.

"Green, you don't think some guy knocked off the old man and then left his vehicle sitting there to show up in the police photos!"

Green cast Sullivan a look of exasperation as he pocketed his keys. "Lateral thinking skills, Sullivan. I'm looking for someone who might have witnessed something. This guy was parked beside Walker. Just a few quick questions, back before anyone even sees I'm gone," he added, already halfway out the door.

The owner of the car lived in an opulent brick house on a quiet crescent close to but sheltered from the crush of the city. In the drive a royal blue Buick LeSabre sat sleekly without a speck of slush or salt on its sides. Green examined the side mirror curiously as he passed by. It was also immaculate. Forensics would be little help there, he thought with resignation, because the car had obviously been washed since the storm. But the mirror was rounder and thicker than the wound on Walker's head, and more importantly, Walker's wound was deeper at the hairline than down towards his brow. For a car mirror to have inflicted that shape of wound, Walker would have had to fall onto it from the sky.

That's one for me, Green thought, as he rang the bell. Dr. Kopec had been on call the night before and was not pleased to be awakened, but the word "homicide" brought him clattering downstairs in his bathrobe. He consulted his appointment book to refresh his memory.

"Wednesday was the day of the storm. Yes, I remember, I arrived about noon. The parking lot was quite full, and I had to park near the end."

"Do you recall the car on your left?"

Dr. Kopec frowned as he tried to mobilize his brain cells without the benefit of caffeine. Slowly, he shook his head. "Not specifically, no."

"The body was found right beside your car. Between yours and the one on your left. When you pulled in, did you see the old man? Did you see anyone?"

Kopec was shaking his head. "I was late and in a hurry. The traffic on the Queensway had been terrible because of the storm. I just got out of the car and headed straight for the nearest entrance. But there was certainly no body."

"Did you see anyone inside the car?"

Kopec sat at the kitchen table staring at the flowered table cloth and frowning as he focussed his thoughts inward. Then he raised his head slowly. "I do remember something. As I was getting out of the car, I heard voices. Male voices. I glanced at the car—just idly, you know—but I couldn't see inside, because the windows were all frosted over. I didn't give it a second thought."

"Male voices. How many?"

"I couldn't tell. Two, perhaps? It was just a low rumble, but it sounded like different people."

"Could you make out any words?"

Slowly Kopec shook his head.

"What was the tone of the voices—happy, angry, conversational?"

"Something gave me the impression of anger. One voice rose for a moment. I heard several sharp words that sounded angry."

"What did they say?" Kopec was shaking his head. "Think!"

"I don't know. They may have been foreign."

Foreign? Green thought blankly. Eugene Walker was a retired Englishman who rarely left the sanctuary of his country retreat. What the hell would he be doing with a foreigner?

*   *   *

I don't care what MacPhail says, Green thought triumphantly as he left Kopec's house and dashed through the frigid air back to his car. The old man was murdered. No matter that all they really had was a snatch of conversation which could have been the radio and a fresh head wound minor enough to be sustained in the fall. All his instincts cried foul. As a police officer, he'd seen hundreds of beatings, and this looked all the world like a lead pipe brought down on the old man's head. And he'd heard enough evasions and subterfuge in his career to suspect that Walker's family was afraid of something.

He glanced at his watch. He'd told Sullivan he was only going for a quick jaunt, and he had to prepare for a meeting with the Crown attorneys in the afternoon. At this rate, he'd be lucky to get back to the station on time even without one more minor side trip. But he was already out in the west end, already halfway to the Reid house as it was. Half an hour more, that was all he needed.

* * *

"Murder!" Don Reid exclaimed. Green had summoned the family into the Reid living room and had plunged headlong into his theory, hoping to catch their first reactions. The son-in-law leaped to his feet, effectively placing himself between Green and the two women. This blocked Green's view of the widow, but he was able to see the expression of panic which flitted across the daughter's face before she brought it back under control.

"The idea hasn't occurred to you?" Green continued blandly.

"Why should it?" Don blustered. "The old man had one foot in the grave! Even the coroner says so."

"But someone might have helped him."

"Why! What could anyone have to gain?"

"Precisely my question, Mr. Reid."

A shocked silence descended on the family as Don Reid eyed Green, speechless. After a minute, he snorted in derision. "That's ridiculous. Eugene was a recluse, he never saw anyone. He had no friends any more, and he wasn't involved in any activities where he could have made enemies. Right, Ruth?"

Ruth Walker was staring at Green in dismay, and he felt a twinge of pity. He didn't like putting her through this.

"What makes you think he was murdered?"

"I have to investigate all angles, Mrs. Walker."

His evasion deepened her confusion. "Then you're not saying he was or wasn't?"

"I can't."

His bluntness brought colour to her cheeks, and when she saw he was still awaiting an answer, she cast about in bewilderment. "I really can't think what anyone had to gain. Eugene saw no one but the family. He's been retired fifteen years, and even before that he kept to himself."

"Who knew you were going to the hospital that day?"

"No one, except Margaret and Don, of course. But no one would have known he was in the car. Unless…unless it was a stranger—I mean, a robbery, or…"

"It's possible, but for the sake of my paperwork, I'd like to explore some background. First of all, what did your husband do before he retired?"

"We owned a hardware shop in Renfrew. It was a small family business, and it gave us a comfortable living, but nothing more. We sold it when Eugene got too…" She hesitated. "Too tired to handle it. We made enough money from the sale to buy a house in the country. He wasn't especially fond of crowds."

"Did he speak any foreign languages, or know someone who did?"

"Well, he was—" Don began, but Ruth held up her hand. Sharply, Green thought.

But her voice was sweet. "Why on earth do you ask that, Inspector?"

"Because he was overheard speaking to someone in the car before he died."

Ruth grew very still. "Someone foreign?"

"Possibly."

"I have no idea—" she faltered. "No one knew he was in town."

"Ruth," Don burst in, "you don't know the half of what Eugene does. There are lots of Poles and Germans out in the Renfrew area where you live."

"But they're all third or fourth generation Canadians."

"Some of the old-timers still speak their language. And what about that guy who—"

"There must be some mistake." Ruth rose, brisk with purpose. "Goodness, look at the time! Howard and Rachel's plane will be in soon."

Green glanced at Don, who shrugged his apology. Don knows something, Green thought, but now is not the time to pursue it. "Who are Howard and Rachel?" he asked instead.

Ruth sat down with visible relief. "My son and his wife. They live in Montreal—Howard's just finished his residency at the Montreal Neurological Institute—but he's been in Toronto at a conference, and Margaret only managed to reach them today."

Green looked at the daughter, who had been staring out the window as if in a trance. She jerked her head around at the mention of her name, and Green saw her flinch. Something is definitely off-kilter in this family, he thought.

"Just to help me get the whole picture," he said affably, "I'd like some background on the family. Howard's married—any children?"

Ruth answered for the lot of them. Howard and Rachel had no children yet, but Don and Margaret had been married twenty years and had two sons. Don was in business, although she was vague on the details.

Don was sitting in the corner, jiggling his legs restlessly. "I work for a management consulting firm," he interjected brusquely. "Although I don't see what relevance it has."

"Probably none," Green said cheerfully. "Just getting the whole picture. Margaret, do you work outside the home?"

Margaret's eyes were fixed on her husband, and for a moment she merely nodded before finding her voice. "Part time. I'm a nurse at the Civic—casual relief. I'm trying to upgrade myself."

"Try psychiatry. It's a nice, cushy job."

He had meant it as a joke; his four years with Sharon had taught him how mistaken that stereotype was. Psychiatric nursing was intense, emotionally draining work. But Margaret was clearly not up to jokes.

"I wouldn't have the patience," she replied. "Or the emotional stamina."

Green studied her for moment. She was pale, and a shredded Kleenex was wrapped around her quivering fingers. He wondered whether it was simply grief, or something more. She seemed frightened, and Green sensed she was withholding something too. But with her husband and mother standing guard, it would be futile to press her. He jotted the thought down for future use and turned back to the widow.

"Did Mr. Walker have a will?"

He threw the question out quickly, hoping to catch someone off guard, but Ruth did not miss a beat. A woman used to surprises, he wondered? Or used to covering up?

"Yes, he did. It's back at the country house. Once Howard arrives, we'll drive out to get it. Not that there's much in it. We have no real money. Just the house and ten thousand in investment certificates which I'd managed to put aside for…well, for our old age, in case we needed care."

A clatter from the corner of the room startled them. Don

had placed his drink on the table. The guy's tight as a drum, Green thought, and jotted that thought down too for future use before retrieving his line of questioning.

"What about the sale of the hardware store? Didn't that bring in some money?"

Ruth coloured slightly. "No, there were some debts. Those were hard economic times everywhere, and…"

Don roused himself from the corner. "And Eugene drank everything away, Ruth. Why don't you simply say so!"

"Don, please. Under the circumstances…" Ruth tried to silence him again, but this time he shook his head.

"If the cop thinks it might be murder, then he should know what kind of a guy Eugene was. He was a drunk. You know it, I know it, and Howard knows it. Hell, even this cop knows it. He's probably seen the autopsy report! The reason you're stuck with no money now is because the bastard drank it all away."

Margaret leaned forward and reached for the tea pot. "Inspector, some more tea?"

He looked at her in surprise. "No, thanks."

Ruth had not taken her eyes off Don. "You children don't know what he's been through. He's had a hard life."

Don rolled his eyes. "Oh, here we go again. The old war trauma."

"Yes! The war."

"Ruth, the war's been over for almost sixty years!"

"For the men who were in it, it is never over," she retorted.

"My father fought in the war," Don replied. "It didn't turn him into a drunk."

Unexpectedly, Margaret burst into tears. She slammed down the tea pot and whirled to her husband. "He's dead! Can't you let up on him just for once! He's gone now!" With that she hurried out of the room.

*   *   *

Striding through the major crimes squad room, Green caught Sullivan's eye and gestured to his office. Once inside, he dropped the bag he was carrying on the desk and extracted two juicy smoked meat sandwiches from Nate's Delicatessen. He handed one to his subordinate with a sheepish grin.

"Minor detour. Food to feed the brain cells."

"I'd say they're overfed already, at least the imagination part," Sullivan replied, picking up the three-inch thick masterpiece. Chunks of succulent meat tumbled from his grasp. "Cough it up, Green. Let's get this over with. The Crowns will be pacing."

With quick, deft strokes, Green filled him in while they ate. "I tell you, there's a lot more to the Walker family than meets the eye."

Sullivan was sprawled in the chair opposite, his huge feet taking up most of the spare space on Green's desk. "Not really anything that points to murder, though."

"Oh, come on! We've got a long-suffering wife, a son-in-law who doesn't buy the family's pact of secrecy, a daughter caught in the middle and an old recluse slowly drinking his family's savings away. A lot of strange, repressed passions in the air, Brian."

Sullivan chewed awhile, then shrugged. "Just an ordinary day down on the farm, buddy."

Green glanced up from picking stray bits of meat from the wrapper, surprised by Sullivan's tone. "What's that supposed to mean?"

"Nothing." Sullivan shook his head as if to banish an irritation. "Nothing. Just thinking what the hell is normal anyway."

Green snorted. "That's fine, go philosophical on me. But

something is fishy. Margaret's scared, Don's scared, and even the old lady's hiding something. I intend to find out what." He licked the last of the juice from his fingers, then rose and stuck his head out his door. To his relief he spotted the very person he needed. Constable Bob Gibbs had been with CID for over a year but still jumped like a startled rabbit whenever Green pounced on him, which he did with alarming regularity. No one was more obsessive and dogged with details than Bob Gibbs. The young man listened, jotted down the strange request without missing a stroke and disappeared behind his computer.

Sullivan eyed Green warily. "And while you have poor Gibbs running around after old war records, what else do you have up your sleeve?"

Green smiled. "You and I are going to Renfrew."

"Now? Are you crazy? The Crowns are waiting."

"After the Crowns. It's the next logical step in the investigation."

Sullivan picked up his sandwich wrapper, crunched it into a ball and lobbed it over the desk, hitting the basket dead centre. "Forget it, Mike. I've got some statements to review, then I'm going home. Home. Where all good family men should be around supper time."

"How about tomorrow?"

Sullivan removed his feet from the desk and stood up to leave. "Tomorrow's Saturday. My day off, remember? A day when all good family men...you know the drill."

Green followed him out, trying to quell his frustration. Sullivan was right; the meeting with the Crown attorneys would take all afternoon, and it was too late to set up a trip to Renfrew that day anyway. As for tomorrow, Sullivan was also right. Green couldn't run his life as if he were the only one in it. Walker's case would still be around Monday.

But Fate would not let the case slip from his mind for that long. No sooner had he returned to his office later that afternoon when his phone buzzed. Mr. Donald Reid was downstairs in the foyer, requesting to see him, the desk sergeant said.

Surprise, surprise.

Green ushered Don Reid into an empty interview room and took out his notebook expectantly. Don had clearly not relaxed one iota since Green's visit out to the house. He drummed his fingers on his thigh and shifted from one side of his chair to the other as he looked for a place to begin.

"You have some information for me?" Green prompted.

"Yeah. Look, I'm not trying to badmouth Eugene, but if you're thinking he may have been murdered—well, there's a lot Ruth will never tell you. She's so protective, and she can never see the other side of him."

"What do you mean?"

"Well, he's a complex guy, and there are things that went on that Ruth didn't know anything about. I think he could have known people and done things that he kept secret."

"Like what?" Green demanded, getting tired of the vagueness.

"Like talking with someone in his car the day he died. Ruth thinks he doesn't know anybody foreign, but the truth is— before they moved to the country, every Saturday he'd go drinking at this bar in Renfrew. He had a whole life there that he never told Ruth about, and he must have met guys there. Twenty years ago, just as an example, he got in a fight. The police were involved. You guys probably have it on your computer, if you want to check."

Green's ears perked up, but he kept his expression deadpan.

Contrary to common belief, the police didn't have Joe Public's every little transgression on their national database, and each jurisdiction guarded its own cases jealously. "Why don't you tell me about it? Save me the trouble of tracking it down."

Don waved his hand as if to distance himself. "Eugene beat somebody up. Bar fight. I don't know that much about it. Eugene never talked about it, and he never said why it happened."

"Did he get in a lot of bar fights?"

"No, that's the thing. When he drank he usually got morose and surly. He'd say bitter, vicious things, but I never knew him to use his fists." Don's words began to flow faster, as if his pent-up thoughts had just been released. "It was a surprise to me when Ruth called and said he'd been arrested for beating up a man in a bar."

"So tell me what you did learn."

"Well, in those days he was a weekend drunk. The hardware store would close at six o'clock on Saturday, and Eugene would head for Paddy's Bar and Grill on Raglan Street for a couple to unwind. That couple would stretch to seven or eight, and he'd usually roll into the house at two in the morning when the bar closed. He'd spend Sunday nursing a hangover with more booze and Monday sleeping it off."

"Did he hang out with a particular group at Paddy's place?"

Don shrugged. "Eugene wasn't a party animal, but Renfrew's a small town, and it was probably the same crowd of serious drinkers who closed the place each Saturday. They drank, watched the hockey game, argued about sports." He made no attempt to keep the contempt out of his voice. "The night of the fight, one of the local farmers brought along his cousin from out of town—Hamilton, I think—who was visiting the family. This cousin and Eugene exchanged words

40

—no one knows what it was about—and suddenly Eugene jumped him. He threw him against the bar and started beating the shit out of him. The others broke it up as fast as they could, but it put the guy in the hospital. Eugene was charged, but I don't know what happened to the case. He probably got off." Don shook his head, and his lips curled in a curious sneer.

"You didn't like your father-in-law, did you?"

Don shifted in his chair edgily. "Does that make me a suspect?"

"No more than anyone else at this point," Green said amiably.

"Eugene was a cold, self-absorbed bastard. My wife suffered a lot because of him, and I get sick of the whole family making excuses for him."

"What was he like as a father?"

"Unpredictable. That was the worst of it, really. If he had always acted like a cold, disinterested bastard, his kids might have been able to write him off and get on with their lives. But he'd dole out these tiny morsels of love at unexpected times, and it kept them coming back for more."

"That's a classic abuser's technique. Keep 'em guessing, keep 'em hoping, but afraid. It's a powerful way to control people."

Don nodded his head slowly up and down, and his edginess dissipated. "Yeah, that was Eugene. And it left its mark on Margie. She's so goddamn unsure of herself. The least hint of trouble, she crumbles. I don't have the patience for all this love and understanding shit, Inspector. I mean—not that I don't believe in love, but I figure you've got to take what life gives you and get on with it. None of this I-can't-be-a-decent-human-being-because-of-what-I-went-through-in-the-war crap. I mean, if we had that attitude, we'd let all the crooks out on the

41

streets and you'd be out of a job, right?" He grinned, but when Green did not join him, he sat forward as if preparing to leave.

"Did Howard have the same insecurities as his sister?"

Don sat back in the seat again. "Howard was trying to write him off and get on with his life. But Eugene still played him like a trout on the line. Even three hundred kilometres away, the hook is well set. The poor kid is going to kill himself trying to be everything his father was not."

*   *   *

After Reid left, Green ran Eugene Walker's name through the police computer, hoping at least to find out the outcome of the assault charge. But as he feared, there was nothing. The Canadian Police Information Centre coughed up no record of the case at all, merely one conviction of impaired driving five years earlier, which had resulted in suspension of his licence. Whatever had transpired between Walker and the visitor from Hamilton, only the Renfrew police files would tell. If they even still existed.

It was Friday night, and November darkness had long since set in. Green locked up and hastened out to begin the homeward trek before he was hopelessly late for Shabbat dinner. The trek to Barrhaven took an incredibly long time, he'd discovered in the two months they'd lived there. He called the suburb the End of the Earth and had only moved there as a concession to Sharon, who wanted clean air, safe streets and a house that wasn't falling apart. They'd acquired that, plus a fifty-minute commute across the cornfields of the Greenbelt, then along the congested Queensway that traversed the city.

He hated it. Hated sitting in his car crawling from red light to red light. Hated living in a plastic cookie-cutter house on a postage-stamp sized lot with a few twigs for trees and endless acres of baby carriages as far as the eye could see. He was an inner city boy raised in the crumbling brick tenements of Lowertown. The rooftops had been his playground and the narrow alleys perfect for a pick-up game of hockey. Pick-up hockey was against the law on the back crescents of Barrhaven.

His suburban neighbours were all ten years younger than him, fresh-faced high techies or junior company managers with their foot on the bottom rung of the ladder and their eyes on the top. Unlike him, they didn't have ex-wives and hefty support payments for a teenager who'd been forced into every West Coast therapy her desperate mother could find. All for being the same type of ornery, restless teenager he'd been, Green suspected. No doubt his ex-wife was trying to eradicate even the remotest gene that tied the girl to him.

That night it was brittly cold and the road was a icy sheet as he nudged his car into the traffic jam on the Queensway. Red tail lights danced in the swirls of exhaust that stretched ahead forever. With a sigh he slipped in a Tragically Hip CD and let his mind roam. Usually the Hip put his mind in a mellow, meandering mood. But not tonight. Tonight his mind was like a hound on the scent.

It headed straight back to the case. What had really happened in that bar twenty years earlier? What foreigner had Walker talked to on the afternoon of his death? And were the two events linked? So many questions, and no one interested in the answers but Green.

Saturday was his day off as well as Sullivan's. Tony's first birthday was coming up later in the week, and Green had been planning to spend the weekend getting ready for the big celebration, to which Sharon seemed to be inviting half the neighbourhood. The house sported a few pieces of furniture from their old one-bedroom apartment, but it was entirely without decor. Sharon had a long list of chores for him to perform, which included painting and picture hanging to be completed in time for the birthday party. He knew she was right, and he owed her that much, despite his aversion to the Dreaded Vinyl Cube. But given his facility and enthusiasm for household chores, he suspected Tony would be married and moved out before he made it to the bottom of the list.

Given a choice between painting walls or chasing murder, if it were up to Green, there would be no contest. Renfrew beckoned. And the lure of a puzzle waiting to be solved.

Four

February 10th, 1940

In my mind the bayonet pricks me still.
I've cleared rubble from the square for three days,
barehanded and hatless in the bloodied snow.
German orders pummelled my ears, their bayonets spurred me on.
As I lie against the soft swell of her belly,
her fingers probe, her tongue clucks.
She will not lose me to German sport, she says.
Already fear and death have taken half of us.
Henryk arrives with bread stolen right off a Nazi truck.
He roams everywhere, hears everything.
As she feeds me, he smiles
And tells of a farm in the rolling hills far from town.
The farmer reads the pain in my eyes, takes my hand gently.
By planting time, he says, you'll be strong again.

At eight o'clock Saturday morning, Green and Sullivan were headed west along Highway 17 towards Renfrew. The sun lay pale and cold on the horizon behind them, and the rolling fields and scrub on either side were blanketed with snow.

"I don't believe I'm doing this," Sullivan muttered as he accelerated around a slow-moving pick-up. "What the hell am

I doing here with you, Green?"

"The valley's your turf, and I need your experience. You think they're going to talk to a city boy like me?"

"And what the hell are you doing here? You should be home with your wife and son."

"I promised Sharon and him this evening and the whole day tomorrow. I even promised to paint the living room." Green had practically had to sell his soul, but he didn't admit that to Sullivan. Sullivan loved his home, and to him, fun was a weekend spent finishing the basement or restaining the deck. Fifteen years of listening to Sullivan's do-it-yourself tales had almost put Green off home ownership for good.

Sullivan turned off the main highway and wove expertly down the narrow country road toward Renfrew. After a few minutes of silence, he shrugged. "Well, she'd better not be holding her breath."

Green had no time to think up a comeback before they pulled onto the main street crammed with little shops, and he had to turn his attention to finding the OPP station. The Ontario Provincial Police were housed in the Town Hall, a self-consciously impressive brick building set back behind the town's war memorial. Inside the grand exterior, the reception area of the OPP was little more than a closet. On the other side of a glass window, a huge uniformed officer was wedged into one of the chairs behind a desk, sipping coffee. He glanced through the glass as the two detectives came in, then leaped to his feet, eyes lighting up.

"Jesus, Mary and Joseph! Brian Sullivan!"

"Kennelly!" Sullivan had time to reply before the door flung back, and he was clasped into a thumping embrace. When the two separated, Kennelly looked him up and down. They were the same height, broad shouldered and powerfully built, although Kennelly's midriff sagged even lower than Sullivan's. He grinned with delight.

"What're you doing back here? Thought you hated these parts."

"Back for my adrenaline fix," Sullivan laughed. "I'm with Ottawa CID. This is Mike Green."

Sullivan slipped the introductions by casually, without reference to Green's rank, which would have torpedoed any chance for collegial solidarity. As Green had hoped, Kennelly engulfed his hand in a friendly iron grip, tossed in a greeting, then swung back to Sullivan with a laugh. "Will you look at you! I couldn't believe it when I heard you were a cop! I thought you were going off to the big city to make a million."

Sullivan grinned ruefully. "Well, I made it to the big city, anyway."

"I used to play football with this guy," Kennelly said to Green. "We went to the same high school up in Eganville, and I tell you he was one fine mean ball player. I heard you married Mary Connolly. That still on?"

Sullivan nodded. "Three kids too."

"Oh well, you always were a good Catholic boy. Fell in love with the first girl you laid eyes on and then never looked at another." He shook his massive head mockingly. "Boy, I tell you, it's a small world. So is this a social call, or are you boys here to learn a thing or two?"

"A man named Eugene Walker used to own a hardware store here," Sullivan asked. "Did you know him?"

"No, but maybe my partner did. He's been here since the Great Flood." Kennelly led them inside and bellowed in the direction of the back room. "Tom! Come out and meet a buddy of mine."

A smaller, older man emerged from an office behind the

main desk and came forward, smiling expectantly. Once the introductions were complete, Sullivan explained their mission.

"Yeah, I knew him," Tom Wells said. "In a small town like this, you get to know pretty near everyone. Walker wasn't a troublemaker, he kept to himself pretty much. I'm not sure we can be much help to you up here. When I heard he died, I asked around to see if anybody'd heard from them recently, just out of curiosity, you know? 'Cause I used to get my fishing and hunting gear at his shop. But no one seen much of them since they moved out to the country."

Green spoke for the first time. "I understand he had an assault charge, maybe twenty years ago. Any chance there's still a file on that?"

Tom Wells scrunched his craggy, sun-weathered face in an effort to remember, then shook his head. "We don't keep stuff that long, and in that case, the charge was dropped."

"So you remember the case?"

"Yeah, I was the one took the call," Wells said. "I remember I was surprised. Eugene was a regular at Paddy's place on Saturday nights. There were more than a few times when me and my partner had to bring him home and put him to bed. But he was a quiet drunk. Never got into fights, never bothered anybody. So I thought it was kind of strange. In fact, I asked him about it. I didn't want to lay an assault charge, and I was hoping he'd tell me why he did it, but he never said a word. Just said he'd had one too many, his mistake."

"Why were the charges dropped?"

"The fellow he assaulted wouldn't press charges. I tried to persuade him to—I mean, when Eugene wouldn't give any excuse. The fellow was a visitor, and I had a bar full of drinkers waiting to see if I was going to apply the law. But nobody would say a word if Dubroskie and his cousin weren't going to.

48

In this town, everybody minds everybody else's business, including the cops'."

"Dubroskie?"

"Local farmer, good man. Cousin's name was something unpronounceable. Polish, began with G."

"So what did this Mr. G. say about it?"

"Nothing," Wells said with a shrug. "He was an immigrant, heavy accent, seemed awful confused. Apologizing all over the place if he'd upset anybody."

Immigrant! Green hid his excitement as another possible piece of the puzzle slipped into place. "And Dubroskie? Did he or anyone else in the family have any idea what was going on?"

Wells shrugged his shoulders. "I've known the Dubroskies all my life. Family's owned a farm west of town since the pioneer days. I went to high school with Karl, and my kids went to high school with Karl's kids. We never been close friends, because here in the valley, the oldtimers tended to stick with their own. Poles with Poles, Irish with Irish. And people kept the secrets within their own group, you know? I mean, the Poles might fight like cats and dogs among themselves and one family hate another's guts, but a Protestant Welshman like myself is never going to find out why."

"So you think people are hiding something about this assault, but only a Pole is going to find out what it is. But Walker's British—why would he keep an insider's secret?"

Sergeant Wells' eyes widened. "Walker? Are you kidding? He was Polish!"

It was Green's turn to be surprised. "Are you sure?"

"Of course I'm sure! He had an accent thick enough to cut with a knife. He came here after the war."

"But his wife… And his name…"

"The wife's British, you're right. Fine lady. We always

figured he took her name. When he first came, there was quite a stir in the Polish community. I remember my father talking about it. Back then, the communities around here were very traditional—you'd know that, Brian—everyone had their place. Walker fitted nowhere. His wife was British and a Protestant, and the Poles thought he'd turned his back on his Polish roots when he changed his name. Plus he would never talk Polish. He would never talk about the old country. He was one of them, but he avoided them. Him and his wife didn't really fit in anywhere."

Green turned to Sullivan. "Call Gibbs. He's looking into Walker's war record. Get him to check immigration too and have the reports ready when we get back."

*   *   *

"Why are you so interested in a twenty-year-old barroom brawl, Mike?" Sullivan took his eyes off the narrow country road long enough to glance questioningly at Green. They were on their way out to the Walkers' country house, having left a disappointed pair of OPP officers behind at the station. Sullivan had seen the curiosity in Kennelly's eyes and had tried to persuade Green to let them participate in the inquiries, since it seemed a slow day in Renfrew County, but Green was adamant. He didn't want extra officers he didn't know trampling all over the evidence in the house. The extent of Green's diplomacy had been to assign the officers the task of setting up interviews for them in the afternoon with people who knew the Walkers.

"Because it's out of character with what we've learned about Walker," Green replied, "and it seems to be a mystery. Maybe his neighbours and acquaintances can shed some light on what he was really like."

"They won't tell us a thing, I can guarantee you that. A couple of big city cops barging in out of nowhere? Forget it."

Green grinned at him. "Give me some credit."

The directions Ruth Walker had supplied were clear and precise, but even so, after the fourth turn into progressively narrower back roads, Green was glad Sullivan was behind the wheel. All around them stretched nothing but drifting snow, icy fields and the grey lace of barren trees against the sky. Ruth had been surprised when the two officers had asked her permission to search the house, but she had not hesitated an instant. If she had anything to hide, Green thought, she seemed confident it wouldn't be found.

When they finally turned into the long, narrow lane, they saw the Walkers' white clapboard cottage set in a windswept clearing at the end. It looked shabby and neglected in the harsh morning sun, and as they drew nearer, Green saw it was badly in need of paint. Sullivan plowed up the lane, parked about fifty feet from the house and surveyed the snowy expanse stretching to the house. At first glance, it seemed to be unbroken except for the tire tracks leading from the shed to the front door and then to the lane.

But as they began their approach on foot, Green suddenly held up his hand.

"Don't move!" He squatted in the snow, peered at the tracks, then took out his notebook and glanced up excitedly.

"Come look at this! Carefully! What does this look like to you?"

Sullivan studied the marks in the snow. Inside the tracks, at roughly two foot intervals, the tire markings were blurred in an oval shape. "Like someone has smudged the tire track. To wipe out something?"

Green's eyes narrowed speculatively. "The tire tracks are partially erased by the wind and snow, and that stopped about noon Wednesday. Before Walker was even discovered dead. But these marks are clear. Someone has walked in this tire tread since the snow stopped, and has tried to smudge over the footprint as they went. Which suggests someone has been out to the house since the Walkers left but tried to conceal that fact. Do you still think his death was natural causes?"

Sullivan backed up carefully. "I'll get the camera."

Thirty minutes later, they had a roll of detailed photos of the tracks leading up to the house and of the footprints in the snow at the front door. One set of partially obliterated prints with a deeply treaded sole led from the front door and trampled around in an aimless circle before disappearing at the edge of the tire track. Suspecting the prints were Eugene Walker's, Green made a note to check his boot soles. Inside two of these large boot prints were the remnants of smudged smaller prints again, leading towards the house. These too had been carefully brushed over in an attempt to erase them. Someone had been very, very careful.

Curious, Green bent to scrutinize the front door, but there were no scratches to suggest forced entry. Using a key provided by Ruth Walker, he eased the door open and stepped inside, scanning the hall rapidly for signs of intrusion or disturbance. There were none. The house was quiet and neat. Sullivan took fifteen minutes to photograph every aspect of it before they put on latex gloves and began the search. Methodically they made their way through the small house, sketching and making notes. The front door opened into a small living room on the right with a fireplace at the far end and a door through to the kitchen and pantry beyond. Upstairs were three doors, the first leading into the bathroom and the other two into bedrooms. The furniture in all the rooms was old and frayed, testimony to the Walkers' limited budget, but the slip covers had been assiduously darned and redarned. The bookcases were handmade by an inexpert carpenter, and the piano keys were yellow with age and wear.

Green tapped the keys idly and was surprised that the sound was still rich and warm, evoking memories of his own mother, not withered by disease but vibrant and tireless as she'd been in his youth, coaxing melody from the leaden fingers of the children on the block. Or all alone at night, after the day's work, racing her fingers over the keys for hours for the sheer rapture of the sound.

He moved on to study the titles in the bookcase curiously. There was a large collection of British mysteries ranging from Agatha Christie to P.D. James, an aging leather-bound collection of Dickens, a sampling of Atwood, Shields and Robertson Davies, and a shelf of Romantic poets. These all suggested the refined feminine taste of Ruth Walker. There was a corner of gardening and bird-watching books which Green also intuitively connected to Ruth, and another small shelf of best-selling spy thrillers of a more masculine genre. Wedged in the corner was a faded black Bible, St. James version. Green opened it to see the inscription on the inner cover in quilled black ink. *"To our beloved daughter Ruth, London 1932"*.

The Bible, despite its age, did not look much used. As Green flipped through it, a brittle, yellowed square of folded paper fell out. It was a letter, dated Feb. 26, 1947, and written in the same elegant, old-fashioned hand as the bible's inscription.

Dearest Ruth,
Your father and I received your letter of Christmas time

and although we are delighted that you have found new friends and new purpose in your work down there, we urge you not to move too quickly without ensuring that any relationship is firmly founded in mutual interests and values. You are young now, and full of hope and the desire to heal, but two wars have taught your father and me that there are differences between people, differences in upbringing, outlook and values which may loom large once the initial excitement has had a chance to calm. As well, we don't know what these people have endured and how deeply they may be scarred.

This is not to dampen your enthusiasm nor to deter your generous nature, but rather to temper it with care, lest you suffer again the pain which I am sure is still all too fresh.

Enough said of prudence. Things are still very hard in the city, with long queues and shortages, and people still homeless. The winter has been very hard on your father and his cough is much worse. I only hope that we can come down to see you when spring arrives, for the sun and the sea air would do him good. I don't believe he has ever recovered from Albert—Lord knows I never shall—and the sorrow saps his strength. But we shall manage, my dear, and we count the days until we can visit you. All our love,

Mother

Pensively, Green turned the letter over in his hands. By itself, it was a mere fragment of history, yet it added one small piece to the mystery of Walker's life. He called Sullivan over to photograph it, and then he replaced it and the Bible carefully back into place. He and Sullivan then searched through every book on the shelves. If a book could be used as a storage place once, why not twice? But they found nothing, either there or in the rest of the cluttered room.

Next they moved up to the larger bedroom. It had been intended as a master bedroom, but they found only men's clothing in the closets and drawers. Ruth's clothing was next door in the smaller bedroom.

"Looks like they slept apart," Green muttered.

"It's not much fun sleeping with a drunk. He probably crashed around a lot and got up in the middle of the night to piss."

"Check the desk drawer for those investment certificates Mrs. Walker mentioned."

Sullivan opened the drawer of a battered maple desk and found it crammed full of papers—mortgage agreements, house deeds, sales receipts, most over five years old. He found the certificates inside a folder and counted them carefully.

"Eight."

"Eight?" Green said. "There are supposed to be ten."

Sullivan counted again. "There aren't."

Green raised an eyebrow. "Two thousand bucks. If this was a robbery, why not take all ten?"

"Maybe he was hoping they wouldn't be missed. Remember how careful the person was to erase their tracks."

Green shook his head. "Or maybe they weren't stolen. At least not then. Leave them out. I'll try to get Ident up here for fingerprinting. And I want to check up on Don Reid's finances—"

Sullivan frowned. "Why him?"

Green was remembering Don's reaction the day before when the investment certificates were mentioned. "Just a hunch."

"Two thousand bucks isn't much of a motive for murder."

"Depends on how desperate you are," Green countered,

rifling through the shoe boxes on the floor of the closet. "Remember the junkies who kill for one more fix, or the winos—"

"Yeah, but we're not talking about drug dealers and bums here, Mike. This guy lives in Arlington Woods and drives a BMW. Two thousand bucks is peanuts to him."

"Maybe. But something is wrong. Margaret is scared, and Don's trying to put me on another track. Let's just see what turns up."

They found nothing else of interest in Eugene's bedroom. Ruth's smaller bedroom had another desk with all the recent bills and receipts, neatly bundled and labelled. Their bank balance was modest, but in the black.

Sullivan grunted. "Better than mine. Lizzie wants to take up downhill skiing with the school this winter, but you should see the price of the equipment. And that's just one kid! Wait till my littlest starts wanting to be a goalie like his brother."

"Cheer up, Brian. Look, I'll be sixty-five by the time I pay off that little vinyl-sided cube I bought at the End of the Earth." Green turned for one last glance around the room before closing the door. "Check out the kitchen while I do the basement."

Downstairs he found a ceiling bulb controlled by a chain and turned it on to reveal a dank, cobwebby cellar. The corners were stacked with the relics of a lifetime—old bicycles, buggies, broken chairs, a sewing machine, boxes of old clothes. Green tried to dig through the clutter and immediately began to sneeze.

The hell with this, he thought to himself. No one's been near this stuff in ten years. He was just about to leave when something caught his eye. He had moved some boxes and a card table aside, and in the process uncovered three cartons which looked less dusty than the rest. Pulling them out into the room, he opened them to reveal thirty-two quarts of cheap Scotch whiskey. Surprised, he called Sullivan down to photograph them.

"So this is where the old man kept his stash!" Brian observed. "Jesus, there must be almost five hundred bucks of whiskey in there."

Green closed the boxes and stepped back, dusting off his gloves. "Let's get Ident to fingerprint this stuff too. I'd like to know who brought it in here. It's too heavy for Ruth, even if she did want to feed her husband's habit. And I don't think Walker could have carried it, either, in his poor health."

The two men began back up the stairs. "Find anything in the kitchen?" Green asked.

"It was easy to search," Sullivan replied. "Nice, neat lady. Not a packrat like her husband seems to be. I bet he wouldn't let her throw out one damn thing in the basement there when they moved. Looks like they ate simply but managed okay. I didn't find anything weird. Except this," he remarked almost as an afterthought, picking up a small black box from the kitchen table. Inside were some rusty instruments and a bunch of oversized keys. "I found it at the back of the pantry. Looks like an old tool box that hasn't been used in at least ten years. I found a newer tool box in the cupboard over the fridge with the usual screwdrivers and wrenches in it."

Green examined the pantry from which the box had been removed. A rim of dust and grime marked the spot where the box had long sat undisturbed. It was virtually hidden behind household cleaning equipment, bottled drinks and cans—all dust free, fresh-looking, and neatly arranged by contents. By contrast, the rusty old tool box seemed out of place.

Green carried the box over to the window. On closer examination it looked more like a small metal storage box painted black with a hand-painted border of coloured flowers barely visible beneath the rust and the grime. It had a small lock like a jewelry box, but it was broken. Inside the box was an old rusted screwdriver with a badly worn wooden handle, a hammer of similar vintage, a hand gimlet and a pair of blackened pliers.

"Jeez, these tools look really ancient," Green muttered, turning the hammer over in his hands. "I know the guy owned a hardware store, but was he into antiques?"

"They remind me of some old tools I found in the back of the barn once when I was a kid. My mother said they were used by the early farmers who settled the valley in the nineteenth century. Handmade by a blacksmith—that's what gives them the primitive look."

"Let's take them back to town and see if we can get any information on them." Green turned his attention back to the black box. He turned it over, scrutinizing the metal carefully. On the bottom, in the corner, he found what he was seeking—a name. Kressman, Ozorkow.

"Ozorkow. Sounds Polish," he muttered. Then to his surprise, he felt the bottom shift and as he turned the box over, a false bottom came away in his hand. In the tiny space between the inner and outer plates, he found a small, tattered booklet. Inside, it was covered in cramped, foreign script. He flipped through it, then gasped.

"Fuck! This could be why Walker didn't fit in with the Polish community. This is a goddamn German identity card!"

*   *   *

Back in the car, heading down the lane to the highway, Green sat in the passenger seat and pored over the document. The black metal box and the rolls of film sat on the seat behind them. The Ottawa Ident Unit had been called to come up to dust the house and check out the tracks in the snow.

"Jeez, this language has long words. My German's not the greatest, but it's a lot like Yiddish. I can't understand everything, but enough to tell that these papers belong to a Wilhelm Ganz from Potsdam, and he's some kind of rank in the Wehrmacht. Unterfeldwebel or something."

"Walker a Kraut? Do you think Mrs. Walker would lie about something like that?"

"I wonder if she even knew. If he'd even tell her. After two world wars, the Brits hated the Germans' guts."

Sullivan whistled. "Boy, that would be some secret to keep from her."

"Still think this is just an old stiff in a parking lot?"

Sullivan smiled. "An interesting old stiff, that's for sure." He drew the car to a halt at the end of the lane and scanned the highway in both directions. On one side, a multi-gabled red brick farmhouse could be seen far in the distance. On the other side, nothing but fields of stubbled corn half buried in white. But across the highway, about two hundred yards further west, stood a white clapboard Victorian farmhouse with a sagging veranda and a steeply pitched tin roof. It had never aspired to greatness but had clearly seen better times.

"Where to, boss?"

"Neighbours," Green said, pointing to the Victorian farmhouse. "Let's start right there."

Green and Sullivan mounted the wooden veranda with trepidation as the splintered boards moaned beneath their weight. Black paint peeled from the door, which proudly sported a shiny new brass door knob. Odd the priorities some people have, Green thought.

His knock was answered immediately by a middle-aged woman bent from hard work but still brisk in her movements. She had a broad Slavic face, steel-wool hair forced haphazardly into a bun, and deep-set, sun-parched blue eyes which bored through the detectives warily as they settled on the aging parlour couch. In the corner, a smoky black woodstove was turning the claustrophobic room into a sauna. Oblivious, the woman hugged a cardigan around her and folded her arms across her chest.

"I don't know my neighbours," she stated flatly as soon as they posed the question. She had no discernible accent, but spoke as if communication were a rarely practised art. Perhaps out here it is, Green thought with a glance out the window at the endless vista of fields. "They had a store in Renfrew, this I know. But we didn't see them much, especially not him. He never came out. She came out sometimes to go to Eganville or Renfrew, maybe to shop. Sometimes she stopped here to buy corn in the summer. She'd say hello, very nice, but he stayed in the car. Never talked. That's all I can tell you. I didn't see nobody, nothing."

Green tried a variety of questions about the Walkers' habits, their relationship to the rest of the community, and any rumours about them. Mrs. Wiecowska stubbornly maintained that she knew and had heard nothing.

Finally, Green smiled at her with what he hoped was a mournful air. "Mrs. Wiecowska, Eugene Walker seems to have been a very sad old man, and very lonely. Maybe he brought it on himself, but who can know what life does to a man, eh? Who knows what he's been through? I think it is terrible that someone left him alone to die in the snow. No person at the end of their life should be left like that."

She was frowning at him in bewilderment, as if trying to

60

follow him but wary of traps along the way. He paused to let her catch up, then shook his head sadly. "Did no one ever come to visit him?"

"Oh," she replied hastily, as if somehow she herself were being chastised. "His family, sure. His daughter, her children."

"Son-in-law?"

She shrugged expressively. "Son, son-in-law? I don't know them. Sometimes a car would come and go. I don't know who."

"Same car?"

"No, no. Different cars. Yesterday—no, two days ago—there was a car. Strange, because no one was home. The old man died the day before. I watched, because I thought it would come out again soon. But it was not very soon."

Green's pulse soared, but he strove to keep his tone on the same gentle level. "How soon?"

"Thirty minutes?"

"What did the car look like?"

"A small car. With a flat back." She demonstrated with her hand the shape of a hatchback. "Black, maybe?"

"Did you ever see it going to the house before?"

She shook her head. "But I don't watch everything."

"Oh, I'm sure you're much too busy. But did you see who was in the car?"

She straightened her shoulders and brushed back an errant strand of steel wool. "My eyes are very good, but it was far away. The person had a hat and dark glasses, so it was hard to see more."

"Did it look like a man or a woman?"

"Hard to say. Woman, maybe?"

Once the two policemen had thanked Mrs. Wiecowska for her help and were walking back across the muddy snow towards the car, Green kicked a chunk of ice across the yard with a curse of frustration.

"Well, that's just great, Sullivan. This time we are screwed by our own stupidity. We just completely obliterated that car's tracks when we drove up the lane ourselves."

*   *   *

At the red brick farm house further down the road they encountered a plump, elderly woman in a flowered apron who was only too delighted to talk. She ushered them cheerfully into her kitchen, which smelled of apples and cinnamon. Both men shed their coats as she poured them cups of tea. Without thinking, she added milk to the tea, causing Green to grimace inwardly. Milk in tea was anathema to his Yiddish soul. Sullivan set aside his notebook and gulped at his eagerly, but Green took a cautious sip. The woman, who had introduced herself as Eleanor MacLeod, watched Sullivan with lively eyes.

"I'd make a guess you're hungry, Sergeant. Would you like an apple turnover? Freshly baked this morning. You'll have to excuse the clutter, gentlemen, but I have all these apples picked weeks ago, and if I don't get them into jars or baking soon, they'll spoil." She placed a turnover in front of each of them, which both men pounced on. It was now past one o'clock, and they hadn't eaten since leaving Ottawa at eight.

"What an ordeal for poor Ruth," she said as she busied herself at the stove. Fragrant steam rose from the pots bubbling at her elbow. "I wish I knew where I could call her, just to give her my sympathies. Not that she didn't know it was coming. She's been saying for two years now that she thought he wouldn't hold on long, almost as if she hoped he'd go—" She checked herself. "Although of course she didn't. But I'm glad in a way that it's over for her. It was so hard for her to get out, even to come over here. She always seemed to have one eye on the clock, and she'd be rushing back to Eugene almost before she'd finished her tea. He was all she thought about — I know what that's like, I nursed Arthur through his last five years, and you do find that your whole life closes in around their routine. Is his colour good today, is his mind lucid, is he in pain? She'll have to find new interests now. For me, having this farm kept me going. The apples would ripen, the strawberries kept coming up. I don't farm it the way I did when we were younger, mind you, but there's still plenty for me to do. I think Ruth will sell, though, and move into the city with her daughter. She wasn't raised on the land, and she really doesn't like being so isolated. It was Eugene's idea, and she did it to keep him happy. I kept telling her she had a right to be happy too in her old age, and she said she was, that it took less to make her happy, and Eugene had been through so much—I never knew what, she didn't say. I don't think he was happy, even with his little retirement cottage. The very rare times I saw him, he was half pickled. But I'm rambling too much, I'm sorry. Inspector, you haven't touched your tea."

He was licking the last flakes of the apple turnover off his fingers when she turned around. "Actually, a cold glass of water would suit me just as well. And please go on. I'm trying to get as complete a picture of their life as I can."

She shook her finger at him as if mere water would never meet the needs of a strong, active man. "I know just the thing for you." She reached into the fridge and extracted a large jug filled with a pale amber liquid, which she poured into a glass. It proved to be a delightfully tart apple cider.

"It was the children Ruth worried about most," she continued once she'd returned to her seat. "It was a great hardship for them to drive all the way out from Ottawa and Montreal to check on their parents, in the winters especially. When it snowed Ruth couldn't always get the car out, and last winter she fell and broke her arm. She isn't strong, Ruth, I believe she has that bone disease with the fancy name they talk about nowadays. Her daughter worries about her a great deal, and I think that troubles Ruth. That's the way of it, though, isn't it? Your children grow up and they move out on their own, and you still worry about them." She paused to rest a maternal eye on Sullivan, who was busily picking up every flake that remained on his plate. Then abruptly she went to her pantry and removed a mixing bowl and a large canister.

"My youngest is a sergeant in the army. He'd be about your age. Although of course I don't know if the ranks are the same in the police." She broke an egg into the bowl. "I'm going to make you boys some apple pancakes for lunch. None of my children have stayed on the farm. It's true all around here. All the children have gone to the city for better jobs. Soon there will be no one left farming the land. You can't make a living on a hundred-acre farm nowadays, and the children find the life too hard. I'm not blaming them. I don't think things are the same as when I grew up. When I was a girl, you only knew the towns and the people right around you. Who even got to Ottawa, let alone saw what life could be like in Hollywood or Paris. Today communities are losing that bond. Families are moving out, and incomers are buying up the land to escape the city. Ironic, isn't it? But no matter how long a stranger has been here, he's a stranger if he wasn't born on the land. Silly, really. I liked Ruth, and I was glad for her friendship, but a lot of people wondered about her. They knew she'd grown up in London in a fancy house before the war, and they wondered why she would marry a drunken foreigner and come to live a poor life in a small Ottawa Valley town. People left here, they didn't move here. Folks wondered that they never showed up for church except Christmas Eve and Easter Sunday at St. James Anglican. It raises eyebrows and suspicions, I can tell you. I always meant to speak to Ruth about it, but—well, the time never seemed right."

The sweet fragrance of butter and cinnamon filled the air as Mrs. MacLeod dropped the batter into the pan. Green's stomach contracted emptily, distracting him from the questions he wished to ask. With an effort he forced his mind back on track.

"Did you know them when they lived in Renfrew as well?"

She shook her head. "We did most of our shopping in Eganville, which is closer. Only occasionally did we go into Renfrew, and never to their hardware store. But some of the folks around here knew of them, and that's how the rumours spread."

"What rumours?"

"Oh, I meant about her fancy house in London and them not going to church. There's even a rumour one of the children was not baptized."

Hardly a crime in today's day and age, Green thought but behaved himself.

"What did Ruth tell you about her life in England and about meeting Eugene?"

"Not much. She was very loyal to Eugene and seemed to act like everyone thought the worst of him. She said both her parents had died just after the war, so she really had no reason to stay in England. She had a brother, but he'd been killed in the war. Eugene was the big mystery, though."

Green glanced up sharply. "How so?"

"Ruth confided to me once that he had no idea what his life had been before the war."

Five

May 13th, 1940

Three days three nights blurred together by my fear.
Eyes shut, ears tuned to every sound.
Her screams, the sibilant hush of Marzina's voice,
the squeak of bedsprings and footfalls around the room.
Dimly from down below, the drumming of hooves up to the gate.
Later Marzina weeps in prayer, rosary beads clicking,
And a black terror swamps me.
I drown, washed numb by my liebling's screams
until a thin wail wavers out through the door.
They invite me in to the miracle, swaddled in white,
And she wraps tiny fingers around my thumb.
Smiles and vodka all around, but new sadness in the farmer's eyes.
His own two sons kidnapped to serve the master race.
Deutschland has devoured us, left only the old and powerless.
We must hide you, Tadeuzs says, erase all sign that you are here.
So the farmer and I begin to dig.

"This case gets weirder and weirder," Green remarked as they headed back towards the OPP station in Renfrew. "Now we've got a dead German World War Two vet who claimed he didn't know who the hell he was."

"You don't really buy that crap, do you?" Sullivan asked.

"Maybe he really doesn't remember. The stuff we've learned about sexually abused kids—about them blocking the whole thing from memory—that tells us anything is possible if the trauma is horrible enough. War's a horrible trauma, for sure, but the question is—is it horrible enough? As Don Reid said, lots of men went through the war."

Sullivan grunted but drove in silence, hunched over the wheel, his brows drawn down over his eyes.

Green frowned at him. "You were pretty quiet back there. This is your home turf. You should be full of impressions."

"That's the problem," Sullivan muttered.

"What does that mean?"

Sullivan shook his head. "Nothing. Just brings back memories."

"Come on, didn't you have one of those idyllic, big family, down-on-the-farm types of childhood?"

"You got part of it right." Sullivan glanced over. "Let's forget it. You're right, this is getting weirder and weirder."

"I wonder what Gibbs has unearthed about Walker's immigration record. I want you to call him when we get back to Renfrew."

"Hey! You know Gibbs will run circles for you. Don't ride his ass."

Green let the silence lengthen, but Sullivan's mood piqued his curiosity. "Tell me, are things as bad as people say about these country cliques? About the importance of religion and lineage and sticking to your own kind."

Sullivan nodded. "Especially with the old timers. It's opened up now, with the younger generation coming and going, but when I was growing up, boy, it was the Poles, the Irish and the Protestants, and you bloody well toed the line. But I can tell you, a hell of a lot of nasty, unChristian stuff went on in the name of religion and Christian morals."

Tell me about it, Green thought wryly.

By the time the two detectives arrived back at the Renfrew OPP station, Karl Dubroskie had been waiting for over two hours. The farmer paced the outer hall in his mud-caked boots, which looked ludicrously oversized on his spindly legs. An old army peacoat hung open over his sunken chest, and his blue eyes glowered in his leathery face. Green realized that any chance for a friendly, cooperative interview had long vanished.

"You boys from Ottawa might think I got nothing better to do than sit here watching the clock tick, but I do. I got snow fencing to patch and cows to milk, so you got ten minutes and you better make it good."

Green dispatched Kennelly to bring a pot of coffee and ushered Dubroskie politely into the little interview room at the rear. The farmer looked around the barren room with grim satisfaction. "I sat in this very room the last time I set foot in this station, to talk about Walker beating up my cousin. I don't know why you want to see me about that, I got nothing to say. Everything I know I told Wells, and that was piss all. I got no reason to lie. Walker…he was nothing to me but a drunken old Polack, and I wasn't even sure about that."

"What do you mean?"

"What do you mean 'what do I mean'?"

"What weren't you sure of?"

Dubroskie looked bewildered as he tried to retrace his steps. He grew sullen. "I don't know. Just he didn't act very Polish, that's all."

"In what way?"

Dubroskie fidgeted, then gestured vaguely with his hands. "He didn't act like we were…together. He didn't even seem to like us."

Green kept his face impassive as he proceeded. "What about your cousin? What kind of man was he?"

"He didn't start it, if that's what you're saying. He's a hard-working guy that just wants to stay out of trouble. He had plenty of it back in Poland, and he's just trying to make a good life."

"What kind of trouble did he have in Poland?"

Dubroskie's eyes narrowed warily, as if he'd sensed too late a trap. "My cousin's a good, honest man and a fine Canadian citizen. If you got any questions about him, you go ask him yourself."

"Oh, I'd be happy to, Mr. Dubroskie," replied Green cheerfully. "If you'll be so kind as to give me his full name and address."

Once Dubroskie had left the room, Sullivan turned to Green in dismay. "You're not going to go all the way to Hamilton. Jules will never approve the travel request. He'd kill us if he knew we were out here pounding the pavement. He'd kill us if he knew we've invested good time on a guy MacPhail says died of natural causes."

Green grinned as he shrugged on his parka. "Well, you only die once, right? Besides, it's on our own time, and I'm paid to make executive decisions. I'm making one."

Sullivan had opened his mouth to escalate his protest when there was a sharp knock on the door, and Kennelly stuck his head in.

"We've got a guy here who used to be a good friend of Howard Walker's. You said you wanted background witnesses. He's one of the few we could find."

Green looked at his scowling colleague and shrugged. "What the hell, we're here."

Jeff Tillsbury proved to be a sensitive, articulate man in his mid thirties who had gone to Guelph University to study Veterinary Medicine. He had opened a practice on his return to Renfrew ten years earlier and had kept in sporadic touch with Howard throughout the intervening years. If he thought there was anything odd about two Ottawa police officers making routine background inquiries into the deceased's "state of mind", he gave no sign as he delved candidly into the family's past.

"Howard will be very upset by his father's death," he said. "He didn't get along with him—actually, that's an understatement. By the end he hated his father as much as he loved him. I have never seen Howard so upset as when he'd just been dealing with his father. They hadn't spoken for five years, and Howard told me that as far as he was concerned, he no longer wanted anything to do with his father. He kept in touch with his mother through his sister but refused to call or write to the house."

"Do you know the reason for this rift?"

"Yes." Jeff hesitated as if weighing how much to betray a confidence. "Howard married a Jewish girl he met at McGill. Not only Jewish, but wealthy, and her father was very influential in the Montreal Jewish community. From what he told me, I gathered his father was very upset."

Beside him, he felt Sullivan fidget awkwardly, but Green had long ago learned not to let personal reactions show through.

"Did his father attend the wedding?"

"Oh, no. Howard said his father wouldn't be caught dead in a synagogue. In any case, he wasn't well enough. I went. I was the only one from around here whom Howard invited. It was a beautiful wedding, and his wife seems very nice."

"Were Howard and his father on good terms before the marriage?"

"As long as I've known Howard, Detective—and that's

about thirty years—his relationship with his father has been difficult." Jeff ran his long-boned fingers over his thinning scalp and frowned in search of words. "No one—not Howard's mother, not his sister—really understood how his father used to torture Howard. Maybe if Howard had been thicker-skinned, it wouldn't have been so bad. But Howard was a sensitive kid. He liked poetry and wild birds. He cried when kids picked on him in school. And they sure did. They picked on him for having an immigrant father, because he was half Catholic—we went to the public school—and of course for just being a sissy. They picked on him because he was small and skinny." Jeff shook his head wryly at the memory. "We were both small and skinny."

Green nodded, remembering. He'd been small and slight as a boy too, and the inner city streets had been a cruel training ground in the concept of might is right. It hadn't influenced his decision to join the police, but he had to admit to a secret twinge of satisfaction whenever his rank and profession cowed some swaggering brute into submission. "That can be pretty rough on a boy."

"Yes. Whenever Howard came home from school in tears, his father would throw him back outside with an order to beat the kids up and not come back till he did. He called him an old woman, so Howard learned to keep his hurts to himself and lie to his father about how many boys he'd beaten up. His father seemed to despise all the qualities about Howard that made him really special—his gentleness, his compassion, his moral sense. Howard could never seem to do anything right in his father's eyes. He could never seem to please him. His father was tremendously moody, I noticed that even as a kid. One day he'd take Howard and me into the back of the shop and show us some beautiful new fishing lure. Another day he'd bite our heads off and throw us out of the shop. He scared me. I hated to go over there. I can't imagine living with him! Howard was always trying to second-guess him, to anticipate his moods and avoid at all costs something that would set him off."

Green jumped into the flow of memories. "How did Howard's mother figure in all this?"

Jeff shifted his lanky body in the chair and stroked his bald spot. "She tried to keep the peace, basically. Tried to coach the children on how to avoid aggravating their father. I do remember at times she tried to act as a buffer—you know, she wouldn't tell her husband that someone had stolen Howard's hat or dumped his bike in the ditch. With the bike incident I remember it backfired on her, and he accused her of turning the children against him. There was a scene in the back of the shop that day. I was there helping Howard after school, and I remember his father screaming at her and throwing merchandise around. Everyone was hiding behind the shelves. Howard was mortified. He never would discuss the incident with me."

"Did his father beat him?" Sullivan had been taking discreet notes and spoke for the first time since the interview had begun. Green was startled, not only by the unexpected interruption but also by the tightness in Sullivan's tone.

Jeff, however, seemed to have anticipated the question, perhaps had posed it to himself before, for he shook his head without hesitation. "I never had evidence of it. He punched walls and he swore a lot, but I never saw him actually hit."

Green glanced at Sullivan expectantly, but he sat back, shaking his head. Green retrieved the thread of his questioning.

"Are you aware of any feud, any enemies, any reason why someone would want Eugene Walker dead?"

Tillsbury pondered the question carefully, his frown deepening. "I've been out of touch with the family for a while, but there's nothing I can remember. He was a nasty man, but in recent years he hardly went out. I can't imagine who'd bother killing him now."

"What about Howard? Is he capable of killing his father?"

"Good Lord, no, Howard couldn't kill anyone." Confronted with Green's expressionless gaze, he reddened in dismay. "All those things I told you, they were to help you understand the father. Now I think I've said quite enough!"

*   *   *

Dusk was already creeping in as the two detectives said their goodbyes and headed back along the county road toward the main highway. Sullivan drove with both hands clenched on the steering wheel, staring grimly ahead into the deepening grey. The melancholy which had first touched him yesterday now cloaked him completely.

"Jeff Tillsbury may not think so, but you can bet old man Walker beat his son."

Green frowned. "What makes you think so?"

"Because it goes with the territory."

Green lapsed into thought. Neither detective was a stranger to the parental violence and cruelty that shaped the criminals they saw every day, but Green sensed a more personal struggle. He began to put the mood and the cryptic allusions of the past day together.

"Brian, what's going on?"

For a moment it seemed Sullivan would not respond, but once he started, the words tumbled out. "My old man is a drunk. I never told you that. I never told anyone. You don't tell anyone. Remember the Walker family secrets? Every drunk's family has them. My mother tried to keep it from us at first—Dad's sick, Dad's tired, Dad has business in town. And then when you're tripping over the whiskey bottles in the hall and the truth is screaming at you, you see it. But you don't tell anyone else you see it. You go along with Mom's lies—yeah, Dad's sick, sure he's tired. You don't have friends over, you don't make plans, and then when you're finally good and sick of it and you get mad, you yell at him and you yell at your mother and she tells you the next lies. Dad's had a bad day, the farm's had a bad year, Dad's had a hard life. It's not his fault. It's never his fault. No, it's your fault, because you made too much noise, or woke him up, or asked him at the wrong moment. Anything but admit the bastard's got a hangover, and it's his own damn fault."

Green was shocked. "Jesus, Brian, I never knew a thing. I've met your father, and I never suspected!"

Sullivan's lips were drawn in a tense line. "No, the old man's good at walking the edge. Very few people suspect. But it's why I left home at eighteen and joined the force. Why my sister Pat lives in Cold Lake, Alberta, and my sister Tracy is on her third husband." He looked across at Green. "My brothers Ed and Frank are alcoholics too. Of course, they don't think so. They tell me they can handle it, but I've seen them at family parties, and it's like seeing Dad all over again."

"You've done okay though, Brian. You're one of the most together guys I know."

Sullivan shook his head grimly. "I've had to work at it. Mary will tell you that. I really have to watch myself. Not so much with the booze—I can take it or leave it. It's the temper. The Irish temper, my father used to call it proudly when he beat the shit out of me. I see that part of him in me and I hate it. No one gets off scot free in a family like that, believe me. Walkers or Sullivans—you look inside, it's a fucking Pandora's box."

Green absorbed this in silence, thinking how easy it is to keep a secret even from someone you work side by side with every day. It explained Sullivan's strict two-drink limit even when out with the boys, and it explained his fierce sense of duty to his family. "Jeez," he muttered. "And to think I envied you your big, boisterous family. There I was, an only child of clingy, overly dependent parents, single-handedly trying to make up for the Holocaust." He grimaced. "And failing miserably."

"And I always envied you your relationship with your father. Those Sunday morning brunches at the Deli with just you and him."

"He complains. I read case reports."

Sullivan, studying the road ahead, suddenly chuckled. "That sounds like you. Thanks, Mike. Let's get this show back on track."

The chuckle was a welcome relief, a sign that Sullivan was back. Respecting the curtain Sullivan had drawn, Green turned his mind back to the case. "When we get back to Ottawa, we've got five things to do—"

"Once I tag this stuff downtown, I'm going home to dinner," Sullivan interrupted. "And you're going to spend the rest of your weekend with your wife and son. Remember?"

Green grinned at him. He'd already planned his evening's sleuthing around his son. Sharon was working tonight, so there would be plenty of time to go home, feed Tony and tuck him into bed before leaving him with a sitter and heading out for a little more detective work. But he couldn't resist baiting Sullivan. "Don't worry, mother, I will. It's early yet."

"You'll turn around, and your boy will be eighteen."

"Five things." Green held up his hand in order to check them off on his fingers. "First, we have to interview Ruth Walker to find out the truth about Walker's background.

Second, we have to talk to Howard about the rift between him and his father. Third, we have to run a check on Karl Dubroskie's cousin from Hamilton, Josef…" He flipped open his notebook to tackle the name. "Josef Grys—whatever. Fourth, we have to take this black tool box to an antique dealer who specializes in Eastern European stuff. Someone may have to take it to Toronto on their way to Hamilton. Fifth, we have to see if forensics has come up with anything at the Walker house yet. Oh! And sixth, we have to find out what Gibbs has dug up on Walker from Immigration."

Sullivan laughed. "All of this we're going to do before work on Monday?"

"Not all. Besides, some of it will hardly take any time. A quick phone call to forensics, two minutes to ask Gibbs how Walker got into the country—"

Sullivan shook his head in mock disgust. "I don't know why I bother."

"Okay, I'll make a deal with you. Just so you shut up and get your mind back on the case. Sometime this evening—after I've put Tony to bed," Green flashed him a grin, "I'll go talk to Mrs. Walker and Howard. That's simple—they're both in the same place. And you meet with Gibbs, get his report and get him to keep on top of Ident. Gibbs is perfect, he'll be at them all weekend trying to get their report. Then Monday either you or Gibbs run a check on Grys…what's-his-name, including immigration and CSIS. Old man Dubroskie let it slip that the guy had some trouble in Poland."

"Where do food and sleep fit into all this?"

"Food and sleep? God, the man's never satisfied! I tell you what. When this case is solved, I'll take you to Nate's and treat you to the best smoked meat and coldest draught in town."

Six

December 24th, 1940

Britain has beaten back the enemy,
Now Poland dances under Hitler's boot.
Snatches of song and laughter sift through the straw above our heads.
Festive chicken and onions scent the air.
But in our lair below the barn, in hunger, cold and darkness,
we wait our turn.
We share our warmth, snuggled together deep in the straw.
A whimpered cry, fumbled buttons, the coo of a baby at the breast.
I contemplate in wonder
the bond of family, so deep and primal that I reach out to touch it.
She cocks her head slyly, smiles and shifts her dress.
A pox on the Nazi bastards, she says,
And she welcomes me in.

Sharon had already left for her evening shift at the psychiatric hospital by the time Sullivan dropped Green off at his house at five o'clock. The teenage babysitter was curled up on the couch talking on the phone while Tony, having recently mastered the art of walking, happily removed all Green's CDs from their rack and strewed them over the floor.

The girl unfolded herself guiltily. "I just fed him supper,

and I was going to give him his bath at six."

Green rescued a Rolling Stones classic from Tony's jaws and scooped the protesting baby into his arms for a hug. "That's fine, I'll do that. But could you come back for a couple more hours later?"

The girl shrugged her indifference. "Your wife left your phone messages on the kitchen counter. She said to be sure you got them."

Curious, Green tucked Tony under one arm and went to check. No less than three messages from Superintendent Jules, with Sharon's succinct editorial on the last. "*He sounded pissed.*" Jules' first message was a little more congenial. "*Who on earth is Howard Walker? He's been calling all over the station for you.*"

Well, well, well, Green thought as he headed upstairs to the bath. He had to quell his curiosity while he played with Tony in the tub and read him his favourite story, *Goodnight Moon*. Tony would not allow a single step in the ritual to be skipped and, as he approached his first birthday, he was developing an impressive, if at times indecipherable vocabulary of single words to express his disapproval. Green had long ago learned that in the battle of wills, Tony always won. Your DNA, Sharon was fond of muttering, as if obstinacy and sheer bloody-mindedness could never have come from her end of the gene pool.

It was seven o'clock by the time Green was able to grab his notebook and slip back out the door with one last glance at Jules' unanswered phone messages. It's not that I'm actually avoiding Jules, he told himself as he headed down to the station to sign out the tool box. It's just that I need to know what has set Howard Walker off and deal with it before I can figure out what to tell Jules. Jules almost never called on the weekend unless he'd received some flak from higher up, which was happening more and more often in the new procedurized, bureaucratic amalgamated police force. Howard Walker must have stirred up the brass, either intentionally or by bumbling around asking the wrong people for help.

Jules might also be angry because Sharon had told him about the trip to Renfrew. Normally Sharon knew better than to betray Green's minor misdemeanours to the brass, even Jules, but she hadn't been too pleased with this one herself. His choice of Renfrew over a day of family togetherness had prompted an entire night of the famous Levy silent treatment which hadn't even broken when he'd tried to kiss her goodbye this morning.

She might have told Jules where Green had gone, and Jules, being a detective long before becoming a brass, would have put Howard Walker, Eugene Walker and Renfrew together, looked up Eugene's file, and known Green was off on one of his wild goose chases.

The interesting question now was—where did Howard Walker fit into this goose chase?

To his surprise, half a dozen cars were parked on the street outside the Reid house when Green arrived with the evidence bags casually concealed in a briefcase. As he mounted the steps, he heard the sound of muted voices from within. The funeral, he wondered with a sinking feeling? Eugene Walker had died on Wednesday, so a funeral on Saturday was entirely plausible. Green was about to withdraw out of respect for the family when a thought occurred to him. Whatever had brought Howard Walker down to the station on the afternoon of his father's funeral must be damn important.

Donald Reid opened the door in response to Green's ring, and a welcome died on his lips at the sight of Green.

"You! I told you about that fight so you could check it out, not go accusing Howard of murder!"

"I did no such thing."

Disregarding the chilly air, Reid stepped out onto the porch in his shirtsleeves and shut the door behind him. To Green's surprise, he was red-eyed. "Jeff Tillsbury called Howard and said you were snooping into his relationship with his father."

"Well, I do have some questions for Howard. And for your mother-in-law."

"For fuck's sake, inspector! We've just buried my father-in-law. Can't it wait until tomorrow?"

"It could, but Howard himself seemed anxious to speak to me."

Reid grunted and reentered the house, leaving the door ajar for Green to follow. "Just go back into the kitchen. Be inconspicuous, at least."

In the living room Green passed a cluster of guests clutching tea cups and murmuring solace. He'd barely settled in the kitchen and slipped the briefcase out of sight at his feet before a youngish man appeared, dressed in a charcoal grey suit and black tie which Green noticed with surprise was cut on one side. Howard was small and fine-boned like his mother, but with dark curls and chocolate brown eyes magnified by thick glasses. He had a drink in his hand and a scowl on his face.

"Why are you doing this?" he demanded.

Green played ignorant. "Doing what?"

"I checked with the pathologist. He told me my father died of natural causes. Why are you stirring all this up? You're upsetting my mother, you're upsetting my sister."

Ah, thought Green. The collegial courtesy of one doctor to another. So it was Dr. MacPhail who had talked too much, no doubt fuelled by half a dozen scotches, and MacPhail who had alerted Jules that Green was poking around in a non-case.

"I'm sorry if I've upset anyone, Dr. Walker. I'm simply investigating possibilities. Standard investigative procedure, I assure you."

"But you're saying he was murdered."

"Please sit down, Dr. Walker. Let's just talk a bit."

Howard dropped into a chair, spilling some of his drink. The effort of being belligerent seemed to have drained him, and now his grief showed through. "We've just buried him. I haven't seen him in five years, and he looked so unreal lying in that coffin. At peace. My father was never at peace!"

"What do you mean?"

It was a moment before he spoke. "All my life my father has wanted me to be something I'm not, and I've wanted him to be something he's not. What a waste. What a damn waste! Our whole goddamn life's been a lie! I didn't kill him, Inspector, if that's what you think. There have been times I wanted to, times I prayed he'd drop dead, but I don't have the guts for it. I ran away instead."

"Not such a bad solution," Green observed. "I wish some of the other people I've met in my job had done the same. Tell me about the fight you and he had five years ago."

"What does it matter? I didn't kill him for it."

"Jeff Tillsbury told me it was because you married a Jewish girl."

"What a sin." Howard's face twisted briefly, as if an unwanted thought had passed through his mind. He focussed on his drink to restore order. "And worse, I converted to Judaism. Eternal damnation! What a goddamn hypocrite. I don't care what anyone thinks, I'm proud to call myself Jewish. It's the first time I've been proud of who I am."

Green understood now the meaning of the cut in the tie. It was the symbolic rending of the garment by a Jewish mourner. But he was puzzled by Howard's defiance and wondered if the man thought himself to be in enemy territory. "I'm proud to call myself Jewish too."

The other man's demeanor changed instantly. The defiance vanished, and his eyes widened in astonishment. "You're kidding! You don't look Jewish."

"And actually you do. But the nose." Green tapped his nose, which despite the spray of freckles was classically Semitic. "The nose says it all."

Howard reddened. "I'm sorry. If I'd known, I wouldn't have shot my mouth off like that. I'm still sensitive about it. My wife Rachel says I need to develop a thicker skin. I get upset by the little slurs, the Holocaust, the way all through history Jews got the short end of the stick. It's personal. I say 'hey, that's me you hate. Why? What did I ever do to you?'"

"The thick skin will come," Green replied. "And a sense of perspective as well. Tribalism is as old as mankind. Once you stop expecting perfection, it hurts a lot less."

"So you've given up on people?"

"Not at all. But ten years in homicide has narrowed my focus a bit. People seem to have enough trouble loving each other one on one."

Howard was frowning at him intently. He opened his mouth as if to add something, then seemed to check himself. He straightened his shoulders as if preparing for a confrontation.

"Why do you think my father was murdered?"

Green shrugged. "I'm not sure he was yet. But why are you all reluctant to let me even look into it?"

"How would you feel in my shoes?" Howard replied. "Your father dies and some stranger starts poking into your private lives?"

"But if I had nothing to hide—"

"Everyone has something to hide! Just not murder."

"Okay," Green proceeded carefully, sensing emotions precariously close to the surface. "Then as part of the routine inquiry, could you tell me where you were between eleven and one-thirty p.m. on November 21st, the day your father died?"

To Green's surprise, Howard relaxed and reached into his pocket without hesitation. "At a medical conference in Toronto. I thought you'd probably ask me that, so I brought you the brochure and my registration receipt. You'll see it's dated Nov. 5. The conference runs all week, and I'd still be there if my father hadn't died."

Green turned the receipt over in his hands. In itself it was not much proof, but Howard's attendance at the conference could be checked. He recorded the address for future verification.

"How did you learn of your father's death?"

"My wife reached me at my hotel on Thursday night."

"That's a whole day and a half later!"

"She left messages at the convention on Thursday morning apparently, but they never reached me. There were over a thousand physicians milling around the seminars."

"What about Wednesday night at the hotel? Why didn't she call you there?"

"Mom couldn't reach Rachel till Thursday morning at work. She had stayed over at a friend's house Wednesday night."

It seemed an innocent explanation, yet there was a strange, evasive look in Howard's eyes. Green took a wild guess.

"Male or female?"

Howard frowned. "What on earth are you talking about?"

"I've been a detective a long time. I've seen a lot of less than perfect marriages."

Howard leaned his head back with a laugh that sounded oddly relieved. "Way off base, Inspector. It was all prearranged—a rare time for two friends to get together. Rachel and Maxine had theatre tickets and late dinner reservations."

The evasive look had meant something, Green was sure, but he sensed a direct demand for the truth would get him nowhere, so he jotted the question in his notebook for future use and leaned back with a soothing smile.

"Sorry, Howard, I had to ask. Getting back to your father, I'd like to know a bit more about his background. Where is he from, and how did he and your mother meet?"

But rather than being soothed, Howard tensed. "Why?"

"Well, she's British and he's…what?"

"They met in Surrey, just after the war," he replied curtly. "During the war my mother worked as a nurse, although she never had much formal training, and she was working in a convalescent hospital in the country. My father was a patient there. She nursed him, and I guess they fell in love. When he was better, they came to Canada to start a new life. Neither of them had much left of their old ones."

"What do you know of your father's background?"

Howard rose and refilled his glass with club soda, perhaps to occupy his hands. "Nothing. He had been evacuated to England from somewhere in Germany to receive medical care, but he arrived in England with no memory of who he was or where he came from."

"What language did he speak?"

"No language at all." It was Ruth who spoke, suddenly appearing in the archway to the kitchen as if she had been listening on the other side. She was wearing a soft blue print dress with a silver brooch at the collar, and her curly grey hair was sculpted neatly around her head. Her well-bred smile barely masked her annoyance.

"Why do you want to know, Inspector?"

Green rose and extended his hand. "I apologize for intruding at this time, Mrs. Walker. Had I known, I would have waited, but I received a message that Howard was anxious to speak with me."

"As am I." She sat with great dignity and her eyes held his. "Because if you think he was murdered, I want to know why. You're asking about ancient history, most of which we know nothing about—"

"Why is that?"

"He didn't lie, if that's what you're implying." She paused as if waiting for his explanation, but when he offered none, she seemed to reach a decision. She turned to her son, who was still propped against the sink, drink in hand. "Howard, this may take a few minutes, and I don't like to leave Margaret to cope with our guests alone. She's worn out."

Howard's grip tightened on his glass, and he opened his mouth to protest, but Ruth's steadfast look never wavered. In the end, he set the drink down on the counter, nodded and strode out without a word. Ruth turned back to Green and clasped her hands in her lap as if to brace herself.

"There are things my children don't understand, and right at the moment, with everyone's nerves frayed, it is not the time to add to their burdens. Whatever his background, Eugene was clearly a casualty of the war and remained one until his death. When he arrived in Surrey, he was severely depressed. It happened to people, both soldiers and civilians, who had been traumatized so severely, and for so long that they no longer responded to the outside world. They didn't talk, they didn't move, they just seemed to pull into themselves."

"Your son said he was picked up somewhere in Germany?"

She nodded. "A Red Cross relief unit found him hiding in the mountains near Dresden, in the eastern part of Germany. He was beaten, starving and sick with typhus. He was taken to a hospital in Belgium where he stayed about three months. By that time he was physically on the mend but still would not speak. That's when they decided to move him to our convalescent hospital. There was a great deal of confusion after the war, Inspector. You have to understand it didn't end neatly, and everyone went back home."

Green did not interrupt her to tell her that he was very aware of the chaos after the war, of the hundreds of thousands of homeless refugees wandering the devastated continent. Of concentration camp survivors with no place to go, of families who'd been torn apart by the war and who were hunting for one another across Europe, of German army deserters shedding their uniforms and Nazis fleeing for their lives. Of lies and lost papers and frantic bids for asylum. Green's parents rarely talked about it, but they had been there.

"Eugene was just one of thousands of refugees without papers," she said. "And he wouldn't talk or tell the Belgian doctors where he came from."

He kept his voice casual, as if he were just probing to understand. "Did he have any personal effects? Clothing? Anything to give them a clue where he was from?"

She wavered. "Well…when they picked him up, he was wearing a German regular army uniform. But it was very bloody, and the Red Cross thought it was likely stolen from a corpse. He had no…" She paused, twisting her wedding ring convulsively. "No soldier's tags around his neck. In fact, nothing but a small plain gold cross. That…that was all we had from his past."

Green waited in silence. He wanted her to present

whatever cover story she had fabricated, and he would spring the black box with its identity papers once she was committed to her lie. It was an old cross-examination trick he'd learned watching the local lawyers in court.

She shook her head at the memory. "It took him a long time to speak, even to react when spoken to. But after a while he started coming out into the sunshine to watch the others at play, and eventually he'd join in a game of cards. When he finally spoke, it was in English, with an accent. He never spoke Polish. To this day he only spoke Polish if he absolutely had to. For instance, if an immigrant came into the hardware store who spoke no English."

Green frowned. "Polish? If he was found in Germany wearing a German uniform, why did you even think he was Polish?"

She smoothed her skirt and rubbed the joints of her fingers. Her face reflected pain, but something else as well. She's wondering what I know, he thought. She's a woman used to the necessity of lying, but not comfortable with it.

"He understood Polish at the hospital. Polish is not that common a language. Few foreigners speak it. He understood German as well, but that's not uncommon for educated Poles. And he was clearly educated. He could read and write and do mathematics, even book-keeping. So he was probably from the city. But he didn't understand French or Dutch or Czech or anything else we tried on him. There was just something 'unGerman' about him. He just didn't seem like a German to me, perhaps because I didn't want him to be."

Green reached into the briefcase at his feet and withdrew the plastic bags with the black box and the identity booklet. Even before he could say anything, the widening of her eyes betrayed her. She looked at the things in silence for a moment, then swallowed.

"You were thorough, weren't you."

"Maybe you'd better tell me the whole story."

She rose and began to clear teacups off the table. They rattled in her hands. "I wish Eugene had destroyed those things before we came over. I was always afraid they'd come back to haunt him."

"And did they?"

She placed some cups in the sink and swung around to face him. "That depends on you."

"I'm an officer of the law. If a fraud has been committed—"

"But it hasn't!" She coloured. "At least…not knowingly. Eugene didn't remember anything! The box, the name on the papers were meaningless to him. Was it a crime just to begin anew with a clean slate?"

"Eugene may not have remembered anything, but you knew he might be an officer in the enemy army."

She sat down again opposite him and massaged her joints. Finally she shook her head. "At the convalescent home, when Eugene and I were engaged, he showed me those papers. The Red Cross had wanted to take them away from him in Belgium, and he had hidden them in that secret compartment. Eugene was absolutely paranoid about his possessions. He clung to them as if his life depended on them. He actually believed he was Wilhelm Ganz. He said we had to keep it secret because they wouldn't let us into Canada, and the British would send him back to Germany. He insisted on taking my name. But I couldn't leave it like that. Somewhere in Germany a family was wondering what had happened to their son. My brother was killed in the war, and I saw what it did to my parents. So I wrote to Wilhelm Ganz's address in Potsdam, simply saying that we had a wounded man at the hospital who might be their son, and could they please send a picture." She hesitated, then rose, wringing her hands. "They wrote back that their son was dead. He had been killed in action defending a bridge outside Dresden on May 8, 1945. They had seen the body, and there was no mistake. They sent me a picture of him in his uniform, and it didn't look anything like Eugene."

Another twist in the trail, he thought. "So the papers were stolen?"

She inclined her head slightly. "But perhaps not knowingly. When Eugene, in his state of shock, took the uniform off the soldier's body to clothe himself, perhaps the papers were in the pocket and he only found them later. By which time he had forgotten where they came from and what he had done."

"Did you tell him what you had found out?"

"That he wasn't Wilhelm Ganz? Yes."

"And how did he react?"

She cocked her head in thought. "He didn't. At least not to that. He was cross at me for writing. He didn't seem to care who he was or wasn't."

"Did you believe him?"

"Yes," she replied, too quickly.

"No, you didn't. You thought he was hiding something."

"From himself!" she shot back, then checked herself. Facing him, she propped herself against the sink and folded her arms over her chest. Buying herself time, he thought, and waited. "Honestly, Inspector, I don't know what else I can tell you. I don't know how he got those papers, or why. But I do believe he was as much in the dark about his past as I."

Green slid the box out of the bag and turned it in his hands, letting the tools slide out. "What about these things inside? Did you try to trace anything? Or check out this name engraved on the bottom?"

Her arms fell to her sides as if the tension had drained from her. Something about those papers bothers her, he thought. Some fear, some remnant of doubt. Her colour returned as she turned her mind elsewhere. "Before we emigrated to Canada, I wrote to the Polish embassy in London asking them to check the existence of such a company in Ozorkow. It took a long time, but eventually they informed me that there had been a tool and blacksmith shop in Ozorkow run by a man called Kressman. The Kressman family, however, had disappeared during the war, and no one had yet turned up to claim the shop."

"Disappeared". Green grimaced inwardly at the euphemism. No one had turned up because they were probably Jewish and lying at the bottom of a lime pit somewhere. Ninety per cent of Poland's Jews had perished in the Holocaust.

"Did the Polish authorities give you any details on this man Kressman? His full name or age?"

She frowned in dismay. "At the time, yes, but I'm afraid I can't remember much." Her delicate brows drew together as if in an effort to concentrate. "Joseph, I think that was the shopkeeper's name. He'd been in business for over thirty years, so he had to have been middle aged."

"And you didn't try to find out if there was a connection? There was a whole chunk of your husband's life missing."

He had tried to sound gentle, but when she looked up, she was flushed and her tone was defensive. "There was chaos in post-war Europe. It took years for the dust to settle and for the fate of people to be uncovered. And Poland was in Stalin's hands. You didn't simply ask for information."

"But later. In all this time, did you never check?"

"Eugene was a fragile man, Inspector. I helped him to live again, but I never made him whole. Whoever he was, he was a victim of this war, and he had suffered dreadfully. I wanted to put all that behind us—the papers, the box—and try to help him turn towards the future."

"He had no desire to know his past?"

She shook her head. "On the contrary. Whenever I broached it, he'd become very upset. In fact, the merest hint of Poland and his youth would send him over the edge. I decided if the past was so terrible that Eugene couldn't face it, it was better left alone."

He laid his notebook down and reached out a soothing hand. "I didn't mean to be critical, Mrs. Walker. I'm just trying to find out as much as I can, and we've got a huge chunk of the picture missing."

To his surprise, she didn't soften. She pushed the box away with distaste. "I don't see how it's relevant. After all this time, to dredge up all these questions seems needlessly cruel. He was probably just some innocent peasant or handyman living out a quiet life in the Polish countryside, and then the Nazis came along and turned his world upside down. Whoever he was and whatever he had done during that time, it had no bearing on who he was today."

Her vehemence surprised him. He had merely asked about the black box, but she had reacted as if he had accused her husband of something heinous. Of what? Of stealing a dead man's ID? People had done far worse in the middle of war.

*   *   *

The puzzle still tugged at him as he left the Reid house. He glanced at his watch and saw it was nine-thirty, still early yet. A quick phone call to the babysitter revealed that all was quiet on the home front. Tony was fast asleep, and Sharon wouldn't be home from work for at least two hours. There was still time to pursue one more small lead.

He stopped for soup and coffee at Tim Hortons and asked to borrow the Yellow Pages from the acne-faced teen behind the counter. About a dozen phone calls later, he finally roused an antique dealer in Centretown willing to take a look at the black box. The man lived above his shop, and after much grumbling agreed to come down. Green drove past the shop twice before spotting the tiny, lead-windowed door wedged in between a photographer's studio and a Chinese take-out. The old English lettering on the door read "Fine Antiques and Jewellery, Harry Fine, Prop."

The door activated a small bell as he pushed it open and stepped inside. Shelves overflowing with china dishes and knickknacks ran the length of the narrow room, and Green had to negotiate carefully to avoid knocking over the tables and stools that blocked the aisles. Dusty curios occupied every surface.

A stubby, barrel-chested man emerged from the back and rolled towards him.

"Mr. Fine? I'm Inspector Green."

Fine ignored the outstretched hand and peered up at Green over his half-glasses. He nodded at the box tucked under Green's arm.

"That it?"

Green removed the box from its bag and held it out. Fine snatched it without a word and lumbered back down the aisle to the rear of the store. When Green caught up, he had already spread the contents out on his battered desktop and was adjusting the beam from a lamp. Slowly he turned the keys over in the light. Then, with a grunt, he peered through his jeweller's magnifying glass.

"I'm not making any promises," he muttered as he focussed the glass. "I'm not saying I know much about Eastern

European antiques, or tools and locks. I just know more than the rest of the clowns in this town."

"Can you tell me where it's from?"

Fine turned the box over impatiently and rapped his fingers against the bottom corner. "Orzokow. The box is made by this fellow Kressman. Handmade." Fine studied the bottom with the glass and nodded. "This Kressman knew his trade. Nothing shoddy about this piece."

"What else can you tell me?"

"If you stop asking stupid questions, maybe a thing or two." Fine turned abruptly and disappeared through a curtain. He reemerged two minutes later with an armful of musty books. Keeping one eye on him, Green browsed through the store in a bored and distracted way. Although he loved the crumbling landscape of the inner city, that sense of history had never extended to bits of dented kitchenware. Half an hour crept by. On a dusty mahogany tabletop in a corner, he found a small pair of silver candlesticks and was checking the price when Fine appeared at his elbow, scowling.

"Those are special ceremonial candlesticks. I won't sell them to you."

"I know what they are, Mr. Fine," he replied with a smile. "Shabbas candles. I wouldn't buy them at that ridiculous price anyway."

Understanding flickered in the dealer's eyes, and Green thought he even looked sheepish. "They're from Poland. An old lady brought them to me last year before she died. They were all she brought with her out of the Holocaust."

Green turned them over curiously, noting the delicate engraving of a bygone era. Neither of his parents had brought anything with them out of the Holocaust. He felt oddly reluctant as he set the candlesticks back down on the shelf.

Fine's scowl returned. "You want to know about your box or not?" He held up the hammer and the set of keys. "I can't tell you much. This is not my area. Maybe in Toronto or Europe you'll find a dealer who knows more. It's an interesting item. With its false bottom, no ordinary tool box. And the things inside were not made at the same time. The tools are older, solid iron, hand forged by a blacksmith. Good job. Probably this guy Kressman. See the small 'K' at the base? The keys are machine cast and not very good quality."

"What kind of locks?"

Fine shrugged and held up the keys, which measured four to six inches. "Big locks. Padlocks, maybe?"

"Like a peasant might have for his barn or gate?"

Fine consulted his pages of keys and shook his head. "These keys are mass produced, and the metal seems very poor quality. Very porous. And I think that's an old German company. If I had to guess, I'd say they were made during the war, when they used lots of recycled metals. Likely for some big buildings like warehouses or storage depots. A peasant would probably have older locks, made by the local locksmith. Just a guess, but for *bopkes* in the middle of the night, that's all you get."

*　　*　　*

By the time Green had returned the bags to the property room, he knew he was in trouble, for what had begun as a minor line of inquiry had taken up more than three hours. Sharon might be home by now and would have found out from the sitter that he'd spent a grand total of two hours with his son before rushing out again. At least he had cleared up the kitchen and collected the CDs Tony had scattered on the floor.

When he arrived home, however, he found all the lights out and Sharon just settling down to sleep. She gave him a bleary frown as he greeted her.

"Just kiss me goodnight and I'll give you hell in the morning, Green. I'm dead."

Contrite, he leaned over to kiss her. "Everything okay, honey? Brian or Adam call?"

"Lots of people called, except of course my husband. I had a nice long talk with Brian Sullivan."

He sized her up warily. She was languid and half asleep, cuddled among the pillows with the duvet up to her ears. With her eyes half closed, she looked too weary to be much of an adversary.

"Did Brian say anything?" he ventured.

One eye opened fully, and for a moment Green caught a glint of triumph. She smiled.

"Yes, he said to give you two messages. First, that he's found out something really exciting. And second, that he was taking his phone off the hook till nine o'clock tomorrow morning."

Seven

February 20th, 1941

We rock to the swaying of the truck,
stranger pressed against stranger to stay warm.
Heads droop, eyes close as the truck drones on.
Ahead to the east, an endless ribbon of grey,
Behind us, a horror burned forever in my soul.
Tadeuzs' farm seized for the superman in our midst,
A neighbour with Prussian ice in his veins.
We woke to shouts, jackboots overhead.
The neighbour counting hens,
inspecting his bounty,
lifting the straw…
Gestapo guns herded us on the truck.
Driving away, I turned to wave good-bye.
Saw Tadeuzs and Marzina roped to the old pine,
spinning slowly in the wind.

"Green, I don't think at seven o'clock on a goddamn Sunday morning!"

"So take another sip of coffee. I'll wait."

Sullivan hunched over the plastic table and cradled the mug of Tim Hortons coffee in his large hands. He glared across at his colleague, who sat clean-shaven and smiling opposite him. Green had come knocking at his front door at six-thirty in the morning.

"How do you do it? How much sleep did you get?"

"Enough. We've got a lot of work to do today, and we have to start early because I also have to paint the living room." He took an impatient gulp of his coffee while he waited for Sullivan to stop laughing. "Come on, Sharon said you found out something exciting."

Sullivan sobered. "You've landed yourself quite a woman this time. Just don't fuck it up." He let the silence lengthen as long as he dared then returned to safer ground. "Okay. First, Ident's been working their butts off on this non-case. I tell you, after this is over, you'll have to buy Lou Paquette a bottle. He lifted dozens of prints off the key surfaces of the Walker house—the certificates, the booze, drawer knobs, that kind of thing—and he spent all of his Saturday night going through them. So far, most of them seem to be Mr. or Mrs."

"Most?"

"He lifted some off the certificates and the booze in the basement that don't match the Walkers."

"Tell him to print Donald and Margaret Reid."

Sullivan glowered briefly over his coffee cup. "I'm ahead of you. He's going over to the Reids' today."

"Well, we might get lucky. What about the tire tracks? I suppose we wrecked them all."

"Nope. They have some great imprints of my tires, but at the bend in the road we didn't swing quite as wide, and so the tracks are separate. The RCMP will work on the tire make first thing tomorrow. Lou would like to see some paperwork, though, so he can put in for the overtime."

Green grinned. "He'll get it, once Jules knows we're

investigating the case."

Sullivan took a deep swig of coffee and shook his head wearily. "I don't know how you get away with it. Jules is going to have our heads over this."

"Don't worry. I'll take care of Jules. You just keep working. What about Gibbs and the immigration records? Walker's and Josef what's-his-name's?"

Here Sullivan came alive. Triumphantly he pulled out his notebook and flipped it open. "There, old buddy, we finally hit pay dirt. According to their immigration applications, both Walker and Mr. G. came from the same town in Poland. Ozorkow."

"But Walker doesn't even remember where he's from."

Sullivan shrugged. "That's what he wrote down on his application. Ozorkow."

*   *   *

Superintendent Adam Jules, head of Criminal Investigations, had turned a delicate hue of pink and the nostrils of his fine aquiline nose flared. It was the only outward manifestation of his outrage. That and the thin, tight line of his lips. Green had called on him at home, which had not improved his mood.

Jules placed his fingertips together on his lap and studied them. "Michael, Dr. MacPhail's report lists the death as natural causes. Eighty years old, enough disease to sink an elephant, and according to the blood work-up, nearly twice the legal limit of alcohol in his system. By all means harass grieving widows, tie up the OPP, build up our overtime bill in Forensics."

Green grinned. Nothing got past Jules. "Adam, just because he could have died of natural causes doesn't mean he did."

"Do you have one shred of evidence to point to homicide?"

"Yes sir."

98

"What?"

"A small depression wound on Walker's temple which couldn't have been made as he fell, because nothing in the vicinity matches the shape."

Jules' eyebrows rose, and the thin line of his lips grew thinner still. "This is evidence?"

"It's a shred. That's all you asked for."

Jules studied him in silence for a minute with no hint of expression in the perfectly groomed exterior to betray his thoughts. His grey eyes seemed emotionless, but Green sensed that he was weakening. Jules sighed.

"Do you have a theory?"

Green relaxed. "Some possible ones, all of which suggest premeditation. But I'm going to need to assign some men to the case."

"And given MacPhail's report and the family's complaints, I'm going to need something to justify it, Michael. Shea and our public image, you know." Jules rolled his eyes almost imperceptibly as he mentioned the new Police Chief.

"Do you need it in writing or will a verbal report do?"

Jules gave his approximation of a smile, for Green's aversion to paper was legendary. "In writing when you can. Until then, a verbal report will have to do."

It took Green fifteen minutes to brief Jules on the investigation to date and the leads he was following. Jules listened in silence as the list of procedural irregularities mounted, but when Green mentioned going to Hamilton, he stiffened.

"What's in Hamilton?"

"The mysterious assault victim. Walker was arguing with someone in a foreign language just before he died, and there may be a tie-in."

"Why not get the Hamilton police to do it?"

"Because it's an intricate matter, possibly involving events that took place over fifty years ago. Only Sergeant Sullivan and I know the context."

"Then send Sullivan. I'll authorize that."

"But Adam—" Green raised his eyes in silent hope, but the grey eyes that met his were unmoved.

"You're an inspector, Michael, not a field man. End of discussion."

Green left Jules' apartment with mixed feelings. Disappointed and frustrated that Jules would not let him follow the Hamilton lead personally, but pleased that he had secured Jules' cooperation to continue pursuing the case, however tenuous the evidence was. For there were many questions and no clear-cut idea as to whether any of them were important.

Kressman, Gryszkiewicz and Walker all seemed to come from Ozorkow. Surely that was too great a coincidence not to be relevant. Sullivan would check out Gryszkiewicz in Hamilton tomorrow. That left Green with Kressman, the simple Jewish blacksmith who had never returned from the war. How the hell could Green find out about him, especially on a Sunday morning when all official agencies would be locked up tight?

Fifteen years earlier, the Federal Justice Department's War Crimes unit had begun its quest to prosecute Nazi war criminals with zeal and optimism but had since become mired in bureaucratic and judicial red tape. All of the original team had been replaced, but Green remembered one fiery former prosecutor whose very passion had been his undoing. David Haley had felt the pain of every one of the frail old witnesses he'd tracked down, and the accumulated frustrations and roadblocks had nearly destroyed his health. Green knew that he had left war crimes several years earlier for the more mundane halls of civil law, but he hoped Haley's interest in war crimes was still keen. Maybe keen enough to accept a call to duty no matter the day.

The federal lawyer had probably just settled down to his Sunday morning coffee, because he was initially gruff on the phone, but as Green had hoped, when he explained his mission, the old adversarial passion began to stir. There was a long silence at the other end of the line as David Haley pondered Green's problem.

"There is no central registry that lists the fate of all European Jews caught in the Holocaust," he began slowly. "The Red Cross compiled lists, but mainly of people who survived the camps. You could ask them to check their lists, in case your man Kressman turned up in their care, but you would need to know what camps he might have been sent to. All right, I'm getting some ideas." His voice lost its groping quality. "A Holocaust historian such as Martin Gilbert in Britain or Raul Hilberg in the States could tell you when the Jews of Ozorkow were rounded up and what camps they were sent to. In fact, Peter Marks at the University of Toronto is becoming quite an expert. He could tell you. Then you could check the Red Cross lists for those camps. They might not be alphabetical, and it would be a hell of a job. Alternatively you could ask an archivist at Yad Vashem—that's the Holocaust Museum in Israel—to research their files. They have been gathering witness testimonials of both survivors and victims and have a massive collection of data. It requires slogging through archives and documents and letters and photos."

"It sounds like it could take weeks."

"Months. And cost thousands."

"Hardly the kind of job a city police officer can justify to his bosses."

"Well, it's not a neat, modern computerized database you can search at the touch of a button, like you guys are used to." Haley chuckled. "The only other way I can possibly think of to track down a Joseph Kressman is to check with the Jewish Documentation Centre set up in France by Beate and Serge Klarsfeld. She's a German married to a Jew, and they're both active in collecting information on the Holocaust, with the intention of bringing Nazi War Criminals to justice."

"Yes, I'm familiar with them. They tracked down Barbie, the Butcher of Lyons."

"That's right. It's a long shot, but they might be able to help. And they're terrific people, it wouldn't be beneath them."

That's wonderful, Green thought to himself after he'd hung up. Just how the hell am I supposed to justify a long-distance phone call to Paris or Israel? Jules' generosity had already been tapped dry for that day.

Peter Marks, on the other hand, was in Toronto, and dozens of calls were made between Toronto and the Ottawa force every day. In fact, he approved many of them. The historian might not appreciate a call to duty Sunday morning any more than the war crimes prosecutor had, but Green was counting on his being equally intrigued. A five-minute call, that was all it would take to find out if the search for Kressman was futile.

It took twenty minutes, however, to track down the right Peter Marks in the Toronto phone book. Marks was delighted to be involved in a real life quest which brought him out of the rarefied halls of academia. He consulted his library immediately, and Green could hear his heavy breathing as he flipped through the books.

"How much time do you have? We could take the short cut and say that Kressman's over ninety per cent likely to have been killed. Three million Polish Jews died in the Holocaust, only 225,000 survived. Not good odds. The worst odds in all of Europe, actually. And statistically he probably died in Chelmno, Treblinka or Belzec."

Green knew that, but statistics had never deterred him. "All right, so the odds aren't good. But we think the man's from Ozorkow. Is there any way I can check survivors' lists or something, if we can trace what camp he'd been sent to?"

"Poland is a lot more complicated than David Haley led you to believe. Ozorkow's a town in the Warthegau, the part of western Poland that Germany annexed during the war. The Jews in Western Poland were handled in different stages. First, when the Germans invaded Poland in September 1939, they rampaged through the towns and countryside, randomly torturing and killing Jews and Poles alike—Jews in greater proportion just for being Jews. About five thousand Jews from western towns and villages were killed in this fashion. Others fled eastward, still others were herded from the farms and smaller villages into larger ghettos in the cities so they could be more easily controlled. Ozorkow was one of the towns they were herded into. Let me check here." His breathing hissed in the silence. "There were about five thousand Jews in Ozorkow before the war, and in October 1939 another forty-seven hundred were forced into it. Disease, winter cold and starvation took its toll. Then…I seem to remember, oh, here—yes, it was Chelmno. Between March and May 1942 the Jews of Ozorkow were sent to Chelmno and gassed. Most of Poland's Jews perished in 1942."

"Chelmno. Any survivors from Chelmno?"

"Two and a half years later? Not likely. But I think it's in here somewhere—" Pages began to flip. "Incredible book, this. Every horrible fact laid out in neat black and white. Ah-ha!

Here we are. Two survivors."

"Names?"

Marks snorted. "Three hundred and sixty thousand gassed at Chelmno, and he's asking about two survivors. Talk about odds!" There was some more wheezing, a curse, shuffling of papers and then a grunt of satisfaction. "Zurawski and Srebik. No Kressman. You know, you might have more luck if you approached the problem from the other end."

"What do you mean?"

"Find a survivor from Ozorkow who knew Kressman before the war and ask if they know what happened to him. Ozorkow wasn't that big. Most of the Jews would have known each other."

Green felt his hopes lift. "Are there records anywhere of survivors by city of origin?"

"Israel has the most complete list of survivors everywhere. But we had a survivors' reunion here in Canada back in the eighties, and there's a Holocaust Remembrance Committee that keeps track of survivors. They might have a list. Just a sec, I even have the contact person's phone number somewhere."

Green waited as the man at the other end of the phone went off in search. Even through the wires, he could still hear the man's wheezing. Green remembered the survivors' reunion, which had been held in Ottawa about fifteen years earlier. His father had not attended, citing his heart, but Green had attended some of the sessions and had listened to the tales of triumph and despair. Most vividly he recalled the noticeboard where survivors had pinned notes asking if anyone knew the fate of brothers, sisters or husbands. Green shivered even now at the memory.

Peter Marks came back on the line with the information, which Green jotted down. Marks seemed eager to chat forever.

"You could also check the survivors of the labour camps in central Poland. Some of the internees ended up in camps in Germany because of the forced evacuations. Check Sachsenhausen, Ravensbruck, Theriesenstadt and Buchenwald. Good luck, and let me know if I can do more."

"What books are you consulting?"

Green recorded the titles, by the historians Martin Gilbert and Raul Hilberg whom David Haley had mentioned, and then gracefully extricated himself. His next call was to Naomi Wyman of the Canadian Holocaust Remembrance Committee in Toronto, who Green suspected was a survivor herself, for she had a gentle Yiddish lilt that reminded him of his own mother. His mind formed a picture of wide, patient brown eyes and grey hair drawn back in a bun.

When she heard Green's request, she clucked her tongue in exasperation. "There were hundreds of labour camps in Central Poland, and if Kressman was in one of them, Inspector, he could have ended up anywhere! The SS marched them here, there, all over the place at the end of the war, trying to outrun the Allies on both fronts. Sometimes they shot them all on the spot. Thousands died just days or hours before liberation. What am I saying, thousands died afterwards too."

"I know it's a long shot, Mrs. Wyman," Green replied patiently, then played his ace. "My own parents were survivors, so I know what a mess things were. But if you could just check your records for names of a few survivors of the labour camps, I'd be very grateful. And even more important, if you have any survivor who came from Ozorkow, please let me know."

He heard an irritated sigh, and his image of the gentle, patient Yiddish grandmother began to fade. This one was feisty and anything but patient.

"It will take me a couple of days."

"As quickly as you can, Mrs. Wyman. It's very important for a case we're working on."

Suddenly her voice perked up. "A war crimes case?"

"I'm afraid I can't say any more at this time."

Afterwards, Green gazed at the notes he jotted down. Holocaust, war crimes, concentration camps—what was he getting himself into? He had three old men, Walker, Kressman and Gryszkiewicz. All born in Ozorkow, all tied together in some way. Was the whole thing a coincidence, or was there a connection somewhere in Poland, deep in the lost events of the Second World War?

* * *

By the time Green arrived home from the university library with three books under his arm, Sharon and Tony had disappeared. They had both been asleep when he'd left to meet Sullivan earlier, and now the only sign of them was a note from Sharon on the kitchen counter.

Green, I'm off shopping for Tony's birthday. When you get home you'd better stay there, or your ass is toast.

He grinned with relief. Sharon was annoyed, but on a scale of one to ten, this ranked only a six. She still had a sense of humour. With Tony's first birthday bash only days away, maybe she was too excited to whip up much outrage.

Grateful for the peace and quiet, he took the books into his new study, spread them on his makeshift desk, picked up a pen and paper, and began to read.

He thought after all his years of wading through human depravity in Major Crimes, he would be inured to the horrors of the Holocaust, but as he worked his way through the coldly factual chronicle on the fate of Poland's three million Jews, he felt his comprehension fail him. He sat at his desk with a forgotten cup of coffee at his elbow and forced himself to write down the grim and twisting trail which had led most of the five thousand Jews of Ozorkow to the gas chambers. His first discovery was that the killing of Jews in Poland had not begun with the Nazi invasion in September 1939. Throughout the 1930s, there had been escalating acts of anti-Semitism, terrorism and murder across the country. Between 1935 and 1937 alone, seventy-nine Polish Jews had been murdered in random attacks, but this fact had become insignificant in the overwhelming slaughter that followed.

Sept. 1939—Hitler invades Western Poland, random killing of 16,000 civilians, 5,000 of them Jews.

Sept. 28 1939—Poland partitioned at Bug River, 250,000 Polish Jews driven or fled east across the Bug into Soviet-controlled territory. Unlikely Kressman among these, because Ozorkow too far west to reach river easily.

Oct. 1939—Jews in Western rural Poland herded into larger cities. Ozorkow ghetto swells to 9,600.

Dec. 1939—Nazis decree 2 years forced labour for all Jewish males ages 14-60.

1940-1942—in general two trends: 1) gradual deportation of Jews eastward out of annexed Poland, collecting them in massive ghettos like Warsaw, many die of starvation and disease. 2) rounding up of able-bodied young men for hundreds of slave labour camps, especially along Soviet border.

-no way to know if Kressman taken from Ozorkow, and if so, where went.

June 1941—Nazi elite decides on its "Final Solution", the extermination of all Jews in Europe.

Early 1942—2,500 Jews from Ozorkow ghetto sent to be gassed at Chelmno death camp.

May 1942—800 "able-bodied" Ozorkow Jews sent to factories in Lodz, a large ghetto nearby (162,000 Jews).

Green stopped to consider the implications. The city of Lodz had been a major armaments manufacturing centre during the war. If Kressman were a blacksmith by trade, and if he were a relatively young and healthy man, his skills would have been useful in a munitions factory making planes and tanks for the war effort. So he might have been among the eight hundred chosen for slave labour in Lodz. It was a slim hope, but it was all he had.

Keeping track of both Ozorkow and Lodz now, Green continued his search.

Jan.-Aug. 1942—40,000 Lodz Jews gassed at Chelmno.

Sept. 1942—Lodz declared "working ghetto", all those under ten or over 60, sick or weak, sent to gas chambers in Chelmno, 16,000 total.

Aug. 1944—last 70,000 Lodz Jews sent to Auschwitz to be gassed, except 500 selected for slave labour in Germany and 800 left to clean up.

June 1945—Lodz liberated by Russian army, 877 survivors.

He paused again in dismay. He had lost all track of Ozorkow, but it appeared likely from the general pattern of deportations that the Ozorkow ghetto had been emptied by the end of 1942, and most of its residents sent either to Chelmno death camp or to the ghettoes, then to Treblinka death camp. In either case, they were gassed. A select few able-bodied ones had been sent to Lodz, but the entire Lodz ghetto had been deported to the gas chambers of Auschwitz in 1944, with only a few strong ones being spared. But after almost five years in slave labour, would Kressman still be strong enough to be selected? Unless he had been a very strong, healthy young man at the outset of the war, there was no way. Kressman's age was an essential part of the puzzle. But tracking that down required cooperation from authorities in Eastern Europe, assuming the records from sixty years ago were still around. Which was a faint hope.

With a sigh, he returned to his place among the dozens of slave labour camps surrounding Auschwitz. But a few minutes later, he laid down his pen again in frustration. The trail had become too fragmented. Depending on which labour camp Kressman had been sent to, he could have met a dozen deaths. He could have ended up in the ovens of Chelmno or Auschwitz. He could have been massacred by the SS in the last days of the war or died of typhus in the DP camps afterwards. It seemed futile to try to track down one lone Jew in this twisting criss-cross of fates.

Futile. "So why am I trying so hard to find him?" Green wondered aloud. The mystery Pole who had come to be known as Eugene Walker had probably bought a tool box from Kressman in the years before the war. That was probably the extent of the connection between them. There was no evidence that Walker was even from Ozorkow; this may have been assumed for immigration purposes because of the black box in his possession. Even if Kressman were still alive and Green could find him, what light would he be able to shed on Walker's identity and on the conflict between him and Mr. G.?

Perhaps, Green thought, I'm just trying to find him because I want to know the fate of one humble, small-town

Jew caught up in the maelstrom of Nazi terror. Because he was one more nameless, faceless victim marched to his unremembered death. Is that all it is? An ancestral tug through time? Perhaps a search for the story my mother and father would never tell me?

He found himself too numb to think reasonably, so he rose and went downstairs to prepare a cup of tea. Cradling the cup, he slipped a CD of Chopin Polonaises into his player, sank back in the easy chair and shut his eyes. He rarely played classical music nowadays, preferring the raw pulse of rock, but the lyrical piano brought with it the presence of his mother, bent over the keys of their aging Heintzman and swaying to the melody beneath her hands. Chopin had been her greatest love.

As the warm tea spread through him, he felt some return of perspective. No, there was more to this search than personal curiosity. Intuition had always been a powerful ally in his detective work, and his intuition told him the black box was important to Walker. It was all that remained of his pre-war life, and he had clung to it even when he could no longer remember what it had meant or what he had endured.

A simple tool box, purchased from an unknown blacksmith years ago, could hardly have had such meaning.

Just as he had gathered the energy to return to the history books, the front door opened and Sharon and Tony spilled into the hall.

"Da-da-da-da," Tony crowed.

"Yes, Daddy's home. Incredibly," Sharon said. "Let's go find him."

Green poked his head through the hall archway just as Sharon was pulling off the baby's boots. She gestured to him to take over and disappeared back out to the car, returning with an armload of shopping bags. Among them, he noticed with a sinking feeling, one from the local paint store. As much as the old wartime mystery beckoned, he knew he owed Sharon some time. He'd promised her Sunday, and now Sunday was half over.

Home improvement had never been his forte, and by the time he had the gallon of blue paint up on the living room walls, he had nearly half of it on himself as well. Sharon had left him alone so that he could swear in peace, but she'd come downstairs briefly to snap some pictures of him perched precariously on a chair as he stretched to reach above the window. "I need some proof for the skeptics at work," she said. Green knew that his domestic antics provided comic relief in the staff cafeteria of the Royal Ottawa Hospital.

By the time he had finished the first coat, the early winter darkness was already descending, and the house was uncharacteristically silent. No baby babble, no whining, no background bustle. It must be Tony's afternoon nap time, and perhaps Sharon had slipped into bed for a brief rest herself. Feeling very virtuous and not a little sore, he washed up and went in search of her to collect his brownie points. Four hours of hard labour ought to be worth something.

But the master bedroom was empty, and as he passed by his study, he saw Sharon hunched over his desk, engrossed in his notes. She raised her head, looking as dazed as he must have earlier.

"Mike, what are you doing here?"

Normally Green tried to keep the grim realities of his police work separate from his home life, especially since the baby's birth; he needed his home as a haven to which he could escape. Sharon too needed a haven, because psychiatric nursing drained the soul as surely as investigating death. But today, still raw from his own glimpse into his past and sensing a rare

111

moment of intimacy in the house, he told her the whole story.

Sharon was not a child of survivors. Her own parents had spent their childhood in Toronto during the war and raised her in the safe, antiseptic suburb of North York. But her empathy was what had first drawn him to her and now, as she sat listening with her chin propped in her hands, her eyes narrowed astutely.

"This is a lot closer to home for you than your average gang execution, isn't it, honey?"

"Well, Kressman is, yeah. I mean, it's just a box, and the rest is just some big fairytale I've made up, but it feels real to me."

Her dark eyes were gentle. "Because of your parents."

He shook his head, pushing sentiment aside. "Maybe, but I feel it's connected to this case. If I'm going to find out who Walker really was, so I can figure out who killed him, I might have more luck by tracking down Kressman. At least I have a name."

"And you think this Kressman might still be alive?"

"Think?" He paused to consider. No, he didn't think Kressman was alive. He hoped, against all reasonable odds. He flipped the books open and bent over to show her the charts and maps depicting the last days of the war. "It's possible. In the spring of 1945 the Allies were pushing eastward across Germany towards Berlin, liberating the camps in West Germany. Now, we know that the Nazi camp commanders were in a panic, so some of them killed all the inmates before the Allies arrived, but some of them forced them to march eastward to camps deeper inside Germany."

"That's nuts!"

"Well, they were desperate to destroy all the evidence and witnesses to their atrocities. And at the same time, the Red Army was advancing across Germany from the east, overtaking all the work camps and death camps in Poland along the way.

112

Some of those inmates were also driven westward towards central Germany."

"On a collision course."

"Right. And that's what led to the eventual partition of Germany. On May 9, the advancing armies converged in the middle, Germany surrendered, and the partition line was drawn right down here. But the ending wasn't neat, like these charts. German soldiers were deserting in droves, Nazis and SS officers were trying to escape the country, civilians were fleeing the fighting, and right in the middle of this were all these half-dead camp inmates milling around. If Kressman was strong enough to survive, he could have ended up in one of the camps right around the partition line." He drew his finger through the map of Germany and in the process passed right through Dresden. He stopped, his throat suddenly dry.

"My God."

She leaned over the map. "What?"

"Two days after Germany surrendered, Eugene Walker was found wearing a German army uniform, hiding in the mountains just south of Dresden."

"You think he was a German deserter?"

He shook his head vigorously. "Let me think this through. No, the uniform and the papers were stolen from a German soldier who actually did die in the battlefield at Dresden. If Walker'd been a German deserter, or even an Allied soldier who'd escaped from a German POW camp, he'd never have concealed his identity by putting on a German uniform. He risked getting shot either as a deserter by the German military police, or as an enemy soldier by the Allies. That makes no sense."

"Maybe he was just a civilian—a simple peasant from Poland or Germany—who got caught in the fighting. Maybe he put on the uniform to keep warm, or because he didn't know the Germans had lost and he wanted to protect himself."

Green forced himself to consider her idea, to disprove it before allowing himself to face the theory that had first leaped to his mind and set his heart racing. Her theory fit the facts well enough, but it didn't feel right.

"Walker was in a state of complete mental and physical collapse," he said. "He was sick, wounded, starving—"

"Well, he could have been bombed, or he could have been driven hundreds of miles from his home."

"But he didn't talk for months, and he seems to have blocked out forever his past—and what happened to him."

"If you believe that."

"Yes," he admitted, "if I believe that."

She looked up at him, pushing her dark curls out of her eyes. "So what are you saying, Mike?"

"What if he was a concentration camp survivor himself? What if he was one of those force-marched across Germany, and on the day of surrender, he was let loose or escaped right at this juncture. Dresden."

Her eyes widened. "A Jew?"

He pondered that. Something didn't fit right. "No. A Pole."

"Why?"

Green didn't know why. Walker just didn't feel like a Jew. "He was big and blonde, for one thing—"

She waved her hand in dismissal.

"He was an anti-Semite," he added. "He threw a fit when his son married a Jew."

"Stranger things have happened, Mike."

"By the end of 1942, almost three years earlier, most of Poland's Jews had already been killed, so the odds of a Jew surviving are incredibly slim. And the way he was found…" Green groped to put his intuition into words. "What Jew, no

114

matter how confused, would put on the uniform of their most hated enemy and hide from the Allies who came to liberate them? The Jews welcomed the liberators with open arms."

"I don't see why a Pole would be any different," she observed.

"He might have been afraid he'd be accused of helping the Third Reich."

"Helping?" She looked skeptical. "How?"

"By working in one of their labour camps. Walker would have been eighteen years old when the Germans invaded Poland. A young man just entering his prime. We know that the Nazis exterminated or incarcerated millions of non-Jews as well as Jews, usually for assorted political or religious reasons, and they were especially harsh towards the Poles, because they wanted to assert the superiority of the *Volksdeutsch*—the ethnic Germans living in Poland. But what is less well known is that the Nazis seized two and a half million able-bodied young Polish men to work in their labour camps. They needed that labour to run their war industries, to build planes and tanks, to make bullets and guns. First they used Jews, but by the end of 1942 they'd worn out or killed off many of their able-bodied Jews, so they had to find another source of slave labour. Young, strong, healthy Poles."

"And you think Eugene Walker was one of them."

He nodded. "It feels right. He was a big, strong ox of a man even at the end, and because he worked to supply their war machine, he might have thought he'd be called a traitor. In fact, maybe people even did. As you said, in torture situations, stranger things have happened."

She ran her hand through her hair, making her curls stand on end. She looked unconvinced. "But you'd think in the fifty-five years since, surely someone would have noticed the prison number tattooed on his arm."

*　　*　　*

Thirty minutes later, with the paint flecks still in his hair and a yellow ski jacket thrown hastily over his jeans, Green mounted the Reid porch. The Walkers' old Dodge sat alone in the driveway, and Green was relieved when Ruth herself answered the bell. He didn't relish another verbal joust with Don Reid.

Ruth was filling out the endless forms that seem to follow death, and to his surprise she set aside the chore without protest to fix them both a cup of tea in her daughter's spotless kitchen. When he explained his theory, she remained quiet a minute, eying him intently. Wisps of grey hair framed her face.

"A concentration camp victim," she murmured finally.

"It never occurred to you?"

She gestured vaguely. "There were so many possibilities. Dresden was horribly bombed. Civilians lost their houses, whole families, even whole neighbourhoods were demolished. Lots of people were wandering around Europe in shock."

"But I thought you assumed he was Polish, not German."

"Well, yes, but—" She broke off, flustered. "It was an assumption. He could have been a DP from anywhere."

"What made you think he was a DP and not a camp survivor? Surely you were seeing lots of survivors, or at least hearing about them."

"Yes, we were." She coloured. "And yes, the thought did cross my mind, especially later when people began to document the emotional after-effects of the Holocaust. Eugene was literally one of the walking dead for a long time."

"Did he have a number tattooed on his arm when he arrived in England?"

She shook her head. "Obviously, if he'd had one, I would

116

have been sure, wouldn't I?"

"He had nothing? No marks?"

"Well…" She vacillated. "Actually, he had dreadful scars on his arms. The doctor said he probably got them on barbed wire. The wounds were on the mend when he came to us, but certainly the skin had been ripped away in strips along his arms and wrists."

"So it is possible there had been a tattoo."

"Yes, it's possible. It is possible." She repeated the assertion with more vigour, her eyes clearing. "I had thought the barbed wire rather supported the wounded soldier story, perhaps that he'd escaped from a German POW camp. Many Poles did fight under British command. But if he were a survivor, a number of other strange behaviours would make sense."

He hid his excitement. "Like what?"

"For a long time after he came to our hospital in England, he huddled in the dark in his room with that wretched black box. He hated to come out into the light, as if he only felt safe unseen. And the strangest things would set him off—a dog barking, the scream of another patient, the whistle of a train. He'd fly into these fits, and we'd need a straitjacket. Didn't they patrol the camps with dogs? And they brought the prisoners in on trains. He could never stand to ride on a train."

"Did he ever go back to Poland or Germany?"

She looked shocked. "Goodness, no. I would never have put him through that. You must understand, Inspector. Eugene didn't remember what he'd been through, and I wasn't sure it would be a blessing for him to remember. Sometimes even the sound of German or Polish being spoken would make him tremble."

"What did you tell your children about his past?"

Her lips tightened in a firm line. "Nothing specific. They

knew he'd been through hardship, but what good would it have done to upset them?"

"It might have helped them to understand him."

"Eugene would have hated the pity. He was old world, the man of the house. One endured one's own burdens."

And you endured them for everyone, he thought. "Do you have a picture of him when he was young? A wedding picture or…?"

She stiffened at the abrupt change of direction. "Why do you want that?"

"I'd like to borrow it for a few days," he replied vaguely. He was hoping to show it to any Ozorkow survivors Naomi Wyman managed to unearth for him.

He could sense from her frown that she was not satisfied, but she tried a more oblique approach. "Frankly, I can't see how all this ancient history has anything to do with his death. All it does is stir up pain."

He could have soothed her with some vague platitudes, but he was getting tired of family secrets. Perhaps it was time to cast a lure and see what he caught.

"I'm a stickler for the whole picture, Mrs. Walker. Did you know, for instance, that the man Eugene brawled with twenty years ago was from Ozorkow, too?"

For an instant, he thought she froze before she pulled the veil firmly down on her emotions.

"No," she replied. But he didn't believe her.

Eight

March 4th, 1941

Lodz. City of legend, of vice and opportunity.
Wide-eyed, we feast on its cobbled streets, grand balconies,
shop windows overflowing with wares.
Furs and bright fashions fill the streets.
She smiles at me. Resettlement, the Germans called it.
Maybe even a small apartment, a bed and stove.
The truck lumbers on
deeper into the city, into grime and crumbling stone.
Faces in the street follow us, toothless and bleak.
Ahead, barbed wire and a massive gate,
Policemen everywhere.
Papers, stamps, permits, questions, lines.
More lines.
Just say you have a trade, whispers a beggar at my side.
Metal worker or bootmaker are the best.
So the poet becomes a tinsmith.

Monday morning dawned blustery and grey, with a
northeast wind that whipped the snow across the fields, iced
the roads and snarled the traffic on the way into town. Green
spent over an hour fuming in bumper to bumper gridlock and

missed the early morning meeting he'd scheduled with Sullivan. He'd spent an hour on the phone with Sullivan the evening before, going over questions to ask the mysterious Mr. G. in Hamilton, but a few more had popped into his head over the course of his half-sleepless night.

This ridiculous commute won't work, he thought as he finally pulled into the station. I'm in charge of Major Crimes, I can't be an hour away from command central when a crisis strikes. He had a dreary committee meeting scheduled for most of the morning, and he didn't dare stretch Jules' magnanimity by skipping it. But he had a list of tasks he needed to address before he went to the meeting, and very little time in which to address them. Now that the case was officially a homicide investigation, courtesy dictated that he at least let the Major Crimes staff sergeant know that it was on the books.

When he reached the second floor, he found Sullivan already gone to the airport and Detective Gibbs hovering outside his door. The tall, lanky young officer was all spit and polish in his new grey suit, and he brightened like an eager puppy at the sight of Green.

"Oh, Gibbs, I've got a job for you." Green opened his office and strode around his desk.

Gibbs followed him in. "Yes, sir? I've got the forensic reports Sergeant Sullivan asked me to get, and he said to give them to you right away. He said it's a whole new ball game."

Green looked up from his drawer. "What did he mean—a whole new ball game?"

"He didn't say, sir. Just that you'd know what he meant."

Green sighed. Sullivan and his riddles again. He'd be laughing all the way to Hamilton as he pictured Green's face. "Tell me what you've got," he said.

Gibbs perched on the edge of the visitor's chair, his back

rigid at attention as he rifled through his notebook. He cleared his throat, his Adam's apple bobbing.

"First the RCMP lab. They identified the tire tread from the Walker laneway. Umm—it's a motomaster SR175 all-season radial made by Canadian Tire. They said you'd be thrilled."

Green knew next to nothing about cars and cared even less, his view being that a car was a box that got you from point A to point B. Preferably without breaking down. "Why?" he asked.

"It's probably the most common tire on the road, sir. But the lab said there's about fifty Ks wear on it, and there are enough accidentals on the tread that they should be able to give us a positive ID on the vehicle if we bring it in."

"Which doesn't help us find it. Did they make a guess at the type of vehicle? Big or small?"

"Judging from the wheel span, a subcompact. And they said Canadian Tire is a replacement tire, so they guess there's a hundred and fifty thousand kilometres on the car, give or take. That makes it likely five years old or more. On probability."

Green checked his notes of the Renfrew visit. The old woman on the neighbouring farm had described the car she'd seen as black and flat-roofed. "That means we're probably looking for a not-so-new black subcompact hatchback."

"Yes, sir, do you want me to start looking—"

"No, I need you working on the black tool box. Did you look into it?"

"Oh yes, sir." Gibbs sat up straighter, if that was possible, and flipped back through his notebook, in which Green caught a glimpse of meticulous rows of tiny script. "I checked the antique dealers in the city, and I also called the Canadian Antique Dealers Association. No one really knows about

European tools, but they gave me the name of a dealer near Toronto who specializes in collectible tools and locks. Do you want me to call him?"

Green shook his head sharply. "Take it to him."

Gibbs blinked. "What, sir?"

"If you hurry, you can just catch the plane Sergeant Sullivan is on. I want you to ask the dealer about the keys. I'm not interested in the tools, just the keys. Who made them, when, and for what purpose."

Gibbs was gaping at him. As a detective, Gibbs was meticulous and thorough, perhaps to a fault, but he didn't handle curve balls well. Green stood up to herd him towards the door.

"But sir, I have the fingerprint report from Sergeant Paquette as well. The one Sullivan says makes a whole new ball game."

"I'll get it from Lou myself."

"But I—I—what about travel authorization, sir?"

"I'll phone the airport and buy your ticket myself. Just go. The box is in Property."

Green was still grinning when the flustered young detective disappeared into the elevator, trailing his parka behind him, but the grin had faded considerably by the time he'd wrestled with airline red tape and managed to book the flight. He glanced at his watch, swore and scanned the squad room impatiently. Two detectives were just strolling to their desks with fresh cups of coffee in their hands. Green knew they were just tying up loose ends on a big file they'd worked, which meant they were free for the picking.

"Watts, Leblanc! I want you to check the make and colour of the cars belonging to the relatives and friends of Eugene Walker." Seeing their blank faces over the rims of their coffee cups, he snapped his fingers impatiently. "The stiff in the Civic parking lot Wednesday. I'm looking for a dark subcompact hatchback. When you find it, match it to the tread the lab has." He held up his hand to forestall their bewildered protest. "I'll explain later. Just check family members, neighbours, whatever. Start with the Reids."

Afterwards Green went down the hall and found Sergeant Lou Paquette in his fingerprint lab, shrugging on his parka. He looked bleary-eyed and grim, and when he saw Green he groaned.

"I gotta go out on a call, Mike. Didn't Bob Gibbs give you my report?"

"No time. I figured I'd get it from the horse's mouth."

The Ident man sighed and sat down again. "I don't know why I keep doing this for you. I must be crazy. I tell you, if I'd had any place to go on the weekend, you wouldn't have seen me for dust."

"What have you got for me?"

Lou Paquette gave him a long stare, then shook his head. "You never were a guy to waste words on thank yous. I've got a suspect for you, if that's what you mean. Don Reid. Boy, was he pissed off when I showed up to take his prints Sunday. Said he was going to call the commissioner, the mayor, his MP. Anyway, his prints were all over the investment bonds. All over the booze in the basement too, but I don't see how that makes him a murderer."

"Anyone else's prints on the booze?"

"Yeah, the stiff's and his wife's. Plus an unidentifiable. But every liquor store clerk from here to Seagram's could have touched those things."

"It doesn't matter. What matters is that Don Reid did." Green swung around, pausing in the doorway to grin. "Thanks, Lou.

Go out to your call. And then maybe try your bed."

Just as he was leaving Paquette's room, he heard his name being paged. When he glanced at his watch, he saw that he was fifteen minutes late for his committee meeting. Fuck, he thought, Jules sure was giving him no margin for error this morning. Obediently, he ducked into the stairwell and descended to the first floor, where he joined the cross-section of officers on the Building Planning Committee, which was at that moment planning the new Far East station. Green had tried to wiggle out of it, citing the exigencies of his job as well as his complete lack of qualifications for designing buildings, but Jules had been adamant. They needed an inspector, and his number had come up.

But as the discussion of toilets droned around him, Green found himself drifting back to the case. Sullivan should soon be arriving at Gryszkiewicz's Hamilton house. What would he learn there? Where did Mr. G. fit into the saga of concentration camps and stolen identities? And what would Gibbs learn about the keys? Mass produced during World War Two for storage depots or the like, Mr. Fine had said. "Or the like…" Like what? In the story of the three old men, there might be enough intrigue and hatred and secrecy to last a lifetime.

But was there murder? Or were Sullivan's more pedestrian suspicions right? He obviously thought that the motive lay among the missing investment certificates and the hidden whiskey in Walker's cellar, and that the killer was from Walker's present life, not his past. Certainly something didn't seem right about Don Reid. He was hiding something—too edgy, too secretive, too eager to divert the blame elsewhere. He might be a thief, he might even be the clandestine whiskey supplier. But how did that make him a killer?

When Green finally managed to liberate himself from the

committee meeting, it was past noon, and he hurried back to check whether there had been any calls from Sullivan or Gibbs. None. But there, sitting at the top of his list of incoming e-mail, was a report submitted by Detectives Watts and Leblanc, brief and to the point.

Dark grey 1994 Honda Civic hatchback L.P. Ont.149 XOA, registered to Donald Reid, 92 Riverbrook Road. Ident is working on a match right now.

*   *   *

"Aw, come off it, Inspector! Am I the suspect of the day? Yesterday Howard, tomorrow…maybe even Ruth?"

"Standard police procedure, Mr. Reid," Green replied blithely. "I'm simply taking a statement of your whereabouts on Wednesday between eleven and two p.m."

"Should I have my lawyer?"

Green shrugged. "That's your right, of course. In fact, although I'm not charging you with anything, there are some formalities we should cover." He went on to recite the standard Charter caution about Reid's rights. Because of the official nature of the visit, he had brought along Detective Leblanc, who had the misfortune to be in the squad room when Green read her memo. They had found Don Reid at work in a glass office tower ten floors above the noon-time bustle of Queen Street. His lunch of a shwarma, coke and Danish was spread out on his desk, and the reek of garlic permeated the room.

Reid had not been pleased to see the two police officers, and, as the precise and official-sounding caution droned on, Green detected a hint of panic beneath the veil of indignation. At the end, Reid leaned back in his swivel chair and surveyed

Green across his black lacquered desk. His eyes were slightly pink, and a pen twirled restlessly between his fingers, belying his casual pose.

"I was at lunch with a colleague, Mason Whitmore. His office is on the seventh floor."

"From when to when?"

Reid looked bored. "About twelve fifteen to two. We ate at Daly's. That's in the Westin Hotel," he added, as if a mere police officer might never have heard of it. In fact, Green had once questioned a suspect as he ate his goat cheese fettuccine at the discreet rose-linened table. The memory caused him to smile, but only briefly before briskly requesting Whitmore's address and telephone number. He signalled to Leblanc, who slipped her notebook into her pocket and left the room. Green turned back to Don's defiant stare.

"Did you know Ruth and Eugene were coming for tea that day?"

"Oh yes, that's why I worked late that afternoon."

"Why?"

Reid shrugged. He was now working the pen slowly up and down through his fingers, the restlessness abated but not gone. "Margaret had to play the dutiful daughter for her mother's sake—to help ease the burden—and she was used to Eugene's mean streak. I couldn't stand the guy. I used to try, for Margie's sake, but when he started taking his meanness out on my boys, yelling at them, shoving them around, I drew the line. Now I stay as far away from him as I can."

"Is that why you bought him five hundred dollars worth of whiskey to hide in his cellar?"

Reid's fingers stopped. "What the hell are you talking about?"

"There are three cases of twelve with your fingerprints all over them."

"Oh." Reid leaned back into his chair, and for some curious reason, Green thought he looked relieved. He shrugged. "I bought the old bastard some booze to keep him happy. Is that a crime?"

"Weren't you aware that in his physical condition, that was tantamount to killing him?"

Reid sneered. "Oh, come on, I didn't pour the stuff down his throat. No way you can pin a murder on me for that."

"No, you're right." Green smiled. "Embezzlement might be a better charge."

Reid's sneer vanished. "What?" he managed.

Green leaned forward quietly. "What did you do with the other fifteen hundred?"

"What the hell—"

"I should warn you I have a man speaking to your bank manager right now, so choose your answer carefully." He doubted the bank manager would divulge a thing without a subpoena, but Don Reid didn't have to know that.

"My bank manager?" Reid half-rose from his chair. "Where the hell are my rights!"

"Taken care of, I assure you."

Reid sat back, regrouping his thoughts. "I made a deal with Eugene. I buy the booze for him, I take a cut of the money."

"Pretty big cut, Reid. Five hundred bucks worth of whiskey for him, fifteen hundred cash for you. Maybe Walker found out you'd ripped him off, threatened to tell Margaret about your money problems, and you killed him to keep him quiet. Better sooner than later anyway, eh? He was drinking up all your inheritance money."

"It was a lousy fifteen hundred bucks! Who the hell would kill for fifteen hundred bucks?"

"A desperate man. A man in so deep a hole he has nowhere

to turn. A man with an image to protect and a lifestyle to maintain." Green took a gamble. "A man with some kind of problem that uses up money faster than he can make it. What is it, Reid? Blackmail? Gambling? DotCom investments?"

Reid sputtered briefly before his gaze dropped, and he lifted his hands in defeat. "I—I just needed a little to tide me over. Hell, who doesn't sometimes? I lost a bundle when the Nortel stocks went in the toilet, but the boys still want designer clothes and all the latest snowboard equipment. I didn't want to worry Margie because she gets so nervous. I didn't like squeezing the old man, but I sure as hell wouldn't have killed him over it." The pen quivered in his hands. "Goddamn it, Green, a little fucking privacy…"

"Why were you at your mother-in-law's house in the country the day after Eugene's death?"

Reid raised his head again, frowning blankly.

"Your car was seen at the house on Thursday."

Reid's eyes shifted from Green's face to the notebook in his hand. Green could sense his thoughts scurrying as he tried to assess this new threat.

"So what?" he blustered finally. "Is it a crime to take a drive?"

"Not at all. I'm just trying to complete the picture. What were you doing there?"

Reid wiped his temple with a trembling hand. "I…I went to pick up some clothes for Ruth. She needed things, but she couldn't face the place. What's the big deal?"

"What time was that?"

"How the hell should I know? That day was such chaos. Margaret was trying to organize everything, and Ruth was trying to find Howard."

"How long did you stay?"

"I don't know—five or ten minutes?"

At that moment the door opened, and Leblanc reappeared. After an exchange of whispers, Green turned back to Reid sharply.

"What time did you say you met Mason Whitmore at the Westin hotel?"

Reid blinked at the shift in focus. "Twelve-fifteen. Perhaps a couple of minutes later."

"How did you get there? On foot? Car? Bus?"

"On foot. It only takes ten minutes. I always walk from the office to the Rideau Centre."

"Even on that day? If you recall, there was a snowstorm."

"All the more reason to walk. Traffic was at a standstill."

"What time did you leave your office?"

"I'm not sure."

"Your secretary says before twelve. She tried to find you for an overseas call."

"Oh. Yes, well, I had to go to the bank."

"What bank is that?"

"Look—" Reid's voice squeaked, and he cleared his throat, trying to recapture some bluster. He looked battered. "I think I'd like to talk to a lawyer."

Green smiled affably. "Sure, no problem. Although, as you said, if you have nothing to hide, you should just answer my questions and save yourself the money."

"I have nothing to hide, But you keep throwing things at me, and I'm not sure where you're going."

"Where I'm going, Mr. Reid, is that I'm trying to figure out what you did with the extra thirty minutes that are missing from your story. Whitmore says you were twenty minutes late and out of breath."

"There was a line at the bank!" Reid retorted, half-whine

and half-defiance. "I waited fifteen minutes in line, almost gave up. The Toronto Dominion Bank on Metcalfe Street. Call them if you like. And I knew I was late for lunch, so I rushed. Nothing sinister, Inspector. Nothing guilty."

*   *   *

Half an hour later, confronting the fear in Margaret Reid's eyes, Green wondered what it was about him that compelled others to defend themselves even before he had accused them. It was an idle question, of course. He knew the answer. He treated everyone as if they were guilty, and he shifted moods so unpredictably that witnesses never felt secure about what he was thinking. It had begun as a natural character flaw which had scattered friends and lovers over the years, but he had learned to use it to his advantage. Now he smiled at Margaret Reid to take the sting out of the question he had just posed. They were sitting in her kitchen, and he had sent Detective Leblanc away so that he could speak to Margaret more gently. Unlike her husband, who needed bullying, Margaret needed kid gloves.

"It's merely routine, Mrs. Reid, just so I have everyone's whereabouts for my files. I can assure you I honestly don't think you killed your father."

Margaret rallied slightly, twisting her purse straps through her fingers as if to give herself strength. Her look was almost plaintive. "But I don't...I don't really have an alibi. I was expecting Mom and Dad for early tea, so I was out shopping. The grocery store and the drug store, then I mailed a parcel at the post office, a Christmas present for a friend in Toronto. I started about eleven, and I got home about one. But I have no one who could say 'Yes, she was with me from this time to that time.'"

"Did you save any of the receipts? They often say the time

on them."

She shook her head. "After I've checked off the items at home, I throw out the receipts. After all, it's not like clothing, which I might return."

He smiled inwardly. Margaret Reid's methods were like her house, neat and rational. Unlike his own, where a bag from the drug store might lie on the counter for weeks, unnoticed by either Sharon or him.

"It's not important," he soothed. "Were you looking forward to your parents' visit?"

"Looking forward?" She spoke as if that were an alien concept to her. "Yes, of course. Mom enjoys the boys so much."

"Did your father?"

She hesitated. "He loved them, of course, but they tired him. Dad was never very good at...at showing his affection. You had to look for the little things—a wink or 'that's my girl'. Sometimes he'd get embarrassed by his feelings, and he'd get angry, but even then you knew it was because of his love. But the boys weren't used to that. Don—their father—is so different. Affectionate, up front. What he feels, he shows." Her eyes glowed.

"Quite an adjustment for you, then."

"Don's been my rock. I know I'm not a very strong person, Inspector. Not like my mother. I lean on him a lot. Too much, in fact. It's hard on him. His father left them when they were small, and he always had to be the strong one in his family, take care of his mother and little brother. And now me. It makes him tense sometimes. I know he's seemed...moody to you, but underneath he's really a wonderful man." Her eyes pleaded. "Don't misjudge him."

"How long has he been moody?"

"He's not moody all the time. Sometimes he's very happy and relaxed. In fact, I've been wondering if it isn't something physical. He's been getting nosebleeds."

Nosebleeds! That was it! The reason for Don's financial problems and his bloodshot eyes. Not grief, not family responsibilities. The next question was, did Margaret know?

"Nosebleeds," he interjected. "You know what causes those?"

"Hypertension," she replied, a little too quickly. "I'm a nurse, remember?"

"And snorting cocaine."

Her colour fled, but for a moment she didn't speak. Didn't breathe. "Don's a respectable, professional man, not some…"

"Even respectable professionals get caught up in it."

"Ridiculous," she snapped, beginning to rise. "My father was an alcoholic. I've seen what that's like. Do you think I'd put myself through that again?"

It happens all the time, he thought grimly, but he didn't say so, since she was fleeing behind the barricades and he needed her back.

"I'm sorry," he said humbly. "Sometimes my job gets unpleasant. Please sit down."

She perched on the edge of her chair.

"We'll change the subject. What I really need to know is what you were doing at your parents' country house the day after your father's death."

She had just begun to unravel the purse strap from her fingers with a sigh of relief, which changed abruptly to a gasp. The strap went taut.

"The next day?"

He nodded, still encouraging.

"My—ah…my mother wanted me to check the house. She was afraid she might have left something turned on, or the door unlocked, or some food out." Colour returned as the excuse took form. "It doesn't really make sense to travel all that way, I know, but I was trying to humour her."

"Did you take anything out of the house?"

"Like what!"

"Clothes, personal items for your mother."

"Oh! I'm sorry, you've got me all rattled. Things for my mother? Yes, yes, I did. She had nothing with her. I packed a small suitcase."

"How long were you there?"

She hesitated. "I'm not sure. Time seemed to stand still. It gave me an unpleasant feeling being in the house Dad would never again set foot in."

"I'm curious…" Green began slowly, shifting his position on his chair so that he could look fully into her face. He did not want to miss one twitch of her reaction. "I'm curious as to why you so carefully wiped out your footprints in the snow on the way in and out."

It was difficult to decipher the first emotion that flitted across her face, but the closest he could come was surprise. Surprise followed by bewilderment. And finally, as the implications set in, fear.

"I—I didn't do any such thing," she protested, but Green barely heard her. His thoughts were already racing afield, wondering why surprise had been the first reaction. And why fear the third.

The question nagged at him as he made his way down the drive to his car. Lunchtime had long since come and gone, but he barely noticed the gnawing in his stomach. Puzzle pieces floated through his head, disconnected and elusive. What's going on? Why are they lying? Which one was in the car!

The answer came to him just as he was negotiating his way

133

across three lanes of Queensway traffic towards the Metcalfe exit and the police station. Perhaps it was neither of them! Perhaps the figure the old farm wife had seen in Reid's grey Civic was neither Don nor Margaret. He had thought from Don's confused answers that he was simply protecting his wife, which was probably a life-long habit. But Margaret's reaction had not made sense. Her explanation had been shaky, certainly, but it was her genuine surprise and bewilderment over the footprints that had given her away.

Yet who would Margaret care enough about to lie to the police? She was a moral woman, bound by tradition and society's dictates. The list of people for whom she would break the law was very short. Her children, her husband, her mother…

And her brother.

But that did not make sense. At the time the car was spotted, Howard had not even known his father was dead.

*   *   *

Green strode across the squad room in search of Leblanc, who should have arrived well ahead of him. But there was no sign of her.

"Three-thirty in the goddamn afternoon, and everyone's on break," he muttered. "Ah, Watts! Finally. Listen, I need you to check out some information for me. It will mean some calls to Montreal and Toronto."

The detective was wrestling with a computer drawing program designed to make life easier for police officers, and he looked decidedly unenthusiastic about being summoned. Green handed him the details regarding Howard Walker's medical convention. "Check specifically if anyone saw him at the convention on Thursday afternoon."

He watched Watts slouch back to his desk and pick up the phone. Delegating grunt work was one of the rare perks of being an inspector. Green hated the committees, the statistics and the memos, but he loved being able to issue orders and have the plodding minutiae of a case fall into place. Making sense of those minutiae, interviewing witnesses and pulling it all together—those were things he hated to delegate, even when he should.

It reminded him that he had not yet met with the Staff Sergeant, whose job it really was to coordinate the major crimes cases, and who would no doubt be offended that Green had so completely overstepped him. Egos needed nurturing, Green was learning in his new management sensitivity seminars, and every now and then he actually remembered to try. So he spent an hour with Staff Sergeant Capelli patiently reviewing the case and other major cases before he spotted Watts through his half-open door, returning from the fax machine with a sheaf of papers.

Green gestured him into his office. "Did you manage to check out Toronto?"

Watts nodded. "The hotel and the convention people. You're going to really love this. Or hate it, depending on whose side you're on."

"What have you got?"

"Statements from colleagues, a copy of his hotel bill." Watts handed Green the fax. "He was registered there all right, but his alibi is full of holes."

Green had been scanning the hotel invoice and gave a cry of surprise. "That's not all that's wrong. Look at the goddamn phone calls!"

*   *   *

Green sat in his little blue Corolla just down the street from the Reid house, where he hoped Howard was still staying. The November chill was gradually seeping through his worn-out boots, but still he didn't hurry. He needed to sort out his plan of attack carefully. Howard had a lot of explaining to do, but he was no fool. If Green were to breach the wall of family silence, his approach had to be very subtle. Almost soundless.

Green was still probing possibilities when the front door flung back, and a young woman appeared on the doorstep, wrapping a long, trailing scarf around her neck. She glanced quickly up and down the street, passing over his car without a flicker of interest, and then set off briskly down the street in the other direction. She was well dressed in a bohemian way, with a loose, brown wool skirt swinging above her ankles.

Ah-ha, he thought. A plan of attack. On impulse, he jumped from the car and ran to catch up with her, startling her as his footsteps pounded up behind her. Hastily, he produced his badge.

"Sorry," he said breathlessly. "Rachel Walker, isn't it? I'm Inspector Green, Ottawa Police. I was about to call for your husband at the house when I saw you."

Her eyes narrowed warily. They were fine eyes, rich amber, widely set and thickly lashed.

"Howard's not here. He took his mother up to the country."

"Oh. Can I have a word with you then?"

"I'm not sure if I…"

"I don't bite, I promise. How about I buy you a hot cup of cappuccino somewhere?"

She said little as she climbed into his car, merely arched her eyebrows at the clutter of McDonald's wrappers and Tim Hortons cups that he tossed into the back seat. Her hands were folded demurely in her lap, whether out of natural poise or aversion to his grimy car, he could not tell.

Hoping to relax her, he grinned. "Don't you dare say a word. I happen to be very fond of Queensway dining."

"Howard warned me you had a way about you."

He cast her a surprised glance. "Warned?"

"He said people could say more to you than they had intended."

He smiled. "I'll take that as a compliment. What did he not want you to tell me?"

It was her turn to smile, turning to him with her flashing amber eyes. For an instant he felt his thoughts scatter.

"Now, I'm not that dumb, Inspector," she was saying when he could focus again. "Howard has nothing to hide. He's not afraid of anything incriminating. He just meant he opened up more to you than he intended. Howard doesn't open up easily—one more legacy from Daddy Dearest."

"I've heard a lot of secrets from people over the years. I don't shock easily, and I guess that's reassuring to some people."

She waited until they were seated across from each other in the Trattoria, a little Italian café on Preston Street. There was only one other customer at the other end of the room, an elderly labourer reading his Italian newspaper over a cup of coffee. The tables were brightly set with red and white checkered cloths in preparation for the dinner crowd. Once the waiter/owner had taken their orders, he disappeared into the kitchen to prepare them.

She fixed her amber eyes on him. "And what secrets do you want from me, Inspector?"

In an interview, control was essential. His years as a police detective had taught him that. But his years as a detective could not prepare him for the look in her deep, laughing eyes.

Women had been his weakness since his youth. An impish smile, dancing eyes, soft, sweet-scented limbs—the slightest hint sent his hormones flooding. Marriage had not changed his chemistry, merely his attempt to control it, and if he continued to look into those eyes, he would not be able to think at all. Studying his notebook, he gathered his forces.

He could not tell what she was thinking nor what she was feeling. He sensed anxiety, amusement, mockery—even fondness. But in this panoply of impressions, hostility was absent. He wasn't sure why. Perhaps Howard had told her he was Jewish, and she felt a natural kinship. Or perhaps she felt no reason to fear him. Whatever the cause, he sensed that he could make her an ally and give himself entry into the closed family secrets. But he had to play his cards right, and for that he had to be able to think.

He raised his eyes to meet hers again and willed his thoughts to remain in focus.

"Right now I'm just trying to get all the facts straight," he began humbly. "I always like the pieces to fit, no matter how irrelevant they might turn out to be. Today I've been working on the activities of the family in the past few days, since the death on Wednesday. I know your husband was at a medical conference at Mount Sinai in Toronto, and he told me you were staying overnight at a girlfriend's. Was that Wednesday or Thursday?"

She smiled, not fooled. "Wednesday. We had tickets to the National Ballet at the Place des Arts. Her name is Maxine Melanov, and her number is 689-2634, if you really want to know."

"And you stayed there how long?"

"Just the night. I went there from work on Wednesday, and went straight back to work from her place Thursday morning."

"And no one knew of this?"

"Howard did. I don't usually submit my schedule to my mother-in-law."

He grinned boyishly. "Of course not. So when did you get the call about your father-in-law?"

"Thursday morning. I checked our answering machine when I got to work and found a message from Ruth about a family emergency, so I tried to call her."

"What time was that?"

"A little after nine. But I had trouble locating her because she was at Margaret's. One of the problems with having in-laws who don't talk to you is that you don't have phone numbers. I did get through later in the morning."

"Why didn't you just call Howard in Toronto?"

Here for the first time, she wavered. "I did call, and I left a message at his hotel, but he was busy at the convention. I finally drove home and rummaged through his papers until I found his sister's address."

"And when did you reach Howard?"

"About six in the evening. He finally returned my call."

"Six in the evening!" Green feigned incredulity. "Why didn't you have him paged at the convention?"

She hesitated. "I did, but he didn't return my calls."

"Was he even there?"

She was a good actress, he had to grant her that. She had clasped her hands before her and was resting her chin on them in apparent nonchalance. He thought her knuckles whitened slightly, but it was the only sign she gave of the tension within.

"Inspector," she rebuked, "there were over a thousand physicians there. He could have been anywhere—the washroom, the coffee shop, outside for a breath of fresh air—and not heard the page."

"Did you try again or leave a message on the board?" he pressed relentlessly.

"Yes, I did, and he finally got it."

"None of his friends and colleagues saw him at all on Thursday," he said quietly. "One of his friends looked for him all day to tell him about the pages, and he couldn't find him anywhere at the convention."

She shrugged. "For all I know, he could have skipped the afternoon and gone out for a three-hour lunch on the town with some colleagues. Isn't that what people do at conventions?"

"My man asked the friend that, and he said it wasn't likely because they were having a luncheon address by a highly respected neurosurgeon whom everyone wanted to hear. This friend looked all over for Howard to sit with him, but he was nowhere to be found."

She finally relinquished the excuses and flounced back in her chair. Now he could sense hostility. "This isn't routine. Just what are you implying, Inspector?"

"Only that it seems he didn't attend the convention on Thursday. In fact, no one remembers seeing him most of Wednesday either. I don't know what that means, but I find it curious."

Her eyes snapped. "I suggest it just means no one could find him. It doesn't mean Howard killed his father. Howard was very mixed up about his father, but he would never have killed him. He was just trying to stay out of his life."

Their cappuccinos arrived, and she gratefully took advantage of the diversion to regroup her forces as she fussed with her coffee. Green did the same. He knew he'd get nowhere by pushing her to the wall, other than losing whatever kinship she might feel for him. He needed that more than he needed her speculations on Howard's activities, and he was beginning to suspect that Howard had kept her as much in the dark as everyone else. Howard was the one he needed to confront.

Taking his first delicious sip of coffee, he held up his hand in truce. "I agree with you. I don't think Howard killed his father." Green had known several sons who'd killed their fathers, but he wasn't going to tell her that. "However, I do think he went out to his father's house the next day—maybe to get something or look for something—and he is trying to hide that fact. I think perhaps he discovered something about his father that he's keeping to himself. And if so, he could be in danger."

Her amber eyes reflected her surprise. The hostility faded. "What are you talking about?"

"I think there's a dangerous secret here dating back to the Second World War. Possibly a secret someone would kill to protect."

To his surprise, she did not react with shock or disbelief, but with fear. Knowing fear. Her eyes narrowed, and her voice grew soft. "What have you found out?"

"I think Eugene Walker was a Polish labour camp survivor."

She dropped her eyes quickly, as if to hide their reaction. "Howard's mother rarely talked about it," she said. "But from what little I pieced together, I couldn't help wondering what he did during the war. That's certainly one explanation."

"What do you mean—one explanation?"

She coloured. "I mean it's one explanation for the way he was when Ruth found him. I know a lot of young Poles were interned by the Nazis."

She had fixed her gaze on her coffee, swirling the foam with a spoon which trembled in her hand.

Carefully, he probed deeper. "One thing puzzles me, though. If he had been a camp survivor, you'd think he would be more sympathetic to the Jews. But I understand he threw a fit when Howard married you."

Briefly her eyes lifted to his, and he caught a flash of what she had been trying to hide. Fear. "Polish anti-Semitism can run pretty deep," she countered. "Both sides hated and feared the other, justifiably or not. I imagine a Pole might react with the same panic as a Jew to intermarriage."

"Is that what Eugene did? He panicked?"

She nodded. "Howard said he was absolutely distraught. Occasionally you hear of Jewish parents being afraid and upset, but for a Gentile it seemed odd. It made me wonder."

"Wonder what?"

"What was he afraid of from a Jew? What he was hiding—" She caught herself and tightened her grip on her spoon.

In a flash of insight, he understood. Throughout occupied Europe, the Nazis had been aided in their round-up of the Jews by hundreds of local citizens. Some collaborated out of fear and self-preservation, but many had welcomed the chance to vent their own hatred and gain recognition in the eyes of their new masters.

Green's eyes narrowed. "You thought he was on the other side of the fence, didn't you? A Nazi collaborator."

She put her spoon down with a clatter. "I didn't think anything. I just wondered. Or rather, my father wondered."

Green recalled Jeff Tillsbury saying her father was influential in the Jewish community. "Does your father know something about war crimes?"

"He's a lawyer, and he used to be an advisor to the B'nai B'rith Anti-defamation League."

"What's his name?"

"Ben Lowenstein."

As he sipped his coffee, Green digested that news in silence.

The Anti-defamation league was a watchdog group that monitored and combatted racism across the country, mainly anti-Semitism. Green had heard of Ben Lowenstein, whose zeal in fulfilling his mandate had made him controversial in the Jewish community, which was anxious to build bridges rather than burn them. That Eugene Walker's son had chosen to link himself to such a family was the ultimate irony.

"That must make for some interesting dinner conversations," he remarked with a smile.

She had some of her father's fervour, however, and she was not easily deflected from her train of thought. Her coffee had remained virtually untouched at her elbow. "But my Dad's right," she said, as if she was used to having to defend him. "What do we really know about Eugene? He was found wandering around in the forests of Germany wearing a stolen army uniform and claiming he didn't know who he was or what language he spoke. Pretty damn convenient."

"So your father thinks the whole amnesia business was faked?"

"Brilliantly."

"But the shape Eugene was in—the typhus, the starvation. You can't fake that. He took months to recover."

"Even villains can fall ill. Look at his life!" She was animated now, her dark eyes sparking. "He picks a quiet farming community with a mixed ethnic make-up including Germans and Poles. He lives a reclusive existence and does almost nothing to call attention to himself. Cooperative, law-abiding, unobtrusive—that's exactly how war criminals have acted when they've come to North America."

"Did you or your father ever discuss this possibility with Howard?"

"My God, no. It's just a theory. What good would it do to

raise it with Howard? This is tearing him up enough as it is." She suddenly tensed. "What are you planning to do about it?"

He pondered the implications of the theory. It seemed as viable an explanation as his camp survivor theory, perhaps even more viable. His intuition agreed with hers. What would Eugene Walker have to fear from his son marrying a Jew if he himself were a survivor? Why would he have hidden in the country, avoiding human contact and exposure? Camp survivors were scarred in many ways, haunted by fears and blunted of feelings. Many of them were never able to talk about the traumas they had endured. But they rarely hid themselves away for more than half a century as a result.

She looked up in alarm as he rose from the table, pulling on his jacket, and tossed a couple of twoonies beside his cup.

"Where are you going?" she cried.

"To talk to an expert." He paused. "And please, tell your husband that if he knows something, don't keep it to himself. He may be playing in the big leagues."

Nine

June 22nd, 1941

The news scurries through the ghetto on the tongues of youth.
The goose-stepping fool has invaded Russia!
A flea leaps at the flank of a bear.
The flea is doomed!
Returning from the factories, workers hide their smiles
but quicken their step,
to reach home, to share the news, to cheer and dance.
Our apartment brims with talk and merriment.
Brotherhood, solidarity, the triumph of the oppressed.
In the centre, my rebel princess smiles,
her belly large with child again but her heart light as air.
Homemade schnaps is lifted high. To life.
Then in the quiet, my rebel princess adds
Next year in Jerusalem.
No need, we are all comrades in Russia's great socialist dream.
Comrades maybe, she replies, but is the Cossack far behind?

David Haley, the former war crimes prosecutor, had just returned from court and was still charged with combative adrenaline from having lost his case. His office in the century-old Justice Building was dry and over-heated, and sweat trickled down his brow onto his flushed face, adding to his irritation. He listened impatiently as Green explained his request.

"Almost impossible," Haley said immediately. "Ten times worse than your proverbial needle in a haystack."

"But is there a way we can check? Isn't there a list somewhere of suspected war criminals?"

"Sure there is. We've got one, so has the OSI—that's the Office of Special Investigations, the American War Crimes Unit. The Israelis have one, of course. And the Simon Wiesenthal Centre has a file on just about every guy who ever said *Sieg Heil.* There are pictures to go with some of these guys, fifty year-old pictures in most cases, but pictures. Your problem is you don't have the guy's name. Without his real name, how the hell can we check lists?"

"But didn't a lot of these guys change their names anyway?"

"Surprisingly, no. The big guys like Mengele and Eichmann did, of course, but thousands of others—camp guards, Einsatzgruppen members, SS officers—they just walked into the U.S. and Canada as bold as you please. Lied a little on their forms, immigration looked the other way. Often at the request of the CIA or the RCMP, I might add. The Soviets were the big bogeymen after the war, and Nazis were good anti-communists; that was the view of the fifties and sixties. So these guys bought themselves a little homestead in the country and lived happily ever after. They're laughing. Listen, they know damn well that even with names, we can't find them. But without a name, you'll never know."

The heat was beginning to prickle Green's skin, and he rose to remove his parka. He had hoped his question would only take a minute, but nothing about World War II Europe was ever simple. "We do have a picture. We could compare the picture."

David Haley gave a harsh laugh. "Have you got several

thousand more men on the Ottawa Police Force that I don't know about? We're talking thousands of photographs, fuzzy, old and tiny. We'd have to go through them one by one. We don't have nice modern computer technology in this business, Inspector. We're using investigative technology that's fifty years out of date. Old documents, letters, photos, scraps of unsubstantiated eyewitness testimony. It's hard work. We hardly nail any of them, Inspector."

"Mike. And I can see that. What a challenge!"

Haley tilted his chair back and loosened his tie. Some of the tension seemed to drain out of him. He was impeccably dressed in a charcoal, pin-striped suit and silk tie, looking every inch the senior government counsel. Green felt conspicuously shabby in his sports jacket that had long since abandoned its shape and his brown trousers that were rapidly following suit. But Haley seemed to be smiling at him with genuine respect.

"Yesterday you were hot on the trail of a survivor, today it's a war criminal. Can you give me a hint what's going on?"

"I'm investigating a man with a secret from World War II, and I'm trying to find out what it is." Briefly Green summarized the facts surrounding Walker's rescue in Germany and his slow, incomplete recovery in England.

"That sounds more like a survivor," Haley said without hesitation. "The alcoholism and the secretiveness—even they could fit the profile of a survivor."

"But the reclusive lifestyle is more characteristic of the war criminal, isn't it? The survivors I know don't hide out in the country for fifty years, shunning contact with people."

"That's because most of the survivors we hear about are Jewish. Jewish suffering in the Holocaust has gained world sympathy, it has been legitimized. Support groups and networks have sprung up to help the Jewish survivor feel less alone and pursue legal remedies. But we're talking about a non-Jewish survivor, and an anti-Semitic one at that. Where is his support and his legitimacy? Before the war, he and the Jew might have been on opposite sides. He can't feel part of Jewish suffering and mutual support, but there's no support and no place for him. All he can feel is shame. In the eyes of his fellow anti-Semites, in fact of most of the Polish community, he has become like a Jew. I can see such a guy easily finding his support in solitude and a bottle of booze."

Green tried to put himself in Walker's shoes, to imagine how it felt to be so set apart. Who would he identify with? Who would he despise? But considered that way, Green still couldn't make sense of Walker's state of mind.

"But if he were a survivor, I don't understand why the continued anti-Semitism. Almost paranoia. He was very upset when his son married a Jewish girl. The girl said he seemed afraid. Wouldn't a non-Jewish camp survivor feel some affinity towards the Jews?"

Haley shook his head. "You got me there. I'm not a psychologist. But it always seems to me the shrinks can explain anything. Maybe it reminds him of those days in the camp, you know? Of his humiliation."

It was plausible. Each individual fact could be made to fit, but the entire picture just seemed wrong. Green told Haley about the bar fight twenty years earlier. "This is another guy from the same town in Poland. He knew something. But they both refused to say a word about it, even to their own families."

"And your man Walker started it?" When Green nodded, Haley's brows gathered in thought. "Maybe the other guy insulted him. But it could have been anything. It could have been a woman they fought over years earlier in the old country."

148

"But it could have been this guy calling Walker a Nazi. If he was a war criminal and he thought he was safely hidden, that would have freaked him out."

"Or if he was a survivor," Haley countered, "it could have been the guy calling him a Jew-boy. That would freak a good anti-Semite out even worse."

Green grinned at him unexpectedly. "You know something? You're a good devil's advocate."

Haley laughed. He was totally relaxed now, his colour back to normal and the court loss evidently forgotten. "Poking holes in people's arguments is my job. What did your camp survivor/possible war criminal do that you're investigating? Are you allowed to tell me?"

"Got himself murdered. No one else thinks so, of course. And they think I'm nuts to be digging fifty years into the past."

Haley's expression grew sober. "Well, you're not. The bitterness of those times can last a lifetime, believe me. I'll never forget the survivors I dealt with. Their experiences were burned into their memory forever. I remember one woman, survivor of Auschwitz, who couldn't stand to hear "The Merry Widow". Apparently the SS had created an orchestra of young Jewish girls, dressed them up in navy skirts and white blouses, and made them play for the trains when they pulled into the station. For entertainment, like they were arriving at some exclusive spa." He sat thinking for a minute, stroking the crown of his bald head and seeming to be caught up in the incredibility of it all.

Then he shook his head as if to clear it and switched back to business. "You might try a few things. First, if you can find a survivor from Ozorkow—in fact, anyone from Ozorkow—you could show them this man Walker's picture and see if they can identify him as either a survivor or a Nazi collaborator."

"I already have someone from the Holocaust Remembrance Committee searching for survivors for me."

"Naomi Wyman?" Haley nodded. "She's a good lady. If there's anyone out there who's still remotely alive, Naomi will find them for you. The second thing you can do is ask the Simon Wiesenthal Centre to check his picture against all their known collaborators from Ozorkow. Provided there aren't too many."

"It's a pretty small town. There shouldn't be." Green's eyes were alight, and he was already reaching for his parka when Haley held up a cautioning hand.

"Of course, it could all be a complete wild goose chase, you know. If this guy is a war criminal lying about his past, who's to say he's from Ozorkow at all? Who's to say he's even a Pole? He understands and speaks Polish, but lots of Germans do, especially those living near or inside what was then Poland itself. The border between the two countries, and the allegiances of the inhabitants, shifted back and forth over the centuries anyway. Many of the ethnic Germans living in Poland joined the SS and served Hitler admirably. Your man could be a full-blooded member of the master race, hiding out in the midst of a snowy Canadian backwater and hoping everybody passes him by. It would explain his not mixing with his neighbours, rarely speaking Polish and not going to the Polish Catholic Church. He figured the masquerade might not hold up under closer scrutiny."

Green sucked in his breath. What had that old farmer Dubroskie said? "Nothing but a drunken old Polack, and I'm not even sure about that."

The case reminded him of one of those Russian dolls his father had told him about, where you open up one doll and there's always another inside.

*   *   *

By the time Green emerged from the Justice Building, November darkness had fallen. Light snow was sifting through the street lights, and Wellington Street was a snarl of rush hour traffic inching westward towards the suburbs. Green thought of the hour-long crawl awaiting him and felt his spirits sink. In the old days, he would have zipped across the canal and been home in his apartment in ten minutes. Black spots laced his vision, and he suddenly realized he'd forgotten lunch. He'd never survive the drive home in this shape. And besides, he'd no sooner get there than he'd have to turn around and go out again to meet Sullivan at the airport. With any luck, Sullivan might have some light to shed on who the real Walker was.

Pulling out his cellular, he phoned Sharon and told her he was going to stop by his father's on his way home.

"So don't hold supper for me, honey. I'll pick up some smoked meat for him and me as a treat."

He heard her groan. "But Mike, I wanted to talk about the party."

He was tempted to ask "What's to talk about?" The party was Sharon's idea—invite a bunch of their high-tech young neighbours and some of Sharon's friends from the hospital, who all thought Green was cute but hopeless husband material. She had told him he could invite some of his friends, but they both knew it was an empty suggestion; Green didn't fit in any better at the station than he did in the neighbourhood. His father would be his only ally.

Tony, of course, would be the centre of attention, but he wouldn't be much of a judge of whether the party was a success. And would care even less. Give him cake, ice cream and a couple of plants to chew, and he'd be on cloud nine.

"I won't be late," Green said instead. "Just an hour or two. I may have to pick up Brian at the airport."

"Have you bought anything for Tony yet?"

He thought fast. "I could stop at the Billings Bridge Mall on my way to the airport."

"Green…"

"Your parents have bought him everything he's going to need for the next five years," he countered in what had become a ritual between them. "All that's left is a two-wheel bike, and he's only one year old! What's left for me?"

"You're his father. Think of what a father gives his son."

"I don't know," he grumbled, feeling his stomach contract. He was too starved to duel effectively with her. "When I was growing up, my father could never afford anything. A baseball glove? A jock strap?"

She chuckled. "I'm not giving you hints, Green. This is for you to come up with—a special gift from you to your son."

He rang off with a sigh. Perhaps after a few moments with his father and a huge, mouth-watering smoked meat sandwich to fill the hole in his stomach, inspiration would come to him.

Sidney Green was sitting in his brown tub chair watching a rerun of *The Red Green Show* when Green let himself in. The sound was very loud, because Sid was slightly deaf, so he didn't hear his son until Green walked into the middle of the living room and stood in front of him. Sid peered up at him in confusion, as if he were out of time and place. His rheumy eyes blinked into focus to see his son holding out a large paper bag in his hand.

"I brought smoked meat and french fries. You hungry?"

"I ate already, in the cafeteria."

"So keep me company."

Sid's eyes had strayed to the television, but now they flicked back to his son with sudden alarm. "What's wrong? Sharon? The baby?"

Green shook his head, set the bag down and headed for the kitchenette, where he kept a modest store of beer in his father's fridge for his own use. A moment later he emerged with a bottle, as well as a glass of ginger ale for Sid.

"I just dropped by to say hi. I have to do some shopping for the baby tonight."

Sid's eyes lit up. "One year old! Oy, I can't believe it!" He laughed and clapped his hands. His father's laughter was such a rarity that Green felt his own spirits lift. Sid appeared to have forgotten Bernie Mendelsohn and the depressing rate at which his friends were dropping dead around him.

Green sank into a chair and propped his stockinged feet on the scarred coffee table. He held out a smoked meat sandwich to his father, who shook his head.

"Come on, it's Lester's. None of that synthetic stuff."

Still Sid shook his head. "Now I have a grandson, I want to stay alive." Unconsciously, he patted his chest. The reference to his heart condition reminded Green of Eugene Walker and of the past the two men might have shared. Deliberately he leaned forward and switched off the television.

"Dad, do you know anyone who comes from Ozorkow?"

"Ozorkow?" Sid stared at the blank TV, as if wondering where Green had got the idea. "In Poland?"

Green nodded. "Western Poland."

"I know where it is." There was a peevish rebuke in his tone. "Why do you want to know about Ozorkow?"

"I'm investigating the death of an old man who might have come from there."

"What does it matter where an old man comes from?"

"Dad," Green exclaimed in exasperation, "just answer me,

okay? It might matter."

"Give me part of that sandwich. I don't know anyone from Ozorkow. Bernie, Marv and me, we're all from little villages. But no one is from Ozorkow."

"What happened to all of you during the war?"

"Happened? We survived."

Green put down his beer and frowned at his father, who busied himself picking the peppercorns off his smoked meat. Eventually, Sid sighed. "Marv was hidden by a Polish family for a while. Bernie was in three camps, the last one Mauthausen."

"Labour camps?"

"Labour camps, death camps, ghettoes—they were all the same. People died."

"Were any of you sent to Ozorkow or Lodz?"

Sid raised his eyes from his peppercorns in astonishment. "Lodz, Ozorkow! What have you been reading, Mishka?"

Green held his eyes. "I've been reading about the Holocaust, Dad. I'm trying to figure out what role this old man played in it."

"Why?" Then Sid clucked his tongue as if at his own stupidity. "Why should I ask why? Since when does my son need a reason to solve a puzzle? It's enough it's a puzzle."

Green grinned. "You got it close enough."

Sid's eyes lit with affection as they met his son's, then gradually the light faded. "So," he said softly, "you've been reading about the Holocaust."

Green nodded. A strange electric silence fell, as if they stood at the edge of the chasm which had yawned between them all these years. But Green was not sure how far he dared venture to bridge it.

"Dad?" he began cautiously. "Can we talk about this old man?"

Sid studied the carpet, his breathing rapid in the silence. "I don't know anything about Western Poland. I was in the East."

"But you know about the labour camps."

"There was lots of labour camps, Michael."

"I only want to know about what they did to a man. And I want to know about the kind of young men who became Nazi collaborators."

"You can't find this in your books?"

"Not the human part. Not the soul of the man and how it would have changed him."

Sid's voice was barely audible. "And that, of course, is the most important part."

Green set his sandwich aside and leaned forward, fearing to breathe lest he break the fragile bridge being built. As carefully as he could, he sketched what he knew of Eugene Walker's story, ending in the mystery of his death. Sid Green said nothing, but he listened intently, his gaze fixed on his hands. When Green finished, Sid shook his head slowly back and forth.

"Every man is different, Michael. In the camps, some people found God, some lost him. Some found purpose, some lost it. Some felt shame, others anger. I don't know what made the difference. And after the war, you had to live with what you had been through. Not only what was done to you, but what you had done. Some could not. Some kept the guilt and the shame for a lifetime. Shame that they are alive even, when their children are dead. Shame that they played music while the people were being selected—" Sid broke off, devoting his full attention to the straw in his drink. When he resumed, his voice was flat.

"I know it is not an answer to your question about this man, Mishka. And I don't know about a non-Jew put in a camp. Would he go through the same things? His people were not all being murdered—his children, his mother and father. He would not be living with this fear that they want us all dead. I don't know, Mishka."

"What about collaborators? The camp guards, the local Fascists?"

Sid's eyes hardened. "The collaborators—how can I know what was in their heads? I can tell you the ones I knew, they hated Jews. That was the most important reason they joined the Nazis—because Hitler was killing Jews, and they wanted to help. Oh sure, it gave them better food and a fancy uniform and made them feel like big men pushing us around—these were important, but not so important as getting rid of Jews."

"But later, Dad, when they had seen the killing and they'd matured, didn't any of them regret it?"

Sid shrugged. "Some of the young bullies from the town—the little men who wanted to be big men—when they saw the blood, maybe they regretted it. But not for long. They got used to it."

"But today, Dad. Years later. As old men, don't you think they'd look back on the cruelty of their youth and feel ashamed? They killed thousands of people!"

As the memories came back, Sid had become animated. His eyes darted around the room and his colour rose.

"Eichmann, Demjanjuk, Barbie—do you think they feel bad? Not at all. They think they did nothing wrong. It was war, they were strong, they did the difficult things. For the good of the Fatherland. They are proud of this, Mishka."

"So a war criminal would not be living on a small country farm, hiding from people and drinking himself to death."

His father wiped his hand across his balding head on which a thin sheen of perspiration had broken out. His breathing was erratic. "I don't know, Mishka. There may be some of those monsters with a little soul left." He fixed his rheumy eyes on his son. "You think this man was a collaborator?"

"I don't know. He was hiding something. And surely a collaborator has more to hide than a victim."

Sid gave him a strange look. "Maybe not. Maybe the thing you want to hide from most is yourself."

*   *   *

More mysteries, Green thought wryly as he left his father's apartment. The more light I try to shine into the past, the more shadowed pathways I uncover. "Hiding from yourself." Thanks for that cryptic morsel, Dad. More shadows. You couldn't shed a little light, Dad, instead of that classic Yiddish shrug of yours before you changed the subject?

Back on the street, the light snow was tapering off in the darkness and, remembering his promise to Sharon, Green glanced at his watch. It was past eight o'clock. The stores closed at nine, so he had barely an hour to duck into a store, find a gift for Tony and get out to the airport before Brian Sullivan's plane touched down.

The Rideau Centre was five minutes away, and Green dashed through its empty halls towards The Bay, which had been his source of one-stop shopping for years when he lived downtown. Usually he could be in and out in ten minutes. The toy department, however, felt like an alien planet to him as he stood in the middle staring at aisles upon aisles of brightly coloured boxes and plastic toys. He wandered down a pink and purple aisle full of Barbie dolls and impossibly pink furniture. Sharon's feminist sensibilities would be appalled, but his first wife Ashley, being something of a bubble-head herself, probably had no such philosophical qualms about their daughter's identity. In fact, considering the size of the cheque he sent out to Vancouver every month, Hannah had probably acquired an entire room full of pink plastic.

He turned the corner and the colours changed to black, grey and camouflage green. The male domain, full of bulging biceps and weapons that would frighten the guys on the Tactical Unit. He sighed. Where in this combat zone were the toys for a one year-old? Dump trucks and sand pails and big wooden building blocks.

"Yeah, sure we got blocks," the harried clerk told him without even glancing up from tallying her cash. "Last aisle on the right."

He made his way past a pile of plastic bowling pins to Lego land, where he simply stood and stared. An entire wall of boxes confronted him—police stations, battle ships, space stations, western saloons, vehicles and boats of every conceivable variety. What happened to simple blocks? The kind you piled any which way to make things, and chewed when you got tired?

Green wandered along the aisle looking for something Tony might be able to manage before he got his PhD. But time was running out. The clerk was rattling her cash drawer, and the store was dimming the lights. Shaking his head in an admission of defeat, Green headed for the exit. Get me back to my world of mysteries and bad guys, he thought, and let's hope Brian Sullivan has had more luck tracking down the story of an eighty-year-old man than I've had finding a present for a one year-old.

But Sullivan's face as he came through the passenger lounge and caught sight of Green was anything but triumphant. He looked tired and harassed, and before Green could even open his mouth, he cut him off.

"You and your crazy ideas, sending me to Hamilton! Three hours in line-ups in airports. Stale peanuts, lousy coffee and a kid kicking my seat all the way on the flight back. And the guy wasn't even there!"

"Mr. G. wasn't there?"

"Flew the coop, vanished, poof."

"What the hell happened!"

Green's dismay must have shown on his face, together with outrage, because unexpectedly Sullivan grinned. "But I got something. You and your instincts. I got something."

"What?"

"Buy me a beer and a decent steak, and maybe I'll tell you."

Ten

January 15th, 1942

Refugees fill every corner of the room
with their stink, their complaints and their soft flesh.
Rations shrink, and yesterday the last of the chairs was burned.
Winter, thief of hope, steals into the room and into our flesh,
battling hunger for possession of our thoughts.
In our corner, the babies sleep while Sonya roams the streets.
An abandoned string, a cast-off rag, all carted home in triumph,
with magic fingers turned to sweaters, bonnets, embroidery for sale.
Through the thin wall drifts a beggar's cry, a child's wail for soup,
A single gunshot from the wire.
She's late tonight and when she staggers in,
laden with fur-trimmed coat and red satin dress,
there is no triumph.
Don't ask, she says, but I do.
I found a body in the street.
Then a look, to chase away conscience.
We have mouths to feed.

Sullivan had arrived in Hamilton shortly before noon, rented a car and, after paying a courtesy call to the Hamilton Police and procuring a city map, he'd set off into the suburbs.

Gryszkiewicz's cousin Karl Dubroskie had begrudgingly provided an address and no further details on his cousin's life, but Sullivan had pictured a modest home in an older, blue-collar neighbourhood. He was surprised when the map led him deeper and deeper into a wealthy suburban landscape sporting double garages and expensive brick facades.

Josef Gryszkiewicz's house had flamboyant red trim and cascades of withered vines, which suggested life and energy, but when Sullivan rang the doorbell, no one came. He thought he heard feet shuffling in the stillness, so he rang again. The shuffling stopped. Sullivan stepped back to peer up at the house, and a brief flick of the front curtain caught his eye. Someone was watching him, wary and reluctant to answer the door. He cursed his own stupidity. Of course, an elderly person would be afraid to open the door to an unexpected stranger, especially one built like a linebacker. As he turned to go back down the steps, he heard a rush of footsteps and the click of the bolt behind him.

Returning to the car on the street, he pulled out his cell phone and dialled. He heard the distant ringing within the house, and through the glass he saw the hazy shadow of a woman lurking in the corner of the window. The phone rang again, but the figure didn't move. Four rings, five, six. Sullivan cursed again. He'd flown all the way to Hamilton only to be stymied by a frightened old woman! Just as he was trying to work out his next move, a car pulled into the drive, and a stout woman jumped out. Her face had a pinched, preoccupied look, and she barely gave his car a glance before turning her attention to the pile of notebooks and the dog in the back seat. By the time Sullivan drew near with his badge, she had the stack of books balanced in one arm and was struggling to tow the dog out. It was an aging Lab retriever which barely lifted its head, let alone mustered any objection to Sullivan's approach.

Before Sullivan could even speak, the woman gasped, dropped the leash and clutched her throat. "Oh my God, no!"

He reached forward instinctively to steady her, and she recoiled. "What is it? What's happened?"

He retrieved the leash. "Nothing's wrong, ma'am, I'm looking for a Mr. Josef Gryszkiewicz."

"Why?"

"Is this his residence?"

"Yes. No." As the woman recovered her wits, her alarm turned to wariness, and she backed towards the front door, tugging the dog behind her. "What is it?"

Patiently, Sullivan tried to reassure her and glean whether his witness did indeed live there without revealing any details. Finally he was able to determine that Josef Gryszkiewicz was her father, and that he lived with her. However, he was asleep right now, and she was reluctant to disturb him.

"I'm sorry, Officer, but you have to understand my father is old and frail. He's from Eastern Europe, and an official visit from the police would upset him. Can you come back in half an hour when I've had a chance to tell him what it's about?"

Sullivan evaluated the request rapidly. Green would never stand for it, for Green preferred his witnesses unrehearsed. Yet there might be an advantage in giving the elderly man a chance to get his bearings and to gather memories that had been long buried. He glanced at his watch, calculated the time remaining before his return flight, factored in possible gridlock along the QEW, and told her she could have ten minutes.

The woman snapped a thank you before nearly slamming the door on Sullivan's nose. Before he could even turn away, bedlam erupted from inside the house.

"Mama! Mama!" the daughter shouted, and another

162

woman's voice could be heard from deeper inside. Curious, he tested the knob and eased the door open a crack.

"It's the police! He wants Tata!"

A shrill babble ensured in a language Sullivan assumed to be Polish, of which he recognized only one word. Ottawa.

"But what should I tell him? He's waiting for Tata."

"Say he go to store…" More Polish. "…come back later."

"But Mama, maybe he can help."

"No help!" he heard, followed by indecipherable arguing. "Not from police!"

"The police won't hurt him, Mama. Not here in Canada. And I'm scared!"

The two shouted in an excited mixture of Polish and English, and the din even managed to excite the dog, who began to bark. "Well, I'm calling Glen!" the daughter said.

Sullivan hoped he'd be able to hear what she told Glen, but there was no fear of that. The daughter was forced to shout over both her mother and the dog. From the tone of the conversation, Sullivan guessed that Glen was her husband, and not very sympathetic to his mother-in-law's fears. Nor even to his wife's, from the sound of it.

"But can you at least come home?" she pleaded. "Be here while we talk to the cop? Mama won't listen to me, but she believes you… We need to tell someone! Dad may be lost or hurt, and lying somewhere in the snow. Just like that poor woman who died in the snowbank in Winnipeg."

The mother-in-law burst in with a volley of protest, and the woman had to shout her down. "I know that's what he said, Mama, but it's been two days! He wouldn't go for that long without calling us. And with all this snow and ice, he could have slipped and fallen."

More yelling, followed by the slamming of the phone and

the daughter's announcement that Glen was on his way and would solve everything. Abruptly, silence fell. Standing on the porch, Sullivan had a sudden feeling that she had sensed his presence. He beat a hasty retreat to his car and was sitting quietly listening to the radio and making notes when a late model Chevy Blazer rumbled into the drive. Pure, sleek black muscle, the kind of car Sullivan dreamed about while he repatched the rust holes in his Malibu one more time. A large man hauled himself from the driver's seat, and Sullivan stepped out of his car to meet him.

Glen had a salesman air about him. Hearty smile, sporty tie and a loud, friendly voice. He stuck out a beefy hand.

"Glen Louks. Ottawa, eh? So what's this about, officer?"

"I'm here gathering background on an Ottawa matter."

"How'd my father-in-law's name come up?"

Sullivan decided to let a little truth slip by, so he mentioned the cousin in Renfrew.

The man's face, far from clearing with relief, grew more confused. "But he hasn't seen him in years. Refuses to go up there."

"This is about an incident that occurred twenty years ago."

Glen shrugged. "Before my time."

"Your father-in-law's not in trouble. He was the victim. But his assailant has been..." Sullivan paused on the wording, "...in some more trouble, and we're interested in revisiting the assault."

"Oh Christ, is that all!" Glen shook his head in exasperation. "My mother-in-law's all worked up because she thinks he's in trouble. They're from Poland, and over there, you can understand, the police were not always your friend. But come on in, I'll tell her it's just about this old business."

Glen ushered him in the door, and Sullivan was assailed by

the smell of onions, garlic and old dog in the over-heated air. The dog had evidently exhausted itself, because it had subsided into a snoring heap by the kitchen door. The two women were perched tensely on the edge of the sofa in the living room. Seeing them side by side, Sullivan could clearly detect the family resemblance despite the thirty-year age difference. Both had deep-set blue eyes, high slanted cheeks, and identical worry lines across their brows. When Glen explained the purpose of Sullivan's visit, the worry lines deepened.

The older woman shook her head vigorously. "No fight. Mistake."

"Your husband ended up in the hospital," Sullivan said.

"Sick." The woman tapped her heart.

"Mama, the guy who attacked him is in trouble again," Glen interjected. "That's why the officer's asking."

"Trouble? What trouble?" the mother asked. Stubborn as a mule, this one, Sullivan thought. The true immigrant grit with which Canada was built.

"I'm afraid I can't—" He began but was cut off by the daughter's gasp.

"My God! Dad! Could he have hurt Dad?"

"Are you saying something happened to your father?"

Both women exchanged quick looks.

"He's missing," Glen said flatly.

"No, no, no," the mother snapped. "Gone to friend."

Once again, the son-in-law refused to play along. "He left two days ago. He received a phone call Saturday afternoon, got dressed, said he was going out to meet a friend and never came back."

"Old friend," the mother repeated. "He went to help old friend. He come back."

Sullivan did some quick calculations. Saturday afternoon

was the day he and Green had been in Renfrew asking questions about the assault. The day they interviewed the resentful and reluctant cousin Karl Dubroskie.

"What's the friend's name?"

Glen had no idea, but an argument ensued in Polish between the two women which Glen watched with bemusement. The gist seemed to be the mother's refusal to supply the police with any names. Sullivan sighed. With all the fear and distrust, this was going to take longer than he'd imagined. He forced himself to sit back on the couch and be patient. When he could get a word in edgewise, he tried to reassure the mother that her husband was not in any trouble, nor were any of his friends, but it was vitally important that the police know what really happened in the assault.

The woman was unconvinced. "My Josef not want trouble. He's good man, work hard. Good citizen."

Sullivan assured her that immigrants like herself and her husband were the backbone of the country and rarely caused trouble for the police. He wished everyone worked as hard as new Canadians. The flattery worked, and the woman's face finally softened. She began to nod in agreement, and her English improved markedly.

"Canada is wonderful country. Here, you work hard, get better life. Not like Poland, small group of people have power and money, give to friends, keep other people down."

Sullivan quickly assessed how to proceed. He seemed to have hit a roadblock in finding out about Gryszkiewicz's disappearance, but here was an opportunity to explore another important avenue in the investigation. Green thought that Walker's death was connected to events in wartime Europe and that the fight between Walker and Josef Gryszkiewicz had its roots in their mutual past. He needed to know that past, and perhaps here was the small opening he could use.

He began carefully. "I know times were difficult in Poland during the war, and even after. When did you come to Canada?"

"Nineteen fifty-nine." Without further prodding, she launched into her story. It was disjointed and inelegant, but her pride shone through. Her husband had been an anti-communist, and after the war when the Soviets took over, he'd been blacklisted and was unable to find work. Only those who joined the communist party and had the right connections got ahead. Others like him had been arrested and sent to work camps in Russia, so he decided to escape. They were both young, in love, but as yet without children, so he contacted some friends he'd made during the war who were now in South America and helping dissidents escape. They were smuggled out of the country and across the border into West Germany in the back of a truck. Her eyes shone like a young girl's as she relived their moment of triumph.

"Russian soldiers very stupid. Joined party for job, liked money and vodka. Josef's friends pay money to them, no problem, they never even open truck."

"Why did you choose Canada?"

"Friends in South America find cousin here. Say Canada good place for Josef, he know steel."

"So your husband had a good trade back in Poland?"

Her chin jutted out stubbornly as she shook her head. Josef had been the youngest child of a poor widowed mother. His father had died in the First World War, and his mother did housecleaning for a rich family in Ozorkow. She raised six children in a two-room shack in the centre of the town. There was no money for school, and he'd been forced to drop out after about four grades. He came to Canada with just the shirt on his back, and he sweated it out in the steel mill. But now her children were Canadians, had professions and could live in a house like this.

She rose to pick up a picture from the piano and held it out to him. "Our son. Doctor. In Ozorkow, never."

Dutifully, Sullivan studied the young man in a graduation gown who gazed directly into the camera. Chiselled jaw, steely blue eyes, no hint of a smile. A determined young man, Sullivan thought, perhaps a chip off the old block. But as eager as the woman was to crow about the present, he needed her to stay in Ozorkow a while longer, to give him a picture of the town which her husband and Walker may have shared.

"I grew up on a farm near a small town myself," he said. "All the farmers brought their goods there, there was a creamery and a couple of mills, and most people lived simple lives. No one got rich, but we all stuck together. Was Ozorkow like that?"

She nodded. "Very poor. Some rich people own business like bank, shop, mill like you say. They have big houses. But people stay where born, with own…" For the first time her English failed her, and she turned to her daughter for help.

"People stayed in the communities where they'd grown up," her daughter said. "And with their own kind. It wasn't like Canada, where all the ethnic groups mix together."

The mother bobbed her head vigorously. "Lot of anger between peoples. And in the war, was very bad. Germans, Poles, Jews, Ukrainians, all on different sides."

Sullivan listened with half an ear while he formulated his crucial question. Now he saw his chance to slip it in, casually, as if from idle curiosity. "The man your husband was attacked by, did they fight about something that happened back then in Ozorkow?"

"Oh, no," the woman said, "they didn't even know each other in Ozorkow."

Sullivan waited, keeping his face deadpan. Flustered, she rushed on to cover her mistake. "How could Josef know him? He was son of cleaning woman!"

To that point Glen had been sitting quietly, letting his mother-in-law handle herself, since she was finally being cooperative. Now, out of the corner of his eye, Sullivan saw him rise from the chair and slip out of the room. Sullivan kept his eyes resolutely on the mother. "And who was the other man?"

"I—I not know him. Josef not know. Josef poor boy, not even have shoes, his mother had to clean for Jews—"

"Mama," said the daughter quickly, "the Sergeant isn't blaming Tata. He's just trying to find out information on the assault, remember?"

Sullivan backed off. With the mother now in full retreat and the daughter running interference, he was unlikely to get more, but he had his hint. Eugene Walker and Josef Gryszkiewicz had known each other in Ozorkow before the war, and the division between them ran deep.

"That's right," he said. "But like your daughter, I am concerned that there may be a connection with his disappearance. I think you should report his disappearance to the Hamilton Police."

"No police."

He tried to explain that the police helped with missing persons all the time, especially elderly people who had become confused, but she shook her head.

"No disappear," she insisted. "With friend." But now her eyes were full of tears.

At that moment, Glen reappeared in the doorway, stopping them all in their tracks. He was sickly pale. "Actually, Ma, I don't think he's with a friend."

"Why?"

"Because when he left, he took my target pistol with him."

*   *   *

In The Place Next Door, the waiters were cleaning tables all around them and the last of the other patrons was paying his bill. Sullivan downed the last dregs of his draught and pushed away his plate with a belch of satisfaction. Every gram of meat had been picked from the bone.

"So that's what I got, Mike. Hamilton Police has been notified, over the old lady's protests, and they'll put some men on it right away. His age is a worry, after all."

"So's the gun," Green countered bluntly. His mind was racing ahead. He didn't like the implications. The alleged phone call and Gryszkiewicz's disappearance had occurred on Saturday, which was three days after Walker's death, although as Sullivan had pointed out, it was the day the two of them had been nosing around Renfrew asking about the past. The phone call had probably been a tip-off, which had led Gryszkiewicz to go to ground. The gun may have been simply for protection, but why the tipoff, and why the disappearance?

"And I know it could be just a slip-up," Sullivan was saying, "but the old lady was definitely hiding something. I hadn't told her Walker was from Ozorkow until I asked about the fight, but she was very quick to deny they could have known each other. It's not much, maybe, but it's a little clue that she knew exactly who Walker was, and that her husband and she had talked about it."

Understanding dawned on Green like a slow spreading of light. It was more than a little clue, far more than Sullivan

170

could even imagine. A theory was taking shape in his mind…of Walker, one of the educated, privileged elite. Of Gryszkiewicz, a young man raised in poverty, fatherless and alienated from the reins of power. A young man blacklisted for political reasons almost immediately after the Soviet liberation of Poland from the Nazis. A young man who had escaped to the West through an international underground network of friends.

Not just any friends, Green thought, but a secret, tightly-organized, well-connected international network of ideological sympathizers, with a base in South America and money to spare.

The skull and crossbones, gone underground.

The theory explained why Walker had attacked him thirty-five years later in a bar half way around the world. It explained why Gryszkiewicz had pretended not to know him and refused to press charges. It explained why, three days after Walker's death, Gryszkiewicz had dropped out of sight.

And most of all, in the death of Eugene Walker, the theory provided a murderer and a motive.

*   *   *

When Green arrived home, the lower floor of the Dreaded Vinyl Cube was in darkness, but a light still shone in the master bedroom upstairs. He slipped in, took off his snowy boots and tiptoed upstairs. Sharon sat propped up in bed with a book, looking delectably pink and tousled. Her expression, however, was anything but amorous.

"Strange hours the Billings Bridge Mall keeps these days," she said.

"I sent Brian Sullivan to Hamilton today, and I had to get a briefing from him."

In spite of herself, her chocolate eyes brightened. "On the concentration camp case?"

"I think I've figured out what happened." He summarized Sullivan's report as he undressed. She cocked her head, and he could see her intelligent mind probing the implications.

"Okay, so now you know a lot about this Mr. G.'s past, but I don't see what it tells you about Walker."

"Well, he knew Walker in Ozorkow—the wife let that slip. She also implied that they didn't move in the same circles. That Walker was rich and her husband was poor, and he hated Walker's kind."

"Walker's kind?" She frowned in bafflement.

"I can think of one major reason why Eugene Walker would have attacked Mr. G. half a century later, but the problem is, after all the years of cover-ups, I don't know how to find out if it's true." He reached for his long underwear. "How do you distinguish a Pole from a Jew?"

She stared at him a moment in bewildered silence before her face lit with a wicked grin. "Check the autopsy report."

*   *   *

At eight o'clock the next morning, Green was scrolling through the reports on the Walker case. No autopsy report, which was hardly surprising since sometimes MacPhail's paperwork took days. But when Green phoned up the pathology department at the General Hospital, MacPhail was uncharacteristically brusque.

"Ah, that bloody Walker case," he grumbled. "Well, it's a natural causes, laddie, so I won't be sending the autopsy report over."

"MacPhail, I'm investigating the case. I have to see the report."

"I've told you my findings. That's all you need to know."

Green was puzzled. MacPhail and he had known each other for years, and were long since past the stage of formalities. "MacPhail, what the hell's going on?"

"I'm not getting in the middle of this, laddie. My conclusion is death by hypothermia, end of story. Your boss has already reamed me out for saying more than I should."

To Howard Walker, Green remembered. Probably after he's had a quart or two too many, which would be why Jules reamed him out. "Jules spoke to you about the case? When?"

"Saturday." There was a pause, then MacPhail's voice grew firmer. "Look, to be perfectly honest with you, I don't know what's going on, and I don't want to know. If the family says they want to protect the man's privacy and Jules says there's no reason not to respect that, I'm going to be keeping my head down."

What the hell is he talking about, Green wondered and felt his pulse quicken with suspicion. Someone in the Walker family had asked that the autopsy report not be released. They had obviously complained to the brass—probably about Green's intrusive questioning—and Jules, not knowing on Saturday that Green suspected a homicide, had agreed with them. Which did not say much about Jules' trust in him.

"Well, things have changed," he said briskly. "And Jules is aware of it. I'm not disputing the cause of death. I just want further details on the condition of the body. Can you fax the report over ASAP?"

He stationed himself by the fax machine and waited impatiently for it to hum into action. The squad room was slowly emptying as most detectives headed off to the morning's briefing with the Staff Sergeant, but Green signalled Sullivan to remain behind. As soon as the fax machine had finished spitting the report out, Green seized it and scanned the contents. At the bottom of the first page, he found the physical description of the body, cataloguing all visible marks and scars. Most of MacPhail's attention was directed to the fresh wound on his temple, with brief reference near the end to a half dozen old scars on the forearm. Barbed wire tears, Ruth Walker had said, but more likely desperate attempts to remove the tattooed numbers from his arm.

On the next page he found what he was looking for. "Aha!" he cried to Sullivan. "I'm right! Why the hell didn't MacPhail mention this to us?"

He handed Sullivan the fax and pointed to the second page. As Sullivan read it over, Green could almost see his mind wrestling with the implications. After a moment, Sullivan looked up.

"But that doesn't mean—"

Green nodded triumphantly. "In pre-war rural Poland, that's exactly what it means."

"Okay, so what's our next move?"

"First we check and double check with MacPhail that this is accurate. That he didn't dictate it by mistake, because it's such a routine comment. Sometimes I think the guy's totally pickled when he does his carving."

"MacPhail?" Sullivan chuckled. "He drinks like a fish, but he can drink the whole force under the table and still get up at six a.m. to jog. I don't know where the guy puts it."

"True, but before I set off to harass the widow yet again, I want to be damn sure I've got my facts straight, because this gives us a motive and a killer."

MacPhail's mood had not improved in the twenty minutes since his last conversation with Green. His voice reverberated through the wires so loudly that Green pulled the receiver away from his ear.

"Every goddamn word in that report is accurate, and if you want, lad, I'll dig the old bugger up so you can all have a look at it."

*   *   *

I should phone to give the grieving widow some time to collect herself, Green thought to himself as he headed out once again to the Reid house. Or I could conduct the whole interview by phone, as most normal detectives would. But the subtleties—the averting of the eyes, the paling of the cheek—these were lost over the telephone, and with a reluctant witness like Ruth Walker, that was half the interview.

Ruth Walker herself opened the door, and a delicate scowl spread over her face at the sight of him. She was dressed in baggy wool clothes wrapped high around her neck to ward off the cold, and her hair frizzed in a grey mist about her head.

"Is this really necessary? I'm just getting ready to go back to the country. Howard and Rachel have already returned to Montreal, and I think Don and Margaret need some time for each other."

An astute woman, he thought yet again, a woman attuned to the hidden secrets and unspoken needs of everyone around her. How much had she known, or guessed, but left unsaid? "I won't keep you long," he said mildly. "Just some questions about Eugene's habits. General background."

Her eyes darkened briefly before she waved him in. "Very well. I'll brew some tea."

On the drive over, Green had wondered how he would secure the information he needed without revealing his suspicions prematurely. If he were wrong, he would upset the family unnecessarily—especially Ruth, whom he considered the one truly innocent and selfless person in this saga. As she prepared their tea, he came up with an idea. He noticed that she served her tea British-style, milk first and then lumps of sugar added to the tea. He held up his hand as she moved to prepare his the same way.

"Actually, I prefer it with lemon, if you have any."

She nodded without surprise and went to fetch him some.

"I suppose you're used to that," he commented amiably, "since Eugene was Polish."

"Yes, he preferred it with lemon."

"My father's from Poland too, and he drinks it in a glass through a cube of sugar in his teeth."

In spite of herself, her eyes crinkled with amusement. "I caught Eugene drinking it that way a couple of times when he was alone. He always acted quite embarrassed."

"Was he ashamed of his old-world habits?"

She tilted her head. "I think he was. He very much wanted to be a Canadian, to put all that part of his life behind him. He even hated his accent."

"Is that why he never spoke Polish?"

"Partly, although of course I never asked him."

"But Renfrew County has a very mixed ethnic make-up, and many people still have a strong sense of their heritage. How did he feel about living among people of Polish and German descent? They must have been constant reminders of his past."

She stirred her tea carefully as she weighed her response, and the teaspoon clinked delicately against the bone china. "I think he had very mixed feelings. I think their presence was soothing and familiar, but they also made him uncomfortable."

"Why did he choose to go out there? Canada's a big place. Why not move someplace where there would be no memories to combat?"

"I chose Renfrew, Inspector. I had a friend who had married a Canadian Air Force chap during the war, and she was moving to Peterborough. Renfrew wasn't far, it was a small town and I felt that was all Eugene could handle. I wanted country, peace and wide-open spaces. Eugene still got panicky in crowds and among strangers."

"Yet he never associated with the Polish community."

"He never associated with anyone, Inspector."

Carefully, he took his next step. "I gather it's really important to fit into a group out there, especially fifty years ago, and social activities often revolved around the church one belonged to. What religion did you choose?"

She flushed a little as she busied herself wiping invisible crumbs from the table. "I can't see the relevance of that. Religion was not part of our lives. Both Eugene and I felt quite strongly after what we'd seen in the war that, if there was a God, we wanted no part of him."

"So you attended no church?"

She laid the napkin down, folded her hands in her lap and frowned at him. "What are you getting at, Inspector?"

"Trying to get a picture of his habits and preferences. It might tell us where he's from."

Her frown deepened. "I told you, it doesn't matter where he's from."

"But you have your theories."

"What do you mean?"

He took a wild guess. It would explain her fear and reluctance to unearth the past. "Deep down, you're afraid he might have been a Nazi."

Her hands tightened convulsively, and she dropped her eyes, but didn't speak.

"Rest easy, Mrs. Walker. Your husband wasn't a Nazi."

For a moment she sat immobile, barely breathing. "What do you know?"

"Not much yet. It's what you know that will tell us for sure."

She was beginning to breathe again. After a moment, she leaned forward and picked up her tea, as if she had made a decision. "I was never sure, but I was afraid he might be. The uniform, the stolen ID…and he spoke German, you see."

"What was his German like?"

"Quite fluent. He rarely spoke it, just as he rarely spoke Polish, but he understood it perfectly. And in English he often mixed up his grammar backwards the way Germans do. You know: 'To the shop you are going?' And sometimes…" She hesitated. "When he was drunk, he'd say things in German, like '*Gott in Himmel, Liebling*'. It was like a cold fist closing on my heart."

The pieces all fit. The more she talked, the more certain he became. He leaned forward. "What about his religious habits? Subconscious little things. Poles are Catholics. You're Protestant, so were many Nazis. Did you notice any differences between your ways and his?"

She frowned in thought. "He had a lot of odd superstitions. He knew they were silly and he'd chastise himself when he caught himself—"

"What kind of superstitions?"

"He'd act as if he didn't want to tempt fate. He hated to talk about unpleasant things, as if talking might bring them about. For instance, if I'd say that I didn't think a particular item would sell, he'd tell me to bite my tongue. Not the least a Protestant sort of thing."

"Did he cross himself on these occasions? Or at other times?"

She shook her head. "No, he never went that far. Nor did

he ever seem to invoke any of the saints or the Holy Family."

"What about the cross you told me he was wearing when he was found? Did he keep it?"

"That disappeared in one of his earlier fits of rage at the hospital. He tore it off and hurled it out the window."

He drank the last drops of his tea in silence as he debated how to proceed. For now he was sure. Eugene Walker was neither the Polish camp survivor nor the Nazi collaborator he had earlier suspected.

"Mrs. Walker, did you ever ask your husband why he was circumcised?"

She choked on her tea, her cheeks flooding with red and her cup rattling in her hand. He waited patiently while she mopped up the spilt tea with a napkin and rolled it into a tight ball.

"Surely the question occurred to you. In your work with the wounded, you must have seen a lot of men's bodies. Circumcision wasn't common in Europe eighty years ago."

"It did happen, though. If there'd been an infection or…"

"Or if you happened to be Jewish." His voice was very soft and she looked across at him, wide-eyed and pink. "That possibility did occur to you, didn't it?"

Very faintly, she nodded.

"Did it occur to you that maybe he himself was Joseph Kressman?"

"Why do you think I wrote to Poland to get information on him?"

"When you found out none of the Kressman family had returned after the war, what did you do?"

"Joseph Kressman would have been older, and they said he was a blacksmith and tool maker. Eugene didn't seem to know much about tools, beyond how to sell them. He certainly didn't know how to make them or use them. My experts said that amnesiacs don't usually forget the little habits and the physical skills. And it seemed..." She faltered. "It seemed obvious Eugene wanted to leave that part of him behind. If he was Jewish, he had already suffered so much. I thought it would be kinder."

"Do you think Eugene knew he was Jewish?"

She was beginning to rally with the relief of unburdening her fears. She sat up straighter, no longer defensive, fully involved as she considered the question. "You mean he was pretending to remember nothing, perhaps to hide the fact he was Jewish?"

"There are a number of possibilities," Green replied. "He could have known from the minute he was picked up by the Red Cross and chosen to disguise himself. That's why he wore the cross. Or he could have remembered at some point in his new life and decided to keep it to himself, perhaps for fear of the upheaval it might cause. Or he might never have remembered."

She weighed the alternatives carefully. "It's hard for me to imagine that he was capable of any kind of conscious dissimulation when he came to England. He was barely alive, psychologically. To have had the presence of mind to wear a cross..." She cocked her head as a thought struck her. "He tore that cross off when he'd been at the hospital a bit, as if it were repugnant to him. Perhaps then he had an inkling..." She shook her head. "But on the other hand, he was still so confused. Eugene has always had flashes of torment, as if hidden things were rising up. I can't imagine he knew everything."

"Was his reaction to your son's engagement a surprise to you?"

"Yes and no. Eugene was never pleased with what Howard did, and I already knew he wasn't particularly fond of Jews." She flushed with shame at the memory. "But the intensity of his reaction did surprise me. That's the thing that puzzles me."

"Can you describe the scene? It may give us some clues about his state of mind."

She sighed, as if Eugene's state of mind had always been beyond comprehension. Before she spoke, she poured herself a second cup of tea and took a delicate bite of her biscuit. She looked very frail wrapped in the heavy woollens and curled in the overstuffed chair across from him.

"Howard told us you're Jewish. I hope you don't find this unsettling."

He smiled at her graciousness. "I've been a major crimes detective for fifteen years. I don't unsettle easily."

She nodded in acknowledgement of his point. "Howard came home at Christmas time. He had written us about his girlfriend Rachel, but he hadn't told us she was Jewish. He took me aside one evening shortly before Christmas and told me he was converting to Judaism, and they were going to be married in March. He asked for my help with Eugene." She paused, groping to put her idea into words. "I guess even beforehand we had a feeling Eugene would be upset. It was odd, because he was actually a strong admirer of Israel; he always wanted her to drop an atomic bomb on the Arabs. But he had little admiration for the ordinary Jew—the businessmen, the doctors. He called them rich, cliquey, spineless parasites." She broke off in dismay and he realized that, despite his vaunted equanimity, a flash of anger must have shown. He forced a smile to defuse the tension.

"A lot of people lost themselves in the Holocaust, Mrs. Walker. Don't feel bad, these were not your feelings. Please go on."

"Howard and I chose a moment when we thought Eugene was at his most relaxed. Right after Christmas dinner. Usually

Eugene lit up a cigar and had a brandy with his coffee. When Howard told him, straight out, I must admit that even I was surprised at Eugene's reaction. He turned purple, I thought he was going to have a stroke. He said 'no, never'. Howard said 'Yes, I love her'. Eugene was shaking all over and shouting at him, and then all of a sudden he left the house. He came back several hours later, very—" She broke off, crimson with shame.

"Very drunk?" he prompted gently.

She nodded wretchedly. "He said a lot of nasty things about Howard killing him, and how could he turn his back on us like this, and there was no way he was bringing that girl into the house. He was weeping, and he kept saying 'How can you do this to me' over and over. Howard walked out in tears, and he hasn't spoken to his father since."

"Never?"

She shook her head. "He'd write to me here at Margaret's, but he refused to see or communicate with his father. He never even called me at home for fear Eugene might pick up the phone."

"Did you ever try to talk to your son about his father possibly being Jewish?"

"Oh, no! In fact, when Eugene reacted as he did to Rachel, I was more afraid than ever that he was a Nazi. I was certain he couldn't be Jewish. Even if he'd been keeping it a secret, don't you think he'd be happy deep down that his son was marrying a Jewish girl? It didn't make any sense."

It didn't on first analysis, Green thought as he headed back to the station. But perhaps, deep down in the tangled undergrowth of the human psyche, there was a logic to it. Walker's son was not marrying just any Jewish girl, but the daughter of Ben Lowenstein, whose life was dedicated to fighting anti-Semitism and whose condemnation of spiritual and moral cowardice would be swift and sure. In Eugene

Walker's life, after all he'd been through, nothing could ever be swift and sure.

Perhaps the prospect of moral condemnation by Ben Lowenstein was more than Walker could bear, or perhaps it was something even more convoluted. Green was not an expert in torture, but he'd read of the "Stockholm Syndrome" in which victims identify with their oppressors and adopt the same monstrous beliefs and actions. Although he'd known several Holocaust victims and lived with his parents' scars all his life, he realized with a pang how little effort he had made to understand the fear and secrecy that cloaked their lives.

However, he had worked for ten years with the brutal outcome of everyday deprivation and abuse. He had seen the way it twisted the psyche, withered love and nurtured rage, giving birth to the psychopath. How much more fertile the ground of the concentration camp!

Somewhere in the labyrinth of his tormented mind, had Eugene Walker locked his Jewish soul away, forgetting its existence and living in terror of anything that brought him close to the locked door? Was it humanly possible to keep the door locked and the terror alive for fifty years? Or had he unlocked it years ago, recoiled at the contents within, and slammed it shut again in revulsion? What would be so repulsive? Why was being a Jew so intolerable to him?

Green didn't have the answers. He was out of his depth and suspected even most psychologists would be, except perhaps those who dealt with torture victims. He didn't know Walker's past, but he doubted an old-world Jewish family could be so corrupt and loveless that he would turn against them. To reject his identity under the degradation of a concentration camp was possible, but to maintain that rejection over a lifetime with such ferocity that he cast out his son for marrying a Jew seemed unfathomable.

As Green navigated the Queensway, little facts which had previously seemed random began to coalesce. Walker's antipathy towards his son, who unlike himself was slight and dark. He recalled Jeff Tillsbury saying "Howard's father seemed to despise everything that made Howard so special— his gentleness, his compassion, his moral sense." All traits of *Yiddishkeit*, the Jewish soul. Walker's admiration of Israel, seemingly a contradiction but not so within this new context. Israel represented the new Jew—the Jew who fought back against extraordinary odds and crushed her enemies. The antithesis of the gentle Eastern European Jew whom Hitler had slaughtered by the millions. Stereotypes, Green knew, but widely perceived ones, even among Jews.

He needed someone who could get inside Walker's head. He was comfortable enough with his Jewish identity but had always left it on the periphery of his daily life. In fact, Sharon was fond of suggesting that his choices in life—his anti-authority nature, his decision to become a police officer, his rejection of, indeed, deliberate reaction against material success—represented his own small rebellion against Jewish immigrant expectations. He had not been the dutiful son who fulfilled the aspirations of his immigrant parents. His career and his women had brought them pain and bewilderment over the years. At times, before Sharon had reeled him back in, he had come close to abandoning all semblance of being Jewish, but he had never rejected it. Never would he have turned against his own, and he would certainly fight anyone else who did. This was the crucial difference between himself and Eugene Walker.

But then, he had not lived through the Holocaust.

184

Eleven

September 1st, 1942

I am sick
I am numb
I have no words.
First refugees, then train by train the old, the sick.
Resettled, they said.
Now babies thrown from windows
Parents walking into guns
Nazis making sport.
What madmen are they to want our children?
What madmen are we to give them?
Stay still, my babies.
Stay quiet.
What have we become?
Where have we gone?
Or are we no more.

"Dad, we need to talk about the Holocaust."

Sid was sitting in his brown tub chair, where he spent most of the day, and he looked up in astonishment at his son's appearance for the second day in a row. The television was tuned to a 1940's Bob Hope comedy, but Green had caught his father dozing. At his elbow were the remains of lunch—a glass of ginger ale and a piece of cheese on a hard chunk of pumpernickel. Sid eyed his son reproachfully, perhaps for raising the topic of the Holocaust again, perhaps for simply being where Sid didn't expect him. Green poured himself a coke and came to sit opposite his father.

"The man we talked about yesterday, it turns out he was Jewish, and he was a survivor. I need to understand what made him act the way he did."

"Every man is different, Mishka," Sid protested. "It does no good to ask why."

Green ignored the obvious evasion. "He would have been a young man of barely eighteen when the war started, well-educated, probably from a privileged family. But after the war he never admitted he was Jewish. Worse, he was actually anti-Semitic." Green went on to delineate carefully the facts as he knew them, as well as the extent of his own theorizing. Afterwards, his father sat in silence, chewing his straw. When he was under stress, he chewed straws to combat the urge for a cigar, which he'd given up when his grandson was born.

"Could that happen to a man?" Green prompted gently. "That he would turn against his fellow Jews?"

Sid nodded, his face twisting at the memories. "What do you think? That we Jews were saints? Even in the camps, some turned against their own."

"But that was to survive, to protect themselves. Deep inside, they would not feel that way. But this guy Walker, even after the danger was passed, even sixty years later, he hated Jews."

"After the war, most of us wanted only to forget. You cannot live with that on your mind, Mishka. We could not talk about it, we could not feel like other men, we had only to pretend that we were like other men. I cannot make you understand this."

"Try."

"I do not want to make you understand it. It is like building yourself a new house, a nice fancy house that looks like everybody else's." Sid paused, and Green sensed he was searching for unreachable words. "But it is built on sand, and it doesn't stand. I cannot understand either what would make this man hate his own people. For me, only our people understand. I feel I belong somewhere only because other Jews have suffered what I did. This man has made himself alone. Maybe he feels he doesn't belong, he did not suffer like they did. Some survivors that were hidden by Gentiles or passed as Christians, they feel shame because they had an easier time. And sometimes..." Sid faltered, caught in a distant time. "Sometimes a thing that you love, but that reminds you of those times, like your mother loved the violin... Then the feeling is too strong to face. But it's not hate. Never hate."

For the moment, Walker was gone. Green's mind was caught in a whirl of questions. He'd only ever known his mother to play piano, with such reverence that he thought she'd been born to it. Violin? He thought of her as a young girl still in her teens at the start of the war, pretty and musical, rescued from Auschwitz at the end of the war. A violinist, who hadn't picked up a bow in all the time he'd known her. A modest woman, who'd never worn a white blouse or navy skirt in all the years of her marriage. Had that been his mother's secret? Did he dare ask? Even as he searched for words, he saw the distant glaze in his father's eyes and knew there was an even more important question.

"What about you, Dad? What did you feel?"

Sid was back in the war looking into the chasm. When he spoke his voice was raw, as if dragged over gravel.

"I felt nothing. You lose and you lose and you lose, and

after a while you think there is nothing more they can take from you. Until they take away yourself, and then you don't think any more. You cannot live like that—a body sitting on the ground with nothing inside. But in the Red Cross camp after the war, I met your mother, and I found a little bit of me left inside myself. And so I went on."

"Oh, Dad!" Green murmured, the two simple words all he could manage safely. Surprising himself, he reached forward and took his father into his arms. He felt his father clutch him, as he had so often in the past, and for the first time he understood.

*   *   *

Unexpectedly, Green found himself driving through a blur of tears on the way back to the station. He must have still looked raw when he arrived; Sullivan took one look at him and followed him into his office without a word.

"This fucking case," Green muttered to cover his embarrassment. "I get the feeling no matter what we turn up, there will be no happy endings for anyone involved."

"Hey, it hasn't exactly made for sweet dreams for me either, buddy," Sullivan replied, dropping into the chair opposite and propping his feet on Green's desk. "I've been reading your books on the Holocaust, and I had nightmares all last night. Haven't had ones like that since I was a rookie. So for you, with your father…" His voice trailed off, leaving the emotion unvoiced.

"I've been a lousy son," Green said. "My father was only twenty-three when he lost his first wife and son. He waited nearly twenty years before he felt ready to invest his hopes in another. And look at me."

"Yeah, look at you. You've stayed here close to him, you see him every week, you pay all his living expenses, you've given him a fabulous daughter-in-law and grandson."

"But I don't really give him the time. Even Sharon's better with him than me. He brought me into this world, and I treat him like an afterthought."

"Well, listen, it's a hell of an emptiness you're supposed to fill. No one could do that. Would you expect that of Tony someday?"

Green stared at his desk top morosely. "I hope not. But I'm not much better at this father business either. Sharon takes the lead on that too." He looked up, putting on a smile he hoped would lighten the mood. "You're the guy with all the experience. What's a good gift for me to buy Tony?"

"For a one year-old? Anything, as long as it's safe to chew."

"Sharon's looking for some kind of meaningful father-son thing. Something that stands apart from the two hundred stuffed animals and trucks and riding toys my in-laws have lavished on him. But she refuses to give me any hints."

"I think the important point of the gift is that you think of it," Sullivan replied.

"Some help. The party's tomorrow night, and I'm running out of time. Those toy stores are scary places. Do you want to come tomorrow, by the way?" He hoped the request sounded like a casual afterthought. In all their years of friendship, the two had never gone beyond the bounds of the job. "Be another world-weary cop's voice among all the techies?"

Sullivan made a face. "All the way out in Barrhaven? I've got Scouts tomorrow night, but maybe I'll drop in later if I can."

"Yeah, sure. Whatever." Green leaned forward and knocked Sullivan's feet off the desk. "Now let's stop wasting time here. We've got a case to solve."

Fortunately Sullivan took the hint. "What did Walker's widow say?"

Green summarized his visit with Ruth Walker. Sullivan put his feet back on the desk and chewed a pen as he listened.

"So she thinks he didn't even remember he was Jewish?"

Green shook his head adamantly. "I'm positive at some point he remembered. I don't know exactly when, but twenty years ago when he had that fight with Mr. G., he knew. He remembered the guy from Ozorkow, and my hunch, if I could only prove it, is that he remembered him from somewhere else, too. From the camps or the ghettos. I think Mr. G. was a Nazi collaborator, and that's why Walker attacked him. It's something he would have felt strongly enough about to have provoked that attack. Walker had kept a really low profile all his life, the quiet drunk, then all of a sudden—pow!"

"But Mike," Sullivan ventured, "if Gryszkiewicz was a war criminal, why would Walker cover it up? You'd think he'd be yelling it all over town. Here's one of the bastards getting off scot-free. I mean, it explains why Gryszkiewicz pretended not to understand a thing about the fight, but why would Walker hide it? What's he got to lose?"

"His secret," Green replied instantly, his eyes alight. "Walker would have had to reveal that he was Jewish, dredge up all the past, face the pain and the memories...and for what? Even if he were willing to face all that, twenty years ago no one was prosecuting war criminals. No one wanted to hear about them."

"So you're thinking that this Mr. G. killed Walker to keep him from talking now? But that fight happened twenty years ago," Sullivan pointed out, always the pragmatist. "And if Walker didn't rat on him then, why would Mr. G. suddenly decide he was a threat now? The Justice Department has been turning up the heat on war criminals for almost fifteen years now."

Green hesitated as he searched for an explanation. Sullivan was right. What had triggered the murder almost twenty years later? What had made Walker's secret knowledge so much more dangerous? He seized the phone. "I'm going to see if the War Crimes unit is investigating Mr. G. right now. That would explain why he suddenly decided to bump off a witness."

By a great stroke of luck, when the call went through, David Haley was just settling down to his lunch at his desk, and he was in an expansive mood.

"I've got a name for you, Haley," Green announced. "Josef Gryszkiewicz. Recognize it?"

Silence. Noisy slurp. "Nope."

Green felt his excitement deflate. "The War Crimes Unit has never heard of this guy?"

"Well, remember, Mike, I'm not in the unit any more, and I'm no longer privy to all their comings and goings."

"You're not missing much," Green remarked.

There was a pause on the line, then a chuckle. "No comment. You could always try asking them if his name has come up."

"Would they tell me?"

"Probably not. Seriously though, we looked at over two hundred names, all the guys who were uncovered by the Deschenes Commission, and I don't remember that name. So unless new evidence has come up, stuff nobody knew or reported back in the eighties…"

Green pondered that possibility after he hung up the phone. Justice Deschenes' mammoth inquiry had lasted nearly two years and examined the evidence on eight hundred potential war criminals living in Canada. If Gryszkiewicz had escaped the dragnet, he must have felt home free. Probably figured that the only person who knew he was a war criminal was not going to talk. Had something happened to change his mind? Had he learned something that made him fear he was about to be exposed?

"Brian," Green said, breaking the silence which had hung since the phone call. "What's the word from the Hamilton Police on Mr. G? Any sign of him?"

"Last I checked," Sullivan replied, "there was nothing, and they're getting pretty damn nervous down there about an old man running around with a gun. They've talked to the co-workers he used to work with, and they say the guy could get paranoid as hell. Thought the office phone was bugged and the surveillance cameras were hooked up to the RCMP."

That's one for my side, Green thought. It wouldn't take much for this guy to think the War Crimes Unit was on to him. Maybe just a few more screws loosened by age. "Let's get the Hamilton Police to check his alibi for the time of the murder too. You said the family claimed he was home all that day?"

Sullivan nodded. "For what that's worth. The wife would swear he was at the Last Supper if she thought it would help. But I'm ahead of you, Mike. Once I learned about the gun, I did ask the Hamilton boys to start checking his alibi. We may find a hole." He sighed. "But we're still a long way from building a case. We're cops, not storytellers. What have we really got to tie this Gryszkiewicz—or anybody—to Walker's death? No physical evidence, no prints, no tissue under the fingernails, no murder weapon. No eyewitnesses—"

"I'll get them, Brian. Even if I have to go to the press and get Crime Stoppers to feature it, I'll catch this guy." He raised his voice over Sullivan's protest. "Just because the guy's eighty years old, he's not getting away with any more murders."

Abruptly he rose to his feet and shrugged on his jacket. "We've got to go back to Renfrew. We have to find out where

Mr. G. has gone, even if we have to turn his cousin upside down and shake the information out of him!"

*   *   *

Sullivan took his foot off the gas and let the nondescript police-issue blue Taurus bump slowly down the rutted lane, splattering slushy muck in all directions. The cold snap of the past few days had broken abruptly, turning Karl Dubroskie's front yard into a pond. Unlike Walker's two neighbours, Dubroskie lived in a boxy, fifties-style split level with none of the decaying charm of the original homesteads. Green scanned the surroundings for signs of activity. An old man scurrying for cover behind the barn might be too much to hope for, but he did hope to spot something out of the ordinary. Not just the bored gaze of cows in the paddock, nor the desultory cluck of hens poking in the muddy straw, nor the usual, haphazard jumble of tractors and rusty pick-ups by the woodshed. But something furtive.

There was nothing but soggy snow and mud.

"Pull in out of sight behind the barn there," he said. "Let's nose around a bit first."

Sullivan snorted. "The guy will have seen us the second we turned into his lane."

"Maybe. But our man might be here, and we need to know what we're walking into." Which was partly the truth. The other part being Green's insatiable love of snooping.

The two detectives checked their guns, stepped out of the car and sank ankle deep in mud and straw. Sullivan gave Green a quick grin, but Green kept his profanity to himself. No point underscoring his status as big city wimp. He picked his way around the edge of the barn until the front yard was in view. The stench of manure, hay and livestock choked his lungs, but he refused to cough. How could people live like this!

As if reading his mind, Sullivan grinned again. "You should smell it on a hot day in July."

Barely were the words out of his mouth when two massive black dogs came barrelling around the side of the house, barking wildly.

Green caught the glint of white fangs beneath curled lips. "Holy fuck!"

"Back away. Slowly." Sullivan said.

Green was just calculating the distance back to the car when the barn door banged open, and Karl Dubroskie strode out. At the sight of the two detectives, he hesitated, and worry flashed across his face.

"Puppies!" he roared, and instantly the dogs subsided and retreated to the porch. Dubroskie took in the Taurus half hidden behind the barn and faced the two detectives with frank suspicion. "Officers? What can I do for you?"

"I suspect you already know, Mr. Dubroskie," Green replied. "I suspect your cousin's wife was on the phone to you the minute Sergeant Sullivan left her home."

The farmer's eyes narrowed at the accusation, but he didn't refute it. "Come inside," he said, and turned on his heel.

Inside the kitchen, a large, heavy-bosomed woman eyed them sharply as they filed by into the living room.

"You need me, Karl?"

"Nope."

His dismissal was curt, and she turned back to her work, but Green suspected she'd be tuning a keen ear. She didn't look the submissive type.

"Mr. Dubroskie," Green began before the farmer could take command, "this investigation is now a lot more than idle curiosity about some old barroom brawl. As you know, your cousin has been missing for three days. And as you also no doubt know, he left with a gun."

In spite of himself, Dubroskie showed his surprise. "Didn't know he had a gun."

"How proficient is he with it?"

Dubroskie shrugged. "We haven't been in contact for twenty years."

"Don't play me for a fool. You called him Saturday to warn him we wanted to question him."

"Officer, whether you're a fool or not, time will tell. But I did no such thing."

Green leaned forward urgently and met the man's unwavering gaze. "Be very careful whose side you choose, please. Not for the sake of the police or the authorities, but for the sake of the innocent people he might have set his sights on. He's a frail, paranoid old man who sees spies and traitors behind every bush. If he thinks he's in danger, he'll strike. As he did with Walker."

"Tell him, Karl!" came an urgent voice from behind them. Then Mrs. Dubroskie filled the doorway, her face flushed with apprehension.

"Jeanie, stay out of it!"

"You don't owe him anything!" she shot back, planting herself firmly on the chair beside him. "He came out of nowhere, suddenly some long-lost relative from behind the iron curtain. We couldn't even do a proper check on who he was!"

"Please, that's—"

But she was unstoppable, for which Green silently celebrated his luck. A good three inches taller and fifty pounds heavier, she ran her husband with a practised hand. "He visited half a dozen times, spooky as a cat at midnight, asked a thousand questions about our neighbours, one time he even put black-out curtains on all our windows. Black-out curtains, for God's sake! In the middle of Renfrew County, thirty years after the war! He's more than a few bricks short of a load, I can tell you, and there's no way I'm having anything on my conscience."

Green's suspicions stirred. "When did this black-out incident occur?"

"The last time he was here, after that fellow beat him up. We brought him home from Renfrew Victoria Hospital so he could rest up a few days before making the trip home."

"It was that bang on the head, Jeanie," Dubroskie interjected wearily, as if they'd had this argument many times. "The doctors said it made him confused."

"Yeah," she retorted, still at full tilt. "So confused he started spouting German and insisted his name was Jozef Fritsch, which really gave me the willies—"

"Jeanie—"

"I mean, I lost my father at Dieppe, and when I thought there might be one right under my roof—"

"Fritsch was his mother's maiden name, that's all," Dubroskie amended, but there was little fight in his voice.

"Anyway, that's when I sent him packing. And I said to Karl, Karl, I don't want that man in my kitchen ever again, and I don't think you want to be having anything to do with him either. So Karl, don't tell me you called him Saturday and tipped him off that the cops were looking for him."

Green turned his attention to her husband, who looked wretched.

"No dear, I didn't call him. I wasn't going to fight his battles for him, and if he got himself into trouble, I was going to let the chips fall where they may."

Green looked at him thoughtfully, at the way he barely met his wife's eye, and wondered whether that was the truth. Or just what his wife wanted to hear.

As Green negotiated the bumper-to-bumper traffic back down Highway 17 towards Ottawa, he listened to Sullivan's end of the conversation on the cellphone and tried to piece together the news from Hamilton. It didn't sound good. When Sullivan disconnected, he confirmed Green's fears.

"Still no sign of him. He's not gone to any of his old haunts, or checked with any of his old pals."

"He's gone to ground," Green replied grimly. "Let's just hope he's skipped the country without leaving any bullet-riddled bodies behind."

Sullivan stared out the window a moment at the flat, monotonous snow fields. "You know, you could be wrong. He could just be a scared old man like his daughter said, still spooked from his persecution and escape from the Soviets, distrustful of police and afraid we'll frame him for something he didn't do. So he grabs a gun and takes off. God knows where he'll end up when he stops running."

Green listened impatiently. "What about Walker's murder?"

"Let's face it, Mike, we don't have much evidence to prove Walker was even murdered."

"We don't have much evidence, but we know he was."

"What do we have that we can possibly substantiate in court? A bump on the head that we can't explain? MacPhail will get up on the stand and say the guy died of natural causes. A doctor hurrying past hears a mumble of voices from Walker's car, but he can't even say for sure there was more than one person in the vehicle. A defence lawyer would make mincemeat of him."

Green forced himself to consider the points; much as he hated to admit it, this was how Sullivan and he worked best.

Sullivan provided the sober second thought that kept Green's feet on the ground.

"We've got the dark grey car at the country house and the footprints someone tried to wipe out," he muttered finally.

"What's that got to do with anything? That was Don Reid's car. And if we're looking for a believable murder suspect, there's one I could sell to the Crown. It was his vehicle, his prints on the investment bonds. Two thousand bucks' worth are missing, and Don Reid's finances are the pits. According to Watts' latest report, Reid's house is second-mortgaged to the limit, he owes fifteen grand on his little BMW toy, his credit cards are cancelled and his chequing account is two thousand dollars overdrawn. He's even borrowed from friends. This guy goes through money like water. He must have a hole in him somewhere."

"It's cocaine," Green interjected.

Sullivan absorbed this with a look of surprise. "Nice of you to tell me, buddy. Cocaine. That's perfect. We all know what cocaine does—makes you nuts, you can't think straight, can't control your temper. You get desperate for the next hit. Reid could have stolen the bonds from old man Walker and gotten into a fight with him over it in the car that day. Reid's wife doesn't know about their money problems, and maybe he didn't want her finding out. The old man threatens to blow the whistle, things get out of hand and Reid hits him. The day after the death, he sneaks out to the house and checks it out to make sure there's nothing around that might incriminate him."

Green had been listening intently for flaws in the logic, and now he shook his head. "It was Howard Walker who sneaked into the house."

"What? How do you know?"

"Neither Don nor Margaret drove out there that day. They

both invented stories, but they didn't know the time nor the duration of the visit. I could tell Don didn't even know the trip had taken place. Margaret did, and she was covering for someone. Howard Walker claims he didn't even know his father was dead until Thursday evening, but the phone records from the hotel show that he made a long-distance call from Toronto to Margaret at 5:30 p.m. Wednesday. After the murder but before the trip to the country house. He learned of his father's death, swore his sister to secrecy, borrowed her car, and went out to the house. Probably to get something."

"What?"

"I haven't a clue. Yet."

"You think Howard bumped off his father?" Sullivan asked with disbelief. "Left the convention Wednesday, bumped him off, returned to Toronto, called his sister, and then the next day drove all the way back to get something out of the country house?"

Green made a face. "No, I don't. Howard despised his father, and he never wanted to see him again, but I don't see him as the murdering type. No matter what you say, I still think the paranoid Mr. G. is the one we're looking for."

Back at the station an hour later, however, he made a startling discovery which cast Howard's actions in an whole new light. Sullivan had gone home, and Green was doing a quick review of the accumulated reports before he too went home, hoping for some small fact they could link to Gryszkiewicz. The first reports revealed little new. Forensics reported no fingerprints other than the Walkers' and Don Reid's anywhere outside or inside the Dodge Aries. Bank records confirmed that Don Reid had withdrawn money Wednesday afternoon, but at 1:30, not noon as he'd claimed. But then, coke addicts spent their lives fudging the truth.

Just when Green was beginning to fear the case might never break open, he came across two phone messages near the bottom of the pile. One was a brief memo from Detective Gibbs reporting on his visits to antique dealers in Toronto. The other was a phone message from Naomi Wyman. He was so astounded that he nearly shouted aloud.

Usually keep inquiries strictly confidential but since possible war crime involved, thought should tell you two weeks ago a Howard Walker came in requesting info on survivors Ozorkow.

Twelve

September 1st, 1942

My hands bleed, my arms scream mercy.
Still my liebling digs. Half mad.
It must be big enough for them to breathe.
The walls thick enough to hide their cries.
She clambers in and shakes her head.
Footfalls on the stair, she dives out and shoves the cupboard
 back in place.
No one must know, she hisses. No one.
But we'll need someone to care for them while we work.
No one, she says.
Traitors and madmen are everywhere.
What price a Jewish child these days?
A bowl of soup?
A chance to live another day?
The Darkness has stolen our souls,
but not these children.
Not if it takes a thousand days in this cave until
 the British come.

The drive to Montreal took less than two hours along the nearly deserted four-lane Trans-Canada highway, and

Green arrived at the western outskirts of the city around supper time, happy to see the rush hour traffic heading in the opposite direction for once. Sharon had been working today and he had left her a cryptic message on the answering machine to the effect he'd be home sometime but perhaps not until ten. She'd be annoyed. No, that was an understatement. Tony's birthday party was tomorrow, and Green was supposed to be home tonight to help her get ready. Since he was missing two family dinners in a row, she'd be plotting his demise.

As he drove, Green tried to integrate the new information with what he already knew, but this new revelation about Howard threw a completely different twist into his theories to date. At least Gibbs' report from the Toronto antique dealer confirmed much of what Fine had already said; the tool box had been handmade by a fine craftsman, almost certainly Joseph Kressman himself, who had made the false bottom to conceal something precious. Probably secret papers or jewels, a common enough subterfuge during wartime. The keys had been mass-produced by a German company which went bankrupt after the war, and they may have been used by the military for storage depots, gates and barracks.

Or concentration camps, he thought with a chill. What would Eugene Walker, Jewish camp inmate, be doing with such a key? And what the hell did Howard know about any of this?

Twenty minutes later, Howard Walker stood in the doorway of his modest brick house, his eyes widened in astonishment at the sight of Green.

"What are you doing here?"

"Following unanswered questions," Green replied, and when Howard continued to gape, he inclined his head politely. "May I come in?"

"Is this legal? Aren't you out of your jurisdiction or something?"

"It's done all the time," Green replied patiently. "Have you got a problem with talking to me?"

"Not at all, not at all." Flustered, Howard drew back into the house and gestured for Green to follow. He led him through a vestibule crammed with shoes and coats into a long, narrow living room.

Howard Walker's home created a curious feeling of contradiction. It was a two-storey brick semi tucked into a narrow lot in Lower Westmount, a house much like the one in which Green had grown up in the slums of Ottawa's Lowertown. Also like his, this one was sparsely furnished in aging hand-me-downs, and home-made bookshelves lined the walls. But the similarity ended there. Green knew this modest little home had probably cost the new doctor and his wife three hundred thousand dollars, and represented Howard's first step up the ladder of yuppiedom. Furniture would come later, when his lucrative specialty of neurology began to pay dividends.

As Green entered the living room, he wondered how a penniless shopkeeper's son from Renfrew who had just completed his residency had managed to scrape together three hundred thousand for a house in the gentrified downtown, when he and Sharon could scarcely afford a vinyl cube at the End of the Earth. But in the next instant he had his answer. Curled up in an overstuffed chair in the corner of the living room, her feet tucked under the generous folds of her designer skirt, was Rachel, the picture of Daddy's Girl. The astonishment in her amber eyes mirrored that of her husband.

"I don't understand why you keep on about my father's death," Howard said as he sat down. "My father was not a well man. Since I've studied medicine, I'm amazed that he didn't collapse sooner."

During the drive, Green had planned his approach carefully.

Howard's visit to Naomi Wyman raised a number of serious questions, but they would have to be sequenced carefully lest he send Howard running for cover. A blend of bullying and coddling was in order.

"Dr. Walker, I want to know why you went out to your parents' house last Thursday," he began bluntly.

Rachel uncurled herself in annoyance. "Last Thursday Howard was in Toronto at the medical convention. We've been through this."

"No, he wasn't." Green kept his eyes fixed on her husband. "He wanted everyone to believe that, but actually he flew up to Ottawa, borrowed his sister's car, and drove out to the country house."

"That's ridiculous," Rachel said. "He didn't even know Eugene was dead then."

"His sister told him when he called her Wednesday night." Green pulled a folded invoice from his pocket and turned to Howard. "There's a record of that phone call on your hotel bill."

"Howard!" Rachel cried. "What is this?"

Howard was looking at him in mute horror. "My God. You think I killed him."

"You tell me," Green countered. "What conclusion should I draw from all the lies and subterfuge?"

"That's outrageous, Inspector! Howard couldn't kill anyone, least of all his own father."

"There was no love lost—"

"There was a great deal of love lost!" she shot back. "That was the tragedy."

"Rachel, please." Howard's weary voice caught them both by surprise. He reached for a loose thread on the sofa arm and twisted it in his long, fluid fingers. "I did call Margaret, and I did leave the convention to go out to the house. I had to retrieve something."

"What?" Green demanded.

"It has no relevance."

"What!"

Howard hesitated. The thread came loose, and he crushed it into a ball between his fingers. "I had written my father a letter. A personal letter which had taken a lot of effort to write. I mailed it on the previous Friday, and I anticipated that he should have received it Tuesday or Wednesday. I called Margaret on Wednesday night to see if she'd heard anything, because I expected there would be shock waves. When she told me he was dead, I couldn't believe it. I was afraid—" He broke off, then shook his head as if to banish a thought. "Anyway, I didn't want my mother to read the letter. There was no point in stirring things up now that he was dead. So I arranged to borrow Margaret's car to go and get it."

"Why not send Margaret? Why travel all the way from Toronto?"

"Margaret had her hands full with mother and the funeral arrangements. I didn't see what excuse she could give."

"And you didn't want her reading the letter."

Howard dropped the thread and clasped his hands tightly together in his lap to hide their trembling. "That too."

"Can I see the letter?"

"I burned it."

"What did it say?"

"Just personal things."

"Such as that you knew he was Jewish?"

The young doctor's eyes bulged. "What!"

"Last time we talked, you called him a hypocrite. That's a hell of an understatement, wouldn't you say?"

"Darling!" Rachel cried. "What's he talking about?"

Howard flushed red, his hands shaking despite his grip. "Where did you get this crazy idea, Inspector?"

"That's how the pieces fit. You tried to suppress the autopsy report because you didn't want me wondering why your father was circumcised."

"Suppress the autopsy?" Howard tried to rally some spark. "I did no such thing."

"You were afraid I might put two and two together—"

"I simply asked the pathologist to give us some privacy. Because of Dad's drinking, I knew the autopsy report would be brutal."

Green regarded him thoughtfully. "Howard, it's a hell of a lot more than that. You've known—at least suspected—that your father was Jewish for several weeks. You see," he added quietly, "I have this phone message from Naomi Wyman saying 'funny you should ask about Orzokow, a young man named Howard Walker was just in a couple of weeks ago'."

"Oh…God."

Green's expression softened. "So you wrote him a letter asking him?"

Very faintly, Howard nodded.

"And you thought your letter killed him?"

Unexpectedly, Howard strode to the window and pressed his forehead against the cold pane. It was a moment before anyone spoke. Rachel was sitting rigidly still, but her ragged breathing punctuated the silence. To her credit, it was the first time she didn't rush in to rescue him.

Finally, Howard raised his head to stare into the darkness. "I think it probably did. I found the letter hidden in his drawer. It was open."

"So he had read it."

Howard nodded wretchedly.

"How did you discover your father was a Jew?"

"Anton Gryszkiewicz!" Rachel exclaimed, startling them both.

Green's thoughts began to spin excitedly. "Gryszkiewicz?"

Still Howard was silent, as if casting about for a safe path.

"Darling, tell him! For God's sake, you've got nothing to hide!"

Green remembered Sullivan's conversation with Mrs. Gryszkiewicz, in which she had told him so proudly about her son the doctor. "A young doctor from Hamilton?" he asked.

Howard swung around in dismay. "What do you know about him?"

"Nothing. But his father knew yours." Green's face hardened. "Now I'm not just filling in odd bits of the puzzle. This could be crucial to the case. You must tell me exactly what happened between Anton and you."

Howard's dark eyes searched Green's worriedly. "He's a nice guy," he pleaded. "I don't want to get him in trouble."

"There's trouble enough already!" Green snapped. "I need the truth! Where did you meet him?"

"At the Montreal Neurological Institute. He's a resident in surgery, and I was called in to look at a patient on his floor who had slipped into a coma and begun seizing. It was a hell of a night. We were both scared, out of our depth, wondering why this always happens at two a.m. when there's not a staff man within miles. Anyway, the patient died, and it created a kind of bond. We became friends, and we found out we had a lot in common. We both had immigrant fathers from Poland we didn't get along with. We both found our fathers remote and cruel. It was amazing how similar they were, even down to the anti-Semitism. We got to talking about the war and wondering if they'd lived through something terrible that had twisted them. I told him my father didn't even remember who he was, that all we had was this box from a place named Ozorkow. He said his father was from Ozorkow, and we got really excited. Maybe his father would know mine."

Howard paused, as if debating how much to divulge. Green could barely contain himself, for finally the case was breaking open in front of his eyes.

"So about a month ago," Howard resumed, "when he went to visit his parents for the weekend, he took an old picture of my father with him. At first his father denied knowing him, but a while later he got drunk—another thing he had in common with my father—and he got mad about the government charging some war criminal. He blurted out that the Jews were behind it all, even passing themselves off as Poles to hide their own guilt, like my father. Anton tried to get him to tell him more, but his father clammed up again. Said the picture just looked Jewish. I didn't believe it. Neither did Anton. He said his father's outburst was very convincing."

Green frowned at him. "Why the hell were you reluctant to tell me this?"

"Because Anton's father would be angry with him, and his father could be cruel, even crueler than mine, if he found out Anton had betrayed him."

"Betrayed him? A strong word. How does this betray him?"

"Because his family isn't supposed to talk about the war outside the family, or about Poland, or anything about the past. The father's very secretive and suspicious of outsiders. He says there are still lots of people from the old country—Communists—who have it in for him. There are spies everywhere, maybe even the neighbour next door. Anton thought he'd gone a bit paranoid because of all the years of hiding from Communist persecution."

Or from something else, like Simon Wiesenthal or the Mossad, or even our own rather polite, grey-suited Nazi hunters, Green thought privately, but he hid his excitement. "So you wrote to your father asking if it was true."

"Not right away. I didn't believe it. My father, the anti-Semite who had driven me out for converting to Judaism. Himself a Jew?"

"So that's why you asked my father if there was any record of Holocaust survivors!" Rachel cried. "Darling, why didn't you tell me!"

They had forgotten her presence, and her sudden, vehement interruption caught them off guard. Howard's gaze flickered towards her.

"I don't know," he began lamely. "I needed to be sure, and I needed to understand why he had lied. My father's prejudices had hurt you so much."

"But now! Once you found out, why didn't you tell me!"

"I was waiting for my father's answer. I still don't understand why he lied."

"Howard, what am I here for? Spouses are supposed to share!" Rachel's eyes flashed with reproach that Green suspected would linger far beyond his visit. But as interesting as this slice of domestic discord was, it was irrelevant to his own quest. And the reference to spouses served to steer him back on track. By this time Sharon would be home from work and making serious progress on her murder plot.

"So you contacted Naomi Wyman?" He prompted brusquely, causing them both to stare at him blankly. Howard's eyes were glassy, but with a deep breath he composed himself.

"I asked her if she had records of anyone in Canada who came from Ozorkow. She didn't, but she gave me the names of three people who'd been in Lodz, a large ghetto where many of the Jews from Ozorkow had been sent. Two are now dead, but one lives here in Montreal. I showed my father's picture to him, and he remembered him. Not well, but they'd been in the ghetto together, and he confirmed my father was Jewish. That's when I wrote the letter."

"What was this survivor's name?"

Howard chewed his lip. "Look, I don't want to get him involved—"

"His name!"

Howard recoiled before Green's sudden anger, and his hands shook. "Isaac Perchesky."

"This Isaac Perchesky, did he give you any details about your father? His name? His occupation?"

Howard's head whipped back and forth. "He said he didn't remember much," he stammered. "He didn't want to talk about those times. That's why I don't want you to... He said that the Holocaust did strange things to all of us, and that it was better to leave it all in the past."

"And in your letter, did you leave it in the past?"

He had his answer when Howard abruptly left the room.

*   *   *

Isaac Perchesky's wife was no more pleased with the intrusion than Howard had been, but when Green explained his purpose, she reluctantly went to rouse her husband, who was asleep in front of the TV. Isaac had some initial difficulty recognizing his wife, let alone recalling Howard's visit, but finally the fog began to lift.

"So...the old man is dead?" Perchesky shook his head dolefully. "It's hard to imagine him dead. In my memory, he

210

was so strong. I can still see him over there in the doorway—like Goliath, with shoulders so wide he could pick up a man and throw him against the wall with one hand. I never forget him doing that."

"But he would have been little more than a boy. Barely eighteen when the war broke out."

The old man shrugged. "Boys grew up fast in the ghetto. The man took his blanket. That's the way it was in Lodz. If you didn't have a blanket in the winter, you died."

"You say your memory of him is very vivid. Howard Walker said you hardly remembered him."

Perchesky's face darkened, suffusing his mottled skin with grey. He sucked on his dentures for a moment as if debating. "That's what I told the boy. Why bring up the rest? Better he should think his father was a victim who covered up his past because of his suffering."

Green sucked in his breath. "You're saying he wasn't a Jew? He wasn't a survivor?"

"Oh, he was a Jew. And he was certainly a survivor. It was other people who didn't survive."

"What are you saying? Tell me what you know!"

Perchesky raised his head at the sharpness in Green's tone and focussed his flat grey eyes on him. "What I know is that in 1942, when the Nazis were sending all the Jews over sixty-five and under ten to the death camp of Chelmno, Leib turned his own father and youngest brother over to the Nazis. The boy would have been ten in two months."

The outrage of the act derailed Green's train of thought briefly. It was another era, he told himself, and in 1942 very few knew the full horror of the Nazi plan. Then the rest of Perchesky's words sank in, and Green's excitement rose.

"Leib? Do you know his last name?"

Perchesky shook his head in contempt. "I remember Leib, because it means lion and he thought he was the king of the jungle. More like a sewer rat."

"You're sure it was the same man?"

"Oh, yes. The doctor showed me his picture and even if he was thirty years older, I recognized him. Those cold eyes, they never changed."

Green showed him the wedding picture Ruth had supplied, taken in 1948 outside the little village church in Surrey. Walker looked hunted even then, gaunt and hollow-eyed. He had tried to smile, but it was pasted on like a slash of pain across a frozen mask.

Isaac stared at it a long time. "Look at what the war did to him by the end," he whispered. "He was a big man, strong, proud. But the Nazis got us all in the end."

"What else can you tell me about him?"

Perchesky raised his wizened face to study Green. His eyes were appraising. "I know little about him," he replied finally. "No one is a saint who survived the ghetto. The saints all died. Now he is dead too, and what I know is not important any more."

Quietly, Green removed the photo and laid in its place one that Sullivan had given him. "Do you recognize this man too?"

He heard Perchesky suck in his breath, but the old man said nothing for a time. The picture trembled slightly in his hand as he studied it. Finally, he stared into space, casting his thoughts back in time. "This man is from Poland?"

"Yes."

"From Lodz?"

"Do you recognize him?"

"I think he was one of the SS officers who guarded the entrance to the ghetto."

Inwardly, Green was cartwheeling in triumph. "SS officer?

You mean Polish Police officer?"

Perchesky squinted in his effort to remember, then slowly shook his head. "Maybe. It was the same everywhere—Ukraine, Hungary, Slovakia, Latvia—the local Fascists helped the SS with their dirty work. They helped seal the ghettoes and guard the gates to make sure no one escaped or smuggled things in. If they caught you, the SS shot you."

"And you think this man was one of these guards?"

Perchesky studied the photo again with obvious discomfort. "It looks like him, but I was only in Lodz for a little time when he was there. He came to the ghetto only in 1942, and I was sent to another camp in October. But you could ask the other man Dr. Walker had on his list. He was in Lodz longer. He knew Leib better, and maybe this guard too."

Green had been putting the photo of Gryszkiewicz back into his jacket pocket, and he looked up sharply. "What other man?"

"Another survivor from Lodz. Dr. Walker asked if I knew him, but I didn't."

"What was his name?"

Perchesky shook his head helplessly. "I don't remember," he began, but was drowned out by his wife.

"Bernard Mendelsohn."

Thirteen

September 10th, 1942

The potato peelings look forlorn,
swimming sparse and shrivelled in the watery pot.
She doles them into bowls, splits a slice of bread in three.
You too, I say, but she shakes her head.
Eyes her bag of embroidery, untouched since that dreadful day,
when the ghetto lost all taste for finery.
I'm going over the wall, she says.
Madness but surely mine to do, I protest.
The hole's too small, she says, the rope too thin.
Besides, I know someone.
She has that look, born of an urge stronger than life itself.
Our babies falter, their spirits and bodies shrunk.
So I nod and she picks up the bag.

There was no answer at Howard Walker's house nor at Bernie Mendelsohn's apartment in Ottawa when Green phoned. He sat in his car outside Howard's house, cursing his cell phone and trying to figure out his next move. It was nine o'clock in the evening. Around him the traffic of downtown Montreal swirled in the darkness, and headlights reflected off the slush-slicked streets. Where the hell had Howard gone?

Green couldn't sit in his car indefinitely, hoping the man turned up sometime that evening. Not when there was a panicked old man on the loose with a gun and Bernie Mendelsohn, who was possibly the key to it all, was not answering his phone.

Nine o'clock. No reason to panic, he reassured himself. Mendelsohn might simply have fallen asleep and not heard the phone, just like the other night. Howard had never even mentioned him and probably never bothered to see him once Perchesky had told him what he needed to know. Just because fifty years later an old war secret had erupted into murder, it did not mean that Mendelsohn was in danger.

And yet...old man Gryszkiewicz had clearly gone off after something.

"Damn it," he swore. Just when time was ticking away, he was at least two hours away from Mendelsohn's home. Given no choice, he picked up his cell again and punched in Sullivan's number.

*   *   *

Half an hour later, Brian Sullivan pulled up in front of Bernie Mendelsohn's apartment and sat for a moment in his idling car, mustering some enthusiasm. It was bad enough that Green had caught him just settling down to a rare cuddle on the couch with Mary, bad enough that he'd been forced out into his frozen car on a blustery winter night, but now he had to barge into an ailing octogenarian's apartment and scare the crap out of the poor guy with his police badge and his hulking six-two frame.

Still, Green had his premonitions, and Sullivan had worked with the man long enough never to dismiss them out of hand.

The damn guy was right just too many times. And after Sullivan had hauled himself up to Mendelsohn's apartment and tapped gently on the dingy door, he began to suspect this might be one of those times.

Silence. No creaking floors or shuffling feet. He knocked more loudly, then thumped hard enough to rouse the comatose.

Silence.

The building superintendent, wrenched from an alcoholic stupor by the sight of Sullivan's badge, wheezed heavily as he fumbled the key in the cranky lock. When the door finally gave, Sullivan strode past him into the room. A quick glance around confirmed what Green had feared. The room hadn't been inhabited for several days. The bed was unmade, pyjamas were cast about, food lay rotting on the counter, and the whole apartment reeked of decay. Paint flaked off the ceiling, and the overhead bulb cast a murky glow through its grime.

"Fuck!" whined the superintendent, who remained swaying in the doorway. Probably thinking about the clean-up, Sullivan thought with disgust.

"When was the last time you saw Mr. Mendelsohn?" he demanded.

The man shrugged, a movement which briefly upset his balance. "I don't know," he said. "It's not my job to watch over all these old guys. Not for a couple of days, I think."

Sullivan installed the man on the single kitchen chair and rummaged through the cupboard's meagre supplies. Within five minutes he had a cup of strong coffee in one hand and a flask of cheap cherry brandy in the other. Looming over the man, he repeated his question.

"I was mopping the front hall, one of them fucking freezing days. Thursday? Maybe Friday? He come out the elevator looking tired and leaning hard on his cane, like he was in pain."

Sullivan gave him a quick sip of brandy. "What did he say?"

"He didn't say nothing! Looked right through me like I wasn't there. He don't usually do that, so I thought he must be feeling bad."

"What else?"

"That's all I seen. I helped him with the door and he went off. I didn't like him going off, what with the cold and the ice, but he's stubborn that way."

"What was he wearing? Was he carrying anything?"

"Wearing?" The superintendent wheezed. "Mr. Mendelsohn always dresses like a gentleman, with one of them hats gentlemen used to wear. But with the cold, he had his old parka bundled up to the very top." Sullivan handed him the brandy, and the man took a long pull in his attempt to concentrate. "He was carrying a brown paper bag. I figured he was going shopping—that's about all he goes out for anyways. Specially in winter."

Sullivan took back the flask and leaned forward. "Did he have any visitors the day he left? Or the day before?"

"He never gets no visitors."

"An old man, maybe Saturday?"

"Old man? Well, his friend came by a few days ago, with his son the cop—"

"Besides that. Maybe even the past few weeks?"

The super sucked at his tongue through the gap in his teeth. "Lives alone, no family, just a couple of friends. Sometimes he goes out for a game of cards, but this place is so small and shitty, who the hell would you want to—" He broke off abruptly, light dawning in his bloodshot eyes. "Jeez! I forgot! His son came. Couple of weeks ago, dropped in to see him one afternoon."

Sullivan frowned. Green hadn't mentioned Mendelsohn had a son. "What was his name?"

"Never said. But I figured it was his son."

"What did he look like?"

"Good-looking fella. Dark hair, nice clothes. Got me curious because Bernie never had no money to spare, used to have trouble with the rent, so at first I couldn't figure where this fancy-looking guy would fit in."

"Did Mr. Mendelsohn actually tell you it was his son?"

The super shook his head and shifted uncomfortably. "I was keeping an eye out while the guy was here. I mean, I got a lot of old people here, and I got to know who's in the building. This guy comes, and Mr. Mendelsohn lets him in all pleasant, like he knows him. I don't hear nothing, no arguing, nothing, but when the guy comes back out after about an hour, he starts crying."

"Mendelsohn?"

"No, the son. He shuts the door and leans against the wall and he bawls. So I thought…well, Mr. Mendelsohn's sick, you know. Dying. And I heard he had a son somewhere. So it made sense."

"How did Mr. Mendelsohn seem after that?"

"Well, it's a funny thing. He's been going downhill for a couple of months now. But the visit kind of perked him up, you know. I mean he wasn't happy or smiling or nothing like that, Mr. Mendelsohn's never like that, but he seemed stronger like. That's why I figured it was his son maybe lifted his spirits."

*   *   *

Green was halfway between Montreal and Ottawa when

218

Sullivan's call came through. As Sullivan filled him in, a tiny knot of fear began to form in his chest. His father had never mentioned Irving coming to visit. On the contrary, when his father had suggested contacting Irving about the cancer, Bernie had become annoyed.

In Green's head, alarm bells began to ring. "Did the super give you a description of this guy?"

When he heard the description, the knot swelled to full force. When he'd rung off, Green rammed his foot closer to the floor and shot through the darkness.

An hour later, Sid Green started up in bed, blinking at his son through rheumy, sleep-filled eyes. "Michael! What has happened!"

"Nothing, Dad." Green forced himself to sound casual as he laid a soothing hand on his shoulder. "I just need to talk to you about Bernie."

Sid turned and stared around the darkened room. "What time is it!" he said irritably. "Why are you waking me up in the middle of the night?"

"Bernie, Dad. I need to talk to him, and he's not in his apartment."

"What could be so important at this hour! For this you almost give me a heart attack?"

Green drew back with a placating gesture. "I'm sorry, Dad. It's not that late. I'll go make you some tea."

He was just squeezing some lemon from a plastic bottle into his father's glass when Sid shuffled into the living room, drawing a ragged grey dressing gown around his waist. Green had bought him a new one, but it never seemed to leave his cupboard. Sid sank into his favourite tub chair with a scowl.

"Dad, you know I wouldn't disturb you if it wasn't important. Do you know where Bernie went?"

"Nowhere. Bernie hasn't gone anywhere in years. He just slept through the bell. He takes a lot of pills at night."

Green shook his head. "The place was empty, and the food on the counter looked several days old."

Sid raised his eyes slowly. Alarm replaced the irritation. "So soon," he breathed. "They said he had one or two months left. He wanted to stay out of the hospital as long as he could."

"Hospital! Of course." Green stood up. "What hospital?"

"Civic."

Green dialled, spoke briefly to reception and was informed that no Bernard Mendelsohn had been admitted.

"What do hospitals know?" Sid said. "He's there."

"Dad, have you seen him since Thursday? Talked to him?" His father was shaking his head irritably. "Did he seem any different recently?"

"I don't know, Michael," Sid said peevishly. "He's upset about his cancer, that's all. What is this! What do you want from Bernie!"

"Do you know if Irving visited him recently?"

"His son?" Sid came alive. "His son lives in Philadelphia, never calls. Why should now be any different?"

"Because his father is dying. Perhaps he wanted a reconciliation." Sid was shaking his head skeptically, and Green found himself gritting his teeth. "Dad, it's important! Would Bernie have gone to his son? Do you have his address?"

"No, no. If Irving called, Bernie would tell me. They haven't talked in years."

"But he had a visitor. A younger man. Bernie didn't mention a thing to you?"

Sid stared across at his son, and gradually his expression began to change. The teacup shook slightly in his hand. "The last time I talked to him, before last week, he was very upset.

Very white, talking all the time about ghosts from the past coming back—"

Green leaned forward. "What ghosts?"

The sharpness in Green's tone must have unnerved him, for he shrank back. "I don't know. Ghosts. I thought he meant memories."

"Of the camps?"

Sid nodded. "Of all that happened. And all the people gone."

"Bernie was from a little village, you said. Was he ever in Lodz ghetto?"

"Yes, Bernie was in Lodz, he was with the partisans, he was in Majdanek and Sachsenhausen, he lost twenty-two relatives in the war, and now he has a son in Philadelphia who doesn't call."

Green hid his anxiety until he had stepped into the darkness outside his father's apartment. It was past midnight, and he was exhausted. All he'd eaten since morning was a Big Mac on his way back from Montreal, and he'd been racing around in circles now for nearly twelve hours. What had happened to Bernie Mendelsohn, and why had Howard lied about him? Questions kept swirling in his mind, but reason told him nothing more could be accomplished that night. Perhaps Mendelsohn had gone to visit his son. He was dying, and death tended to change a man's perspective on family.

But what if Mendelsohn were in danger? What if someone was killing to keep the atrocities of the past a secret?

On impulse Green swung his Corolla towards Mendelsohn's apartment. Just one last brief stop, he told himself, before he stumbled home to Sharon.

The search of Mendelsohn's tiny room took less than ten minutes before yielding up the address and phone number of

Mendelsohn's son. At least this one small question could be answered tonight, Green thought as he picked up Mendelsohn's phone. His call to Philadelphia woke a very irate housekeeper who objected vigorously to his request that she rouse her employer. Her protests were cut short by Irving Mendelsohn himself, who took over the line with a grumpy bark.

"Inspector Green, Ottawa Police. Sorry to disturb you at this hour, sir, but we are trying to determine the whereabouts of your father. He's been missing from his apartment for several days. Is he with you, sir?"

"My father?" Mendelsohn exclaimed as if his father were but a distant memory. "No, he's not with me. Why should he be with me?"

"Because you're his only living relative."

"Well, he's got plenty of dead ones to keep him company. Always has."

So great was Green's shock that he removed the receiver from his ear and stared at it in disbelief. His first impulse was to hurl it across the living room, but he knew that would touch the pompous *putz* not at all. Something more pointed was necessary.

"He'll be joining those soon enough. I thought he might have wanted to see you beforehand. Goodnight, sir," he added and hung up just as the first challenging roar surged through the wires.

Green's hands shook with outrage as he stuffed Mendelsohn's papers back into the drawer. Let's hope I at least gave the prick a sleepless hour or two, he thought. Irving Mendelsohn hadn't seen his father in years, had just received a midnight call from the police notifying him that he was missing, and his only reaction was to disparage the man? Green was so appalled that he almost missed the torn scrap of paper lying on the counter half hidden by the phone. A few tell-tale letters of a word scribbled in a shaky hand. He freed the paper and stared at it, and his blood ran cold.

Josef Gryszkiewicz 230

*   *   *

Sharon was asleep when Green stumbled back into his house at two a.m. Balloons and streamers festooned the walls and ceilings of the living room, and more were piled on the dining room table, awaiting his help. In case he had missed the message, she had propped a big card in front of the pile—*Green, take note.*

He lay awake in the darkness, anguishing over what he should do. He'd already filed a preliminary missing persons report on Mendelsohn downtown and alerted the street patrols. He'd also phoned the Hamilton Police and reached some desk-bound detective who was propping himself awake with caffeine and who informed him there was no news. Gryszkiewicz was still missing. The gun was still missing. In the morning, Green knew he'd have to contact the actual investigators assigned to the case, might even have to go down to Hamilton to nip at their heels a bit. But he also had to intensify the search for Mendelsohn, and he had to talk to Howard again. All that would be enough to keep him busy until late tomorrow night, but his wife, curled peacefully beside him, needed—no, deserved—his help, and his son deserved his presence at the first major birthday of his life.

Daybreak had barely touched the eastern sky when Green, after an almost sleepless night, made his way into the police station. First on his list of imperatives was to get an APB out on Bernie Mendelsohn. Second was a call to Sullivan's contact on the Hamilton force. Sergeant Strauss was just signing in and was not surprised to hear from him.

"Yeah, I was getting to you," he said. "We did a check on our guy's activities last Wednesday, to see if he had an alibi for your homicide up there. Well, he does and he doesn't. Usually he and the wife stay alone at the house during the day while their daughter and her husband work, but that day the wife was in town most of the day for some medical tests."

"So how many hours does he have unaccounted for?"

"Looks like at least six."

Green did some rough calculations. He'd have to check with the airlines, but it was theoretically possible to fly to Ottawa Wednesday morning, murder Walker and fly back before any of his family returned home. It was a long shot, but a call to the airlines would tell him if it could have been done. With any luck, Mr. G. had even used his own name to buy the tickets.

"Good work," Green said. "Was anyone in the family nervous that you were asking?"

"Nervous?" Strauss gave a short laugh. "They're totally freaking out down here. The old guy hasn't come back yet, and we've called just about every person he ever said hello to."

"Did you check with his son, Anton? He's a doctor in Montreal."

"Yeah, twice. He's been away at a conference and hasn't spoken to his father in over a week."

"Well, the old man's internationally connected in ways they may know nothing about, so if he's decided to drop out of sight, it's a phone call away."

"The family is scared he's dead."

"Why? Was his health bad?"

"No, he's as strong as an ox, but when you're over eighty, anything's possible, eh? We've plastered his name around and alerted the hospitals, but so far no leads."

"Trust me, you won't get any. He's probably half way to Paraguay."

"What the fuck did you boys unearth up there in Ottawa? Some underworld conspiracy?"

Something like that, Green thought as he rang off and sat staring at his notes. It was a conspiracy of sorts, but he had a sick feeling not everybody was on the same side. Three old men were bound together by a common place at a common time—Lodz, 1942. Two were Jews in the ghetto, the third a Fascist guard. One Jew had been murdered on Wednesday, and the other had disappeared on Friday. The guard had dropped out of sight Saturday, after being tipped off by a friend.

Gryszkiewicz had both motive and opportunity to kill Walker, but how could he have known Walker would be in the Civic Hospital parking lot at that time? Only Ruth, Margaret and Don had known. So had Walker himself, of course, but what sense did that make? Would Walker himself have invited Gryszkiewicz?

Green's mind raced over the idea, ferreting out the implications. Walker had received the letter from Howard on Monday or Tuesday. What had he done? He had not told his wife, that much was clear. He had not called his son. Had he called Gryszkiewicz? Why? If there was a pact between the two men to hide the past, why call him now? To tell him to keep quiet if Howard asked him? Why ask the man to travel over four hundred miles to make a request that could be done over the phone? Why make a face to face meeting? Unless...!

Perhaps Walker had phoned Mr. G., and it was Mr. G. who had insisted on the meeting. Insisted because he was afraid that the truth about his Nazi past was about to be revealed and he needed to eliminate witnesses. So he met Walker and perhaps demanded to know how much Howard knew and how he had found out. At which point Walker might have mentioned another survivor from Lodz who lives in Ottawa. Bernie Mendelsohn.

It would be simple for Gryszkiewicz to call all the B. Mendelsohns in the Ottawa directory. When he found the right one, he would have given him some story about a mutual old friend from Lodz or a search for a lost relative. Mendelsohn would have been easy prey for such a tale of woe. Once Mr. G. had Mendelsohn on the hook, he'd set up a meeting with him at 2:30.

As a theory, it had an elegant simplicity. Mr. G. murders Walker on Wednesday. Tracks down Mendelsohn on Thursday. Murders Mendelsohn on Friday. Tipped off by Dubroskie on Saturday. It fit all the known facts, but its foundation rested on two major assumptions. One, that Walker had indeed contacted Gryszkiewicz when he received Howard's letter. And two, that Howard had talked to Bernie Mendelsohn then told his father about it.

Howard could not confirm the first assumption, but he could certainly confirm the second. Green did not relish another confrontation with the young doctor. He was afraid it was too late anyway, that if his theory was true, Bernie Mendelsohn was already dead. Unlike Gryszkiewicz, Mendelsohn had no place to go and no friends to call on. But if there were even the slimmest hope that Mendelsohn had eluded Gryszkiewicz and was trying to hide, Green had to find him first.

Howard Walker's phone was snatched up before the second ring, and a breathy, urgent voice snapped hello.

"Rachel, it's Inspector Green calling. I need to speak to Howard."

"He's asleep."

"Then please wake him. It's urgent."

"Inspector, my husband has been on duty all night, and I've only just persuaded him to lie down. He hasn't been sleeping, he's exhausted, depressed and near collapse. If your damn phone call hasn't already woken him, I will not wake him just for your convenience."

Green was beyond subtlety. He'd managed less than three hours sleep himself and was now wound up into knots with worry about Mendelsohn. Her outrage took him aback and left him wondering what her own night had been like. Full of hurt and accusations, no doubt. I was only the deliverer of this bombshell, he thought, so don't take it out on me.

"Rachel, I'm not doing this for my convenience. If your damn husband had told me the truth in the first place, I'd be home right now getting ready for my son's birthday. Now get him!"

"Surely for everyone's sake then, it can wait."

"Not if another man's life is in danger!"

He could almost hear her gritting her teeth as she weighed her next move. "I want you to know I'm not impressed with this," she said finally. "Two minutes, and please go easy on him. He can't take much more."

I'm not impressed either, believe me, he thought with a flash of temper which he reined in quickly. For Mendelsohn's sake, he had to focus on the best way to draw the information he needed out of Howard. He thought an appeal to Howard's compassion might be the key, but he was wrong.

"Howard," he began once he heard the doctor's guttural croak through the wires, "I know this has been a difficult week for you, and I apologize for waking you, but I need your help. Bernie Mendelsohn has disappeared, and I'm very concerned for his safety."

"Who?"

"Bernie Mendelsohn, the survivor you met with."

"I met with an Isaac Perchesky."

Green hesitated. The man sounded drowsy, but surely not so drowsy as to forget an entire meeting. "And Bernie Mendelsohn as well. Up here in Ottawa, remember?"

"In Ottawa? I've never heard of him."

Green abandoned all attempt at gentleness. "Dr. Walker, stop playing games. Bernie Mendelsohn happens to be a friend of my father's. He's old, he's sick, he's got nobody in his life who cares about him, and now he's disappeared. He greeted you with open arms, so the least you can do—"

Unexpectedly, he heard weeping at the other end of the line, followed by a crash. Rachel Walker's voice came back on the line.

"Green, that's it. Your two minutes are up!" she said and slammed the receiver down.

"Rachel!" he shouted, then glared at the phone in frustration, swearing.

"You won't reach her by yelling at her," came a voice from his doorway. Rich, precise and British public school. He jerked his head up to see Ruth Walker leaning against the doorframe. "We women in the Walker family are a strong-willed lot."

"How did you get in here?" he demanded.

She stepped through the door into his office and drew back the extra chair from his desk. She eased herself into it stiffly, and for the first time he noticed she used a cane. She propped it against his desk.

"You don't think I negotiated all those hurdles during the war, or tracked down Eugene's past or immigrated to Canada, without learning a thing or two about bureaucracy. Your desk sergeant downstairs is a pussy cat in comparison."

Looking at her sculpted grey hair, her soft blue eyes, and her long woollen cape, he realized she was probably right. Sergeant Simms wouldn't have suspected her of anything nefarious in a million years. She sat back, removed her gloves and folded her hands in her lap.

"Inspector, it's time to stop all this nonsense."

"You mean the way you've all blocked my path at every step of the way, withheld facts, misdirected me, and even tried to convince me your husband wasn't murdered in the first place?"

"No," she countered without missing a beat, "your insistence that he was murdered. You've got my daughter positively scared silly, and my son on the brink of nervous collapse. It's time it stopped."

"It stops when I'm convinced that justice has been done."

"Justice. That's an interesting point." She thrust out her delicately pointed jaw. "Look, for the last time—Eugene had been courting disaster for months. He collapsed that day, but the truth is, it could have happened any day. He'd been racing headlong into death for months. That's what I tried to tell you on your very first visit to the house. I know all about the whiskey in the basement, I know all about the pact with Don and all about the investment certificates."

When Green raised a surprised eyebrow, she nodded. "I don't know what kind of fool Eugene thought I was that I wouldn't notice. He was dragging himself down, and he was dragging the rest of us down with him—Margaret, Don, Howard, even our grandsons. Perhaps this all ended as it was meant to end."

He frowned. "What do you mean?"

"I mean, did it ever occur to you that perhaps God had a hand in it?"

"I thought you didn't believe in God."

"I didn't. Because if there is a God and he has any power over what his creations are doing in their world—if he lets the horrors and the injustices prevail—then his purpose makes no sense to me. But, if at some other time and in some other way, a balance is struck, then perhaps there is a kind of divinity at work after all."

"God doesn't commit murders, Mrs. Walker," he countered flatly. "People do, and for the most prosaic of reasons."

She collected her purse and her cane, then rose to her feet. "You're not listening. Eugene died of natural causes, not murder." She paused in the doorway, pointing her cane at him. "Think about it, Inspector."

Green rose from his chair and stared after her as she walked across the squad room, her cane swinging and her step surprisingly spry. Almost liberated. What the hell was all that about, he asked himself? She was asking him to drop the investigation. Fair enough—it was uncovering a number of shocking truths. She was asking him to stop harassing her children. Again, fair enough—a mother's instinct to protect her children could be a ferocious force. But what was all that business about God, and the cryptical allusion to a balance being struck? What was she hinting? That his death was some sort of divine stroke of luck?

Or that she knew why he had died, and who had killed him? And more than that—she didn't want it investigated. Because a balance had been struck.

Green looked at the notes he had scribbled in front of him. Notes about Gryszkiewicz detailing how and why he could have committed the crime. Surely if a Nazi collaborator had killed her husband, she would not be alluding to some sort of divine justice, but would be demanding a very human kind.

But what if the killer was someone else? Someone she didn't want revealed, or punished.

Howard.

His throat went dry with the sudden realization. She thought it was Howard. It had been good theatre she had enacted in his office just now, brandishing her cane and talking about divine intervention. But the truth was, underneath all the metaphysics, she was just trying to save her son's skin.

The question was what did she know that he, Green, did not?

Fourteen

October 12th, 1942

The quiet is eerie now.
In my mind, I hear the beggar on the curb,
the children at play,
the old men arguing on the bench.
All gone.
Now ghosts scuttle along the street,
living and dead, hollow-eyed and empty.
I push the cupboard aside with a twinge of fear.
Always the twinge of fear.
But they're still there.
I gather them in my arms, caress them back to life.
My princess is over the wall,
To trade for supper, maybe something special again.
An apple, an egg.
I set the Shabbas candles, the chipped cup.
Voices overhead, floorboards creak,
And somewhere,
A single shot.

Green was halfway to Montreal again when his cell phone rang.

"Where are you?" Sharon demanded. He had left the house that morning before she was even awake.

He glanced out at the passing trees. "At work, honey." Not a lie, exactly.

"I tried there. They said you took off like a bat out of hell about an hour ago."

"Oh, well, I'm actually on my way to a meeting that just came up. You know how I await them with bated breath."

"Did you even bother coming home last night?" She was clearly not up to levity.

"Yes, and I saw your note. I'll be home on time to do that, I promise you."

"I hope so, Green. And on your way, could you pick up some more wine?"

"No problem. How about I pick up bagels too?"

"Bagels and wine?" This time she chuckled. "Why not? It's a Jewish party, and there can never be enough food, right?"

He rang off with a sigh of relief that he had survived, then turned his cell phone off to stave off further interruptions. The effort of deceiving her and pretending to be cheerful on three hours sleep and a triple dose of caffeine had left him drained. Thinking ahead to what he had yet to face that day, he wondered where he'd find the strength.

Rachel Walker had obviously gone to work, because it was Howard himself who, after several rings, cracked open the front door with a bleary scowl. When he saw Green, he groaned, dropped his hands limply to his sides, and stumbled back inside without a word. Green followed him in and shut the door. The doctor walked past the living room into the kitchen, which was small and crowded with the latest gadgets.

"Before you even start on me, Green, I need some coffee."

Howard was dressed in an expensive beige velour bathrobe

which gaped open to reveal his naked torso. He seemed oblivious as he measured beans and operated various machines. Soon the fragrant scent of coffee filled the room.

"Rachel had a feeling you'd come," he said. "She wanted me to barricade the house. She was on the verge of calling in her father."

"Well, you've got your own guard dog," Green replied, trying to keep his tone light. He wanted to slide into this interview casually. "Your mother. She's being very protective of you."

Howard flushed. "Yeah, well, I spoke to her last night, after you left, and told her a few things I wish I hadn't."

"Oh?"

"About writing the letter, about how furious I'd been with him," Howard replied vaguely. "It upset her needlessly."

Green wondered how much detail Ruth had learned, and if that was what had aroused her fears. "She knew none of that before?"

Howard drooped over the counter, watching the coffee drip. He looked too tired to make sense of things. "I don't know if she suspected anything. Sometimes I think she did—she never wanted to discuss his past. She'd shut us all up really fast if we got angry at him or started to speculate about him. As if he could do no wrong."

"I think your mother feels guilty now for all the hell your father put you through." Green probed ahead very carefully. "She'd forgive you anything, you know."

He watched closely, but Howard showed not so much as a quiver of guilt. Instead, he raised his head and gazed at Green with blank bemusement. Green debated how to proceed. Howard's activities in the days surrounding his father's death had certainly been suspicious, but Green had very little concrete evidence on which to hang a motive, let alone the actual murder. Without evidence to back up an accusation, he'd accomplish nothing other than tip his hand and give the man plenty of chance to cover his tracks. If there were any to cover.

But if Howard were the killer, his motive was still a mystery. His father had been mistreating him for years and had rejected his wife, but that was nothing new. His recent discovery of his father's hidden identity had shocked and outraged him, but it hardly seemed a motive for murder either. Had Howard discovered something else, perhaps in his discussion with Bernie Mendelsohn? Mendelsohn's building super had said Howard was in tears after his meeting with Mendelsohn. Had Mendelsohn told him something about his father's appalling cruelty—cruelty which began in the camps but continued with his son even fifty years later? And now, to cover up all the information that might give him a motive, Howard was denying the meeting ever took place.

The theory had a twisted logic, far-fetched and tenuous, but it was all Green had.

"Howard," he began, accepting the coffee Walker held out to him, "why did you say you never met Bernie Mendelsohn?"

"Because I didn't."

"But the building super saw you. He described you to a tee."

Howard put his cup down with a thud. "That doesn't make sense."

"He saw you coming out of Bernie's room crying. You must have learned something terrible."

Howard's eyes filled with tears, and for once Green welcomed them. Maybe some of the man's defences would wash away.

"You did see him, didn't you?"

235

Howard fell into a chair, his head in his hands. "I wish I hadn't. I wish I'd never learned any of this stuff. I wish I could just remember my father as the drunken bastard I've always known. I can't ever talk this out with him, find out why, or try to understand."

"So Bernie knew him?" Green asked gently.

"Yes, he knew him. He said he'd never forget him, poor man. Such a sad old man. He invited me in, sat me down and made me coffee, no questions asked, as if just having a visitor was a treat. Then when I showed him a picture of my father, it was like he'd been struck by lightning. He went white, he fell into a chair, he started to shake, and I was afraid he would go into cardiac arrest."

Green's pulse quickened. Something major must have happened to sear Walker so indelibly into Mendelsohn's emotions.

Howard fought for control a moment before heaving a deep sigh. "He wasn't a well man, I could tell that just by looking at him, and I was afraid to push him, but I had to know. I couldn't get this far and then leave all these questions unanswered. But he wouldn't say anything for a while, just sat there staring. I finally got some brandy, and after a bit of that he came around. He apologized and said he'd lost his wife and children in the Holocaust, and recently he'd been thinking about them more and more. Seeing my father had reminded him."

He fell silent, his head bowed, and Green forced himself to be patient. Finally, he couldn't stand the suspense. "Why?"

"My father…my father…" a mere wisp of sound "…was a Nazi whore."

Scraps of conversations raced through Green's mind. *No one is a saint who survived the ghetto… Leib turned his own father and brother over to the Nazis… Maybe the thing you want to hide from most is yourself.*

"Was your father responsible for sending Mendelsohn's family away to their deaths?"

Mutely, Howard nodded. "Them. And thousands more."

Green chose his words carefully. "In the ghettos, the Nazis made the local Jewish leaders run the day to day business of the community and choose the candidates for forced labour and deportation. Some leaders cooperated because they hoped that by maintaining Jewish control, they could protect the entire community better. Slowly, they found themselves in a trap. They didn't know deportation meant death."

Howard had been shaking his head vigorously, and now he burst in. "No! I've been doing some reading, and I know all about the *Judenrat*. That was the Jewish municipal council the Germans set up to run the ghettos. But this was worse than that. My father was part of the Ordnungsdienst, Bernie Mendelsohn called it."

"The Jewish police." Green stifled his excitement as more pieces tumbled into place. The Jewish police had been set up by the Nazis to maintain order in the ghettos. They carried no weapons and were charged initially with enforcing bylaws, checking papers, directing traffic and other petty functions. At first, the ghetto residents saw them as a welcome alternative to the Germans, but when Nazi brutality, starvation and forced evacuation to the death camps increased, the Jewish police became vilified as mere enforcers of the SS. The paradoxes in Walker's life suddenly made sense. His fear of exposure, his avoidance of Jews. His possession of German keys.

"Thugs!" Howard retorted. "That's all they were! Doing the Nazis' dirty work, ferreting out those in hiding, catching smugglers, informing on their neighbours. I had hoped that my father's suffering in the Holocaust was what had made him the cruel, warped human being that I knew. But it appears he was like that all along. Leib Kressman, king of the sewer." Howard's eyes were blazing now, and he shook his head bitterly.

But Green looked up in astonishment. "Kressman?"

"That's what Mr. Mendelsohn said his real name was."

Green's mind raced. Not Joseph, the middle-aged blacksmith, but Leib, another generation altogether! In a flash of insight he understood who Walker was, and what the black box had meant to him. And another facet of the Russian doll was revealed.

Howard was pacing now. "My father, a goddamn collaborator!"

Green forced himself to be calm. "It's not as simple as that," he replied. "It never is. He was still a teenager when the war began. A kid, afraid to die."

"And that makes it okay? Millions died because they refused to betray."

"The Nazis had their ways of persuading, Howard. They wouldn't shoot you, they'd shoot your child. Or hang an entire village for the defiance of one man. They always seemed to know just where the weaknesses lay."

"No, this was more than weakness, Inspector. This was cruelty. Bernie Mendelsohn told me how his family died. One night his wife was trying to smuggle some food into the ghetto for their children, because there were no rations for them any more. My father was patrolling the wall and caught her. He turned her in, and the SS guard shot her on the spot."

"And if he hadn't turned her in, he would have been shot himself."

"Only if the guard found out."

"It's easy for us to say that, Howard, but there, with the machine guns pointing and spies hidden everywhere—"

"You still don't get it!" Howard cried distractedly. "He wasn't just saving his own skin! He was carving out a life of profit and ease—"

"But Howard—"

Howard barrelled on obliviously. "By selling his fellow Jews to the Nazis! After Mendelsohn's wife was shot, my father went into their house, found his two children and brought them to the guard. To set an example, the guard shot them! Two little children, right before their father's eyes!" Howard sagged back in his chair with his head in his hands and the fire of a moment ago quite gone. "How can I look Rachel in the eye? That's the greatest irony of it all. I finally discover that I really am a Jew…and all I can feel is shame."

"Enough to kill him?"

Slowly, Howard lifted his head as Green's meaning sank in. "You think I killed him?"

"Did you?"

"No!"

"Then why did you refuse to tell me about the meeting? Why did you say you'd never heard of Bernie—" Abruptly Green broke off, as the full significance of this latest twist struck him. For here was the centrepiece of the whole puzzle! The moment when the lives of these three old men had come together. And with the placing of this piece, much of the rest of the picture suddenly made sense. Walker's misanthropy and inner torment, his denial of his Jewish identity, his panic at Howard's marriage, his assault on Gryszkiewicz and the pact of secrecy between the two men.

At the edges of his thoughts, Green was aware of Howard's pain as the son struggled to assimilate the picture of pure evil into which he had cast his father. Green knew that it wasn't true, that the human psyche is rarely that black, and that much of Walker's later behaviour was the result of the war within himself. Of the anger, the despair, the self-loathing which tinged everyone around him in black. After the war, the only remnant of himself that he could handle was the special tool box his father had made, probably as a gift to his teenage son with the hope that its secret contents might keep him safe.

The father whom he himself had sent to the gas chamber.

But Green was in no mood to try to explain all this. For as the pieces of the puzzle fell into place, he put together something that the Civic parking lot attendant had said with something Mendelsohn's superintendent had said, and their significance began to shift. A hazy alternative began to emerge, and he felt himself grow cold with dread.

"My God," he breathed, "you think Bernie did it, don't you?"

*　　*　　*

Green drove like an automaton through the farm country between Montreal and Ottawa. Even at noon, the highway was largely deserted, and the boredom of white fields and trees had a numbing effect on the senses. There was little to distract him from his tumbling thoughts. Yet after an hour of thinking, he was no closer to knowing what to do than he'd been when he'd left Howard.

Two old men were missing, their whereabouts a mystery. Mendelsohn had no friends or family beyond an estranged son in Philadelphia and a handful of pinochle-playing cronies at the synagogue. He had no place to go, no one to visit. Gryszkiewicz was a retired, reclusive immigrant who had rarely ventured from his neighbourhood since moving to Canada. His wife was completely baffled about the mystery friend who had invited him to visit. Green had not been baffled. Despite the man's denial, Green had assumed the mystery caller was Dubroskie, warning his cousin about the police inquiry. Gryszkiewicz had every reason to fear a police inquiry into his connection with Eugene Walker, and every motive to track down the sole survivor who could reveal his Nazi past. The theory fit all the known facts. Gryszkiewicz had received a warning phone call from his cousin, had tracked down and assassinated his only witness, and then dropped neatly out of sight into the underground safety net of the party faithful.

But what if the phone call had not been Dubroskie, but a voice from the past? Not arranging safe passage to some Nazi haven in the jungle, but setting up a secret rendezvous from which Gryszkiewicz would never return.

Do I really want to know why he never returned? Green asked himself. I could just walk away from this. Forget Hamilton and Mr. G., drive back to Barrhaven and be all ready for my son's birthday. Let Mendelsohn's form of justice prevail.

After the Second World War, a small underground cadre of Jews had scoured the globe, relentlessly tracking down war criminals and executing them. As an officer of the law, Green knew he was sworn to uphold the system, but he'd battled evil on the streets long enough to understand why others might choose another route. Not simply revenge or redemption, but a swift, effective justice far more efficient than the clumsy legal apparatus over which the Department of Justice presided. So far, the War Crimes unit had managed to charge only a handful of the two hundred potential war criminals living in Canada. Of those cases which had actually reached the courts, one trial had resulted in an acquittal, another had taken more than two years to render its guilty verdict, and the rest had floundered in the legal maze.

Perhaps Bernie Mendelsohn thought he had found a better way. Sixty years later, on the eve of his own death, he had righted a wrong. And now, driving home dizzy from exhaustion, late for his son's birthday, and running counter to everyone else on the case, Green wasn't sure he wanted to argue the point.

His car tires hit gravel and he jerked alert to discover that the car had drifted onto the shoulder. He blinked his eyes and shook his head repeatedly to clear it, but heaviness weighed his eyelids. He pulled off at the Casselman exit and stopped at the Tim Hortons doughnut shop next to the gas station to order the largest jolt of caffeine possible. Slumped in a corner booth, he cradled his cup, leaned against the wall, and let his mind roam in endless loops through the facts. Sometimes, in free fall, his thoughts snagged on facts he'd never seen. Justice, betrayal, dying, balance, strike...

A long, dingy hospital ward stretched before him, where the patients lay on rows and rows of narrow cots. He ran desperately between the rows looking for Sharon, searching the hollow faces and calling her name. The cots transformed into wooden bunks and hands reached out, clutching at him as he passed.

"Mishka!" A voice cried out, loud and firm, and he turned to see his father standing at the side of one of the bunks. He wore pyjamas and carried a stick loosely in his hand at his side. He said nothing more, merely gestured to the figure on the bottom bunk. Green looked and saw Sharon gazing up at him. Her eyes were fevered and her colour grey, but there was a smile of joy on her face. Nestled in the crook of her arm was Tony, tiny and fragile again.

"Sharon! Tony!" Green cried and rushed forward. But as he reached to embrace her, he saw it was not Sharon but his mother, gaunt, hairless and yellowed with jaundice. As he recoiled with a cry, there was a shout from the other end of the ward and a man in black uniform came striding over. The man shouted in a foreign tongue, raised a pistol and fired a bullet through his mother's forehead. Green found himself paralyzed, unable to cry out in protest as the guard raised the gun towards him. But with a roar of rage Sid Green swung his stick with all his might and struck the man, sending the gun clattering. The guard slumped to the floor, and only then did Green feel his movement return.

"Dad!" he cried. "Where is Sharon! Where is the baby!"

Sid had fallen to his knees at his wife's side and had gathered her into his arms, but now he looked up at his son. His face had aged, his eyes grown weary. Slowly, he clambered back to his feet.

"Come, I'll show you." He took his son's arm and led him out of the hospital into the sunshine. Stretched out in front of them as far as the eye could see was a barren, muddy field covered in tombstones.

"This is where we all are."

Green started awake in a clammy sweat. Lukewarm coffee spilled over his hand. His heart was hammering, and his body went limp with relief as he realized where he was. Not in Auschwitz staring at the graves of his wife and child, but huddled in the corner of a doughnut shop on the Trans-Canada. He glanced at his watch. Two o'clock! His son's birthday was due to start in three hours. He had barely enough time to get home and help Sharon prepare the house for the party. He had no time for Hamilton, no time to figure out where Mendelsohn was. Fate had intervened.

The dream had jolted him thoroughly awake, but his limbs were weak as he returned to his car and headed back onto the highway. He wanted nothing more than to revel in the comforts of the present and look ahead three hours to when he and Sharon would cuddle Tony in their arms and give him his first birthday present.

What present? he thought with dismay. What a prize father you are, and what the hell was that dream trying to tell you about that? He let his mind drift back to the images in the dream. And suddenly, one more tiny piece of the puzzle of Walker's death fell into place. The cane! Amazing, even when his conscious mind was too tired to make sense of the facts, his unconscious mind kept right on at work. Somehow, Ruth's brandishing her cane and the building super's commenting on Mendelsohn's cane had come together in his dream. He smiled in spite of himself. "How did you find the solution to this latest murder, Inspector Green?" "It came to me in a dream." Where things are never quite what they seem. Where a stick is a cane, and years collapse into seconds.

Another image came to him, of the field of tombstones, of his father's voice in the dream: "This is where we all are." Of something Mendelsohn's son had said: "He's got plenty of dead ones to keep him company."

Suddenly he knew where Bernie Mendelsohn was.

Fifteen

November 25th, 2001

I am old, a spent and soulless shell,
trapped too long in a web of memory.
Too late, my son, I sit on our street corner,
watching little boys at play.
Hearing you, seeing you,
but unable to reach
Across the dead and the damned
that clutter my world.
A single shot
resounds across the arid decades of my life.
The web is pierced,
And I slip beyond its grasp,
to nothing.
For you are gone.

Green kept his foot close to the floor all the way along the 417, hoping that none of his brothers in blue were waiting in ambush. The little Corolla covered the remaining distance to Ottawa in less than an hour and was slowed only by the trucks and traffic lights along Hunt Club Road. By the time he reached the cemetery, the winter sun was slanting into the western sky, casting a yellowish mist over the graveyard.

Once inside the wrought-iron gates, Green stopped in dismay. The Ottawa Jewish cemetery was huge, and he had no idea where Mendelsohn's second wife was buried. He tried to remember what his father had said about her. It had not been a happy marriage. She had been sickly from the start, and after the one child, she had more or less taken to her bed. She was a kind woman, Sid had said, but no match for Mendelsohn's moods. Green remembered she had finally succumbed to pneumonia around the time his own mother had died, and it had been that bond which had brought the two elderly men together.

Since the two women had died around the same time, perhaps they had been buried in the same general section of the cemetery. Purposefully, Green set off across the snowy slope. He had covered about half the distance to his mother's grave when he heard a slight scraping sound to his right. His eyes strained through the pallid light. It took a few seconds for him to distinguish a light-coloured tombstone in the distance with a dark, bulky shape obscuring one corner. He drew closer until he could distinguish the outlines of a human form huddled against the stone. It took only a second longer to recognize Bernie Mendelsohn.

Green's first instinct was to rush to his side and bundle him in his warm, dry parka, but he stopped himself. Mendelsohn was snoring peacefully, his head resting back against the stone beside his wife's name. He was wrapped in a long, warm parka with boots, mittens and hat. Although he was gaunt and unshaven, he looked at peace. When Green came to stand at his side, he opened his eyes and came to slowly. Focussing on Green's face, he managed a smile.

"*Nu*, Mishka," he murmured. "So. You figured it out?"

"Some of it, Bernie." Green knelt beside him. "Are you in pain?"

Mendelsohn shook his head. "Not now. I have my pills."

"Maybe you should visit your son before you go."

"And say what?" Mendelsohn sighed. "Some things I cannot fix. Would you talk to him?"

Green tried to hold his gaze. Remembering Irving Mendelsohn, he could have said "I don't think he'll listen," but instead he nodded. "Sure I will. And he'll understand, Bernie. Don't you worry."

"I didn't mean to kill Kressman, you know," Mendelsohn remarked in a musing tone.

Green thought of Ruth Walker's comment that things had ended as they were meant to end. That perhaps by some power beyond ours, the wrongs had been righted. "You didn't really," he said. "You were just fending him off with your cane. He died of hypothermia."

Mendelsohn looked at him in surprise. "He was scared I was going to tell the whole story to the police. He still had the same coward's temper he had when he was young. Always his fists was the first way out. In Lodz there was a story that he used to go with the Christian peasants before the war, trying to be one of them because he was tall and blonde. Such a *mensch*, too much a coward even to call himself a Jew."

"Did he call you to arrange a meeting?"

"Him? To face me? Oh no. I called him. I wanted to see him, to see if this Eugene Walker was really Leib Kressman, and also to ask him why."

"And did he remember you?"

"When he saw my face, oh yes. We don't forget those days, Michael. They are burned into our brains like a hot iron. He got very scared. He said he had to do those things or the Nazis would kill him. Hah!" Mendelsohn's eyes glowed in his pale face as he struggled to sit up. "I knew his kind. Whores! They thought they could stay nice and warm by getting into the Nazis' bed. Little men inside, trying to be big. He had an older brother, short and fat but ten times the man, a councilman in the ghetto. People looked up to him. He was trying to protect us by giving false names to the Germans of who should be deported. The SS shot him, and then they had no such trouble with Leib. He sent his own father to the trains so he wouldn't have to see the shame in his eyes. Leib rolled over like a good dog and spread his legs. And worse, Mishka, he got to like it! He stopped being one of us, he thought he could be one of them and make a nice little profit out of both sides."

He stopped to catch his breath, his chest heaving from the effort of his outburst. Spittle had formed at the edges of his mouth, and he wiped it away. "But he was a fool. In the end they sent him away to a camp just like the rest of us. Even now, fifty years later, the fool still doesn't know who to hate. I didn't kill your family, he shouts, and I think he's going to jump over the car seat at me. He's drunk, and he's getting all red. I'm not such a healthy man, so I get out of the car, and he gets out too. He says if I want the real murderer of my family, he is here in Canada living happily with his family."

"And he told you about Josef Gryszkiewicz."

"Gryszkiewicz." Mendelsohn spat the name out. "Called himself Fritsch back then, a Nazi halfbreed who thought his blood was pure enough for the super race. They gave him a fancy uniform and a job at the gate, keeping Jews in their place. He loved it! Thought he was born to catch the young boys smuggling blankets and the mothers sneaking potatoes to their children."

The sun sank slowly, carving hazy shadows across the snow, and on Bank Street the homebound traffic gathered strength. Green asked the question he knew he should leave unasked.

"Where is Gryszkiewicz, Bernie?"

Mendelsohn lay back against the gravestone and gave him a long, searching look. "Michael, I don't want jail. And I don't want hospitals and machines and people not letting me die. I want to stay here with Lydia. This is where I belong. It won't be long now."

Green studied his hands. He could feel the old man quivering beside him, whether from cold or fear he couldn't tell. He sensed Mendelsohn was right, that he didn't have long. In this cold and with the disease closing in, maybe only hours. It took Green mere seconds to reach a decision. "There won't be any jail, Bernie. I wasn't even here. I'll have to report what I learned from Howard Walker, and the whole police force knows I'm looking for you, because I was afraid you were in danger. But no one has any idea where you are, and it may take a day to figure that out."

Mendelsohn stared a long time into the mist. "A day is enough. I have my pills. I want to sit awhile with Lydia. If there is a God, where I'm going I won't see her again. When I have said goodbye, I will take them." He shut his eyes and took several breaths as if gathering strength. "I shot Gryszkiewicz. It was very easy, and I don't feel bad about it. I was afraid I would. Maybe I should be afraid, because I don't. But he showed no regret, Mishka. That was why I did it. When I went to meet him, I didn't think I would kill him. I planned to tell the RCMP when I was sure who he was. They had the name Fritsch, but not his real Polish name. So I phoned Fritsch, I told him I was Walker and we had to talk in secret. I took the train to Hamilton, and I met him behind a small warehouse that was closed for the winter. He looked at me, and he said I was not Walker and so I told him that I was in Lodz and that he had shot my family, and he said 'What do

249

you think you can do about it?' So I said 'This' and I pulled out the gun and shot him. I had the gun for years, I had never shot it, but I didn't give one thought. Just—bang." Mendelsohn shook his head in wonder. "I killed two people, Mishka. I'm eighty-four years old, I just killed two people and I feel…nothing."

Green looked at the gaunt spectre before him and remembered the man he'd known in childhood as Irving's father. A taciturn, unyielding man who sat on his front balcony buried in his newspaper and trading insults in Yiddish with the old woman across the way. A man who shouted at the boys for running over his tiny lawn and who turned off all his lights on Halloween. A man in whom joy had been eclipsed for so long that when the rage was expunged, he felt…nothing.

Green pushed himself to his feet. "Bernie, I promised you no jails or hospitals. But come back to my father's place with me, where you can be warm and taken care of till the end. You can't stay here."

Mendelsohn remained where he was. He was tiring rapidly, and he leaned his head back against the tombstone and shut his eyes. "This is where I belong. Where I want to be."

It took all Green's strength to walk away, not because he was turning a blind eye to murder, but because he was leaving a man to die. As soon as he reached his car, he pulled out his notebook, checked a number, and punched it into his cell phone.

"Irving," he snapped, abandoning all pretense at professional protocol, "Mike Green again. Your father is sitting in the cemetery by your mother's grave waiting to die. If you're any kind of a son—"

"Green!" Irving roared, and his tone stopped Green short. It was brusque but bewildered, like an unaccustomed call for help. "I got a strange package from Ottawa in the mail today.

An old ratty notebook, all scribbled in Yiddish. Looks like a bunch of poems. Did you send it?"

"No," Green replied in surprise. "It must be your father's."

Mendelsohn sighed. "Isn't that typical. No hello, son. No how's my grandson. No explanation."

"He obviously thought it speaks for itself."

"Well, I guess I'll have to get it translated, then."

Green thought of Walker and the grimy toolbox he had hung onto for sixty years. "It's probably the most important thing he owns." He had heard the perplexity beneath the nonchalance in Mendelsohn's voice and was reluctant to help the man understand, when he'd done nothing to earn it. Yet there had already been too much left unsaid. "Maybe his way of explaining."

"Explaining what?"

"Why don't you get your ass on a plane up here and ask him."

*   *   *

Green felt marginally better as he put the car in gear and headed towards home. A balance had been struck after all. Perhaps the only one possible. He knew his decision to walk away from the graveyard might generate some complications once Gryszkiewicz' body was eventually found. He didn't know what forensic or eyewitness evidence the Hamilton police would unearth nor how clearly that evidence would point to Mendelsohn, but their investigation would surely lead back to Ottawa. Several people knew Green considered the two cases linked, but they had only bits of the picture. Howard knew Green suspected Mendelsohn of killing Walker, but didn't know Green had found Mendelsohn in the graveyard. Irving knew Green had found Bernie, but didn't know he suspected him of murder.

The only person with the whole picture was himself, and no one was going to question his call on the case. Mendelsohn was a feeble old man who barely had the strength to raise his cane, let alone kill a man. Never mind that the rage of half a century had probably given Mendelsohn the strength to kill an elephant. Let MacPhail's verdict stand: death by natural causes. God knows Walker's family would be happy enough, Gryszkiewicz' family would be happy enough to leave the past buried, and Mendelsohn would be dead within hours. The crimes, past and present, would remain undetected, and yet in the final reckoning, justice of a sort would have been done.

As for Gryszkiewicz's murder, let the Hamilton police make whatever case they could, without, Green suspected, much cooperation or disclosure from the dead man's family. No one knows about Bernie's confession but me, he thought. The old man is dying, and this is how he wants to die. After all he's endured, that simple wish should not be too much to ask.

With an effort, Green tried to put the image of the dying man aside and turn his mind to the next crisis of the day. He glanced at his watch. Three-thirty. If he broke all the speed limits, he could be right on time for the party. Maybe even on time to help Sharon prepare the house and blow up some balloons. Just what he needed—fun, family and the chance to keep dark thoughts at bay.

He dialled home and a rushed, frazzled Sharon answered. He spoke quickly before she could unleash a diatribe. "Hi, sweetheart. I'm half way home now, on my way to buy wine and bagels."

"Have you bought Tony's present?"

He bit back a curse of dismay. "Just picking it up," he

replied and glanced out the window to get his bearings. Nothing but car dealers and fast food outlets, and up ahead the sign for the airport parkway, which in the other direction led downtown. What the hell could he get at the boutiques and novelty shops downtown? Suddenly brilliance struck.

"What did you get?" she demanded.

"It's a secret," he said and steered the car up onto the ramp.

* * *

Six hours later, the last straggling guest had left, and the centre of the party had long since been put to bed, cranky and exhausted from a surfeit of cake, noisy laughter and mauling hands. When Green arrived back from driving his father home, the stuffed toys, books and trucks had been piled in the corner of the living room, and Sharon was slumping around picking up paper plates and wrapping paper from the floor. Her eyes were at half mast, but they mustered a little sparkle when he took her into his arms and kissed her.

"It was a great party, darling. And all your doing too. I'm sorry."

"You should be, and believe me, I'll collect. But it worked out. Our very first party as homeowners."

"Yeah." He glanced around the living room which, despite its fresh new blue paint, was featureless. His antipathy must have shown, for her enthusiasm faded and she leaned into his arms with a sigh.

"You hate it here, don't you?"

He opened his mouth to deny it, then stopped himself. "Yes."

"They're not really your kind of people, are they?"

"Do my kind of people even exist?" he asked. He'd kept

himself sober so that he could drive his father home, but now he longed for a brandy to stave off the disquiet that was stealing back in. Outside, the chill of night had settled in, and he thought of Bernie. Sullivan hadn't called, which meant neither old man had been discovered. Green prayed Irving had heeded his call in time.

Sharon seemed to read his mind, because she disengaged herself and went to pour them both a small snifter of Remy Martin. "Here's to our little boy. One year old and showing every sign of being a miniature you."

The cognac spread its warmth through him and he smiled. "What a curse."

"You never did give him his present. Did you even get it?"

He feigned insult and went into the front cupboard, returning with a square box elegantly wrapped in silver paper. "I waited till after the guests left, because it's kind of private."

"But now Tony's asleep," she protested. "Shouldn't we wait till morning?"

"We'll put it by his bed. It's not a gift he'll appreciate right away anyway."

She cast him a puzzled look and reached to grab the box, but he held it out of her reach. He led her upstairs to Tony's room, where he opened the box and unrolled its contents from the tissue paper. Carefully he stood the antique candlesticks on the dresser and stepped back to let her admire them.

"There are six million stories to go with these. One day, maybe I'll tell him a few."

She slipped her arms around his waist. "Green, sometimes out of the blue, just when I'm about to lose hope, you get it just right."

Barbara Fradkin was born in Montreal and attended McGill, the University of Toronto and the University of Ottawa, where she obtained her PhD in psychology. Her past work as a child psychologist has provided ample inspiration and insight for plotting fictional murders.

Her dark amd compelling short stories haunt several anthologies and magazines, such as *Storyteller*, *Iced* (Insomniac Press, 2001), and the Ladies Killing Circle anthologies, including *Fit to Die* (RendezVous Press, 2001).

The first Inspector Green Mystery, *Do or Die*, was published in 2000. *Once Upon a Time* is inspired by her husband's work as a war crimes prosecutor.

An active member of Canada's crime writing community, Barbara is currently on the executive of Capital Crime Writers as well as the Ottawa Chapters of Sisters in Crime and Crime Writers of Canada. She resides in Ottawa with assorted pets and children, and in her spare time she enjoys outdoor activities and travelling.